PRAISE FOR LAUREN LAYNE

huge deal

OTHER TITLES BY LAUREN LAYNE

21 Wall Street

Hot Asset
Hard Sell

I Do, I Don't

Ready to Run
Runaway Groom

Stiletto and Oxford

After the Kiss
Love the One You're With
Just One Night
The Trouble with Love
Irresistibly Yours
I Wish You Were Mine
Someone Like You
I Knew You Were Trouble
I Think I Love You

Love Unexpectedly (stand-alone novels)

Blurred Lines
Good Girl
Love Story
Walk of Shame
An Ex for Christmas

The Wedding Belles

From This Day Forward (novella)
To Have and to Hold
For Better or Worse
To Love and to Cherish

New York's Finest

Frisk Me
Steal Me
Cuff Me

Redemption

Isn't She Lovely
Broken
Crushed

The Best Mistake

Only with You
Made for You

huge deal

LAUREN LAYNE

Montlake
Romance

Published by Montlake Romance, Seattle

www.apub.com

Amazon, the Amazon logo, and Montlake Romance are trademarks of Amazon.com, Inc., or its affiliates.

ISBN-13: 9781542093347
ISBN-10: 1542093341

Cover design by Letitia Hasser

Cover photography by Regina Wamba of MaeIDesign.com

Printed in the United States of America

For Anth.
PS: One day, I will win at chess.
For now, my heroines do it for me.

PART ONE

PART ONE

1

"Okay, so where are we with the ice sculpture?"

Kate Henley let the question hang in the air unanswered for about seven seconds longer than comfortable, hoping that the asker would *hear* the ridiculousness of the question and retract it.

Claudia Palmer merely blinked at Kate with eyelashes that may or may not have been real and waited for Kate's response.

Kate let out a tiny internal sigh. She'd mastered it over the years. It was the kind of sigh nobody else knew was happening, but it allowed Kate a moment of silent acknowledgment that she was right, even if the other person didn't realize it. Yet.

If Kate had learned anything in her twenty-seven years, it was that there was a certain power in being underestimated. And at five foot one, with boring brown hair, boring brown eyes, and a penchant for prim clothing, Kate was the queen of flying under the radar when she needed to. Other times, being underestimated wasn't powerful so much as supremely annoying.

Times like now.

"Still working on it," Kate finally replied. "General consensus is that a six-foot ice sculpture in a warmer-than-usual spring is going to be a pricey endeavor."

The other woman gave a practiced, dramatic wave of her hand. "Please. If Givenchy can pull it off in Milan in August, we can do it in Manhattan in April."

Kate surreptitiously checked the time on her iPad: 2:14 p.m. Cue the slow clap for Claudia. Her boss's girlfriend had made it fourteen minutes into their meeting before name-dropping one of her famous designer contacts. A new record.

"Okay, so you'll take care of that," Claudia said, looking back down at her tiny spiral notebook. "I'm still undecided on who we should have supply the oysters. I've heard good things about Oysters XO. Have you worked with them?"

"Sure, several times," Kate said. "But—"

"Okay, maybe I'll hand off this task to you as well," Claudia said, tapping her lip with a perfectly manicured red nail. "I'm thinking a mix of East and West Coast. What do you think?"

"I'm thinking Kennedy's allergic to shellfish," Kate said.

Claudia didn't even glance up. "So? He won't be the only one at this party."

Um. "But it's his birthday party."

Claudia apparently hadn't mastered the silent sigh, because hers was audible and annoyed. "Kennedy will understand that other people like oysters, even if he can't indulge. There'll be other food for him to eat."

And chances are he'll be so horrified by the ice-sculpture statue in his likeness that he won't even notice the shellfish he can't eat, the Maroon 5 cover band he can't stand, the guest list of people he doesn't know . . .

Kate was on the verge of letting Claudia know exactly what she thought of her party plan when the other woman reached across the conference room table and touched her arm. "Thanks again for helping me with this. His mother kept offering, but it's important to me to show Diane that I can do this on my own. That I care about her son as much as she does."

Kate forced a smile in response, even as she privately doubted that someone who'd been dating Kennedy Dawson for all of two months could possibly care about the man *as much as his own mother.* Not to mention, Claudia was hardly doing this "on her own." Kate should have known better when Claudia had asked if she could "run a few ideas" by Kate for a small surprise get-together for Kennedy.

In reality, Kate was spending nearly as much time on this damn party as she was her actual job as Kennedy's assistant, and she was pretty sure she was ending up with the majority of the work for what was turning into a freaking circus.

"I'm sure he'll appreciate it," Kate said noncommittally. "Though if you're open to suggestions—"

"Claudia? What are you doing here?"

Kate went still for just a half second, the way she always did when she heard *his* voice, the gesture as frequent, and nearly as imperceptible, as her internal sighs.

Claudia immediately stood, all graceful movement and long legs, as she slid her notebook across the table to Kate.

Since Claudia's and Kennedy's focus was entirely on each other, Kate allowed herself the gratification of an eye roll at Claudia's hasty handoff. As if Kennedy were really going to make a beeline for a tiny, impractical little notebook that had—Kate flipped through it—*maybe* twenty pages.

Most of the pages were filled with over-the-top party ideas. One simply said *Doves.*

Kate smiled a little at that. It would serve Kennedy right to have doves at his party. In fact, if Claudia asked Kate's opinion on the doves, Kate was happy to lie her little heart out.

Absolutely! Kennedy would love *to see a bunch of creepy birds at the birthday party he doesn't know is happening and probably doesn't want, because he hates surprises even more than he hates parties . . .*

Kate gathered her iPad and Claudia's mini notebook, then turned, which she immediately regretted, because she'd moved too fast and saw Claudia pressing her lips to Kennedy's.

Claudia didn't have to go on her toes, Kate noticed. Even without the heels, Claudia Palmer probably never had to go on her toes to kiss a man. The former model was five foot eleven. Kate knew, because she'd looked it up. Was she proud of her online stalking? Not particularly. But she'd learned over the years that doing a little up-front research on her three bosses' latest lovers came in handy if things took a turn toward the dramatic, which was often the case. And who handled the drama? Spoiler alert: not the guys. *Kate* was the one who dealt with the fallout of her bosses' ill-fated romantic endeavors.

Of course, she didn't have to worry about Ian or Matt anymore. Two of her guys had settled down quite nicely and had become another woman's problem. There was just one left . . .

Kennedy's gaze found Kate's within seconds of his lips leaving Claudia's, and though she'd withstood the force of that glare nearly every day for six years, the effect never failed to jolt her, just a little.

Kennedy Dawson was almost brutally attractive, in the upper-class, authoritative way of *the* Kennedys he'd been named after. His hair was somewhere between dark and medium brown, with a shiny thickness that rivaled the duchess of Cambridge. His eyes were golden brown and fringed with long lashes she'd once dared to comment on and gotten a growl in return. Everything about him was serious. His thick brows frequently tilted down into a frown; he had an unsmiling mouth, a sharp jawline that was tense more often than not.

Sort of like now.

She gave him a mocking smile in response to his impenetrable stare, sensing from the way his eyes narrowed that he'd seen both her eye roll and her smirk.

"What are you two up to?" he asked, the question directed at Kate and not the woman pressed to his side.

"Just girl talk!" Claudia chirped. "Getting to know each other. I stopped by to see you, but you weren't around, so I chatted with Kate instead."

He looked back at Claudia and frowned. Always with the frowning. "I'm around. I've been in my office. Something my *assistant* would know. She could have told you to come on in." He cut an irritated gaze at Kate.

"Spare me," Kate said in a bored tone as she stood and headed toward the conference room door. "But I've made a mental note. Next time you're on a phone call with your biggest investor that took three weeks for his assistant and me to coordinate, I'll let everyone know you're in your office and that it's okay to go on in."

"Oh, I'm sure Kennedy wouldn't mind if *I* went in," Claudia said with a warm smile, pressing her nose to his cheek and giving him some sort of weird Eskimo kiss.

Kate caught Kennedy's eye as she passed the couple and smiled sweetly. He tried to hide his wince and failed. She knew the only thing Kennedy hated more than interruptions while he was on the phone was public displays of affection.

Just wait till you see the life-size ice sculpture created in your likeness, Kate thought as she left the conference room. *It'll be right next to the oysters you can't eat.*

"Ah, there you are." A large, masculine arm dropped over her shoulders as Matt Cannon, one of her other bosses, fell into step beside her. "Don't be mad."

"What did you do?" she asked, already scrolling through the email on her iPad, trying not to be annoyed that her inbox had overflowed in the brief time she'd been discussing shellfish with Kennedy's girlfriend.

"You look so pretty today," Matt said. "And you smell nice. So nice. New perfume?"

Kate didn't wear perfume.

"Matthew," she said, stopping at her desk and batting his arm off her shoulders. "Please tell me you didn't."

"Didn't what?" He picked up her stapler and pretended to study it. Matt was gorgeous, with blond hair and playful blue eyes. He was also utterly brilliant, having taken Wall Street by storm as a "boy wonder" back in his early twenties. He was also kind, charming, and she loved the guy, but the man had one serious shortcoming . . .

Kate sighed. A real sigh, not one of the silent ones. "You did."

"Did what?" This from another male voice. "Managed his own calendar again?"

"*Managed* is a strong word," Kate muttered to Ian Bradley, her third boss, as she dropped into her desk chair and pulled up on her computer Matt's calendar for the following day.

"How bad is it?" Matt asked, craning his neck to see her screen.

"Well, it depends," she said, her mouse already clicking rapidly to repair the damage. "Just how much do you want to meet with Jarod Lanham, at the same time you have lunch with Sabrina, at the same time the Sams scheduled your Q1 review?"

"Cozy!" Ian chimed in with enthusiasm. "Your bosses, your wife, and your top client, who once dated your wife . . ."

"They didn't date," Matt groused at Ian before looking beseechingly at Kate. "Can you fix it?"

"Done," she said, already locking her computer screen and picking up her cell. "I sent an invite to Jarod asking to reschedule for Friday, confirmed the review with the bosses, and . . ." She held up her screen. "Just texted Sabrina to see if happy hour works instead of lunch." Her phone buzzed, and Kate looked down at the message from Sabrina Cross, Matt's wife and one of her best friends. "She says we're good."

"I love you," Matt said. "You are the best. And so, so pretty. Isn't she pretty, Ian?"

"So pretty."

Kate shot Ian a suspicious look. "What'd *you* do?"

He sucked in his cheeks and pretended to think. "Hypothetically, if Lara was feeling a little stressed about the wedding, and I told her to calm down . . ."

She gave him a look. "Please tell me you didn't actually say the words *calm down* to the woman planning your wedding."

"Well . . ."

"Oh my God," Kate muttered, thumbs already at work as she wrote another text message, this time to Lara McKenzie, to do damage control with Ian's fiancée. "At least if you two keep it up, I have unshakable job security."

And she meant it. Of course, on paper, she reported to Kennedy, Matt, and Ian. *Technically*, they were the bosses, she, the executive assistant. But they all knew who really ran the show.

It wasn't a typical arrangement, but the four of them went way back—they'd all started at Wolfe Investments the same year, within a month of one another. Back when the guys were junior brokers and Kate's primary employment goal had been a job that covered vision insurance, contributed to a 401(k), *and* put her over-the-top organizational skills to use.

Though Wolfe had a high burnout rate, with very few junior brokers "making it" to the next level, *her* guys had all been promoted to director. And while protocol had dictated they each pick their own dedicated assistant, they'd all picked, well, *her*.

It had worked out well for all of them. On Wall Street, where douchebags were a dime a dozen, Kate had lucked out not only to have one boss who wasn't a total dick but three who respected her and had become friends.

The result had been a crazy few years, but Kate wouldn't have changed a moment of it. Well, that wasn't true. Kate would happily eliminate Matt's fondness for screwing up his own calendar. And she hadn't exactly relished Ian's pre-Lara days when she'd smoothed out more than one of his awkward *Whoops, I slept with her; Whoops, her, too* scenarios.

As for Kennedy . . .

"Hey, if it isn't my two favorite boys!" Claudia said, releasing Kennedy's arm and coming over to greet them.

Kate knew it was petty, but she couldn't help but relish Matt's ever so slight eye roll at Claudia's over-the-top air-kiss routine.

Claudia slapped Ian's biceps. "Ian Bradley, I haven't seen you in forever! You keep dodging my double-date invitations."

Ian dutifully pecked Claudia's cheek. "Apologies, doll. The wedding planning's been keeping us busy."

"Right! Remind me again when the big day is?"

"It was supposed to be Valentine's Day, but we made a last-minute venue change and pushed it to June."

"Oh, so your darling girl will be a June bride!"

Matt caught Kate's eye and mouthed, *Darling girl?*

She pressed her lips together to hold in a smile, imagining what Lara, a badass FBI agent, would think of the descriptor.

Kennedy caught their exchange and swatted the back of Matt's head, which earned him a curious look from Claudia.

Without acknowledging her silent question, Kennedy asked, "You ready for lunch?"

"Lunch? It's two thirty," Matt said, glancing at his Rolex.

"Congrats, Kate, you finally taught Matt how to tell time!" Ian exclaimed.

"I wish," Kate said.

"You know, I mastered that a few years ago," Matt said. "It's damn dates that seem to trip me up . . ."

"You sure?" Kennedy said. "Because you didn't seem to have telling time mastered this morning when you were four minutes late for our six a.m. run."

Ian turned to Claudia. "It's not too late, you know. Save yourself."

"I think he's adorable," Claudia said, reaching out and taking Kennedy's hand. "Shall we?"

Kate looked away under the pretense of checking her email, but not before she caught the way Matt was looking at her. She looked back for a moment, and Matt gave her a hint of a smile that was just a tiny bit sad.

She wasn't an idiot. She knew her friends all thought she was besotted with Kennedy Dawson. She wasn't. Not anymore.

She didn't know how to explain it to them, though. She could barely even admit to herself that once upon a silly time, when she was far younger and more idealistic, Kate had looked up from her computer, locked eyes with her new boss, and promptly—stupidly—fallen head over heels in insta-love. The kind of all-consuming, butterflies-in-the-stomach, wedding-fantasy type "love" usually reserved for eighth graders and Disney characters. She'd even been so naive as to think maybe, just maybe, the way his eyes darted away when she looked his way meant something. She'd foolishly let herself believe that he'd been quietly watching her, the same way she found herself looking at him more than necessary.

And then reality slapped her. *Hard.*

Five years ago, Kate had inadvertently overheard a conversation among the three guys discussing how undatable she was. Kennedy's exact words were *She's hardly irresistible*, after which he'd suggested they all agree never to date her. Hearing Ian and Matt agree to the pact had stung a little—she was human, after all. But hearing Kennedy's casual dismissal of her had damn near ripped her heart out.

And yet . . . she was grateful for it. Really. Truly. It had been exactly what she'd needed to cure her of her childish visions of love. Not to mention, it had given her perfect clarity on what she wanted: someone who *did* find her irresistible. And he was out there. She just had to . . . wait.

"I'm hungry," Matt announced. "You guys hungry?"

"You *just* gave Kennedy shit for having lunch at two thirty—" Ian broke off when Matt gave him a look. "Yeah, okay, I could eat. Kate, let's go eat."

"I have work to do," she said, even as Ian pulled her chair backward, and Matt grabbed her purse.

In the end, she let them take her to lunch. Not because they were her bosses but because they were her friends. And though they'd never say so, she knew they were trying to make her feel better about the Kennedy/Claudia thing. Which she fully appreciated but was unnecessary. Kate's heart had gotten over its foolish Kennedy infatuation years ago, and her brain was far too smart to still be in love with her boss.

Unfortunately, her body was impossibly, irrationally, annoyingly still in *lust* with the man.

2

Kennedy glanced at the grandfather clock on his office wall, an antique that his friends never failed to give him shit for. It was half past seven, and he wasn't even close to being done with work for the day.

The late lunch with his girlfriend probably hadn't been the smartest decision. Then again, if he *hadn't* taken Claudia to lunch, she'd be planning their dinner date, wondering if he felt like sushi or Italian or whatever new, hip place had just opened in the West Village, where she'd inevitably order a pile of vegetables, regardless of where they ended up.

Instead, she'd eaten half a Cobb salad at three p.m. and then spent the next fifteen minutes telling him she wouldn't *possibly* be hungry for dinner after such a late lunch. One of the unexpected perks of dating a model was that Claudia spent a lot of time deciding when *not* to eat, which meant he was off the hook from the typical early-courtship routine of having to finagle reservations at every hot spot in NYC.

And actually, Claudia wasn't a model—she was a former model, which was even better. She was stunning, but at thirty-three, she'd decided to "give up the life," as she put it, and put her time toward "philanthropic endeavors." Also her words.

He'd had his doubts about her, considering she'd been the result of a blind date set up by his mother, but he had to hand it to his mom.

Now he had a beautiful girlfriend who spent most of her time raising money for charity and who, on the clingy scale, was hanging in there at a respectable seven out of ten, with ten being *I need my space, damn it.*

Though, if Kennedy were brutally honest, and he almost always was, Claudia's clingy score was increasing lately.

He wasn't loving her recent penchant for showing up at his office in the middle of the day unannounced. Today was the third time in a week that he'd had to take Claudia to lunch so she'd quit bugging his assistant with God only knows what variety of girl talk . . .

Kennedy slid his chair two inches to the left, a habitual motion that allowed him to see through his open office door to Kate's desk.

As expected, the familiar sight of the back of Kate's head greeted him. She'd worn her dark-brown hair in the same straight, basic style as long as he'd known her. He liked that about Kate. She was predictable. Steady. Reliable. At least as it pertained to her job duties.

On a personal level, she was a pain in his ass.

And yet, there was a comfort even in that. Kennedy and Kate may have gotten on each other's nerves more often than not, but he also knew they were the same. They both liked calm. Order.

And somehow over the past few years, she'd become his calm. She *was* his order.

Even when she annoyed him. Which was . . . always.

Kennedy glanced at his inbox. There was plenty to contend with, and yet . . .

He stood and walked to his office doorway. He cleared his throat. Kennedy knew Kate heard him, because her fingers paused for a split second before resuming their rapid-fire typing.

"You see my note about George Overby?" he asked. "I need a lunch place for Monday."

"Done," she said, her fingers continuing to fly across her keyboard. "It's on your calendar and confirmed with his assistant."

Kennedy gave a slight shake of his head in amused irritation. He'd just sent the request not five minutes ago, but then, Kate seemed to delight in staying one step ahead of him. She was one of the few people who could.

He tried again to get under her skin. "Well, I hope it's someplace that can accommodate—"

"It's at Augustine. The chef knows he's coming, and they've got a whole gluten-free situation worked out."

Kennedy lightly rapped his fist against the doorjamb. *Damn.* She was good. Really good. "Thank you," he said begrudgingly.

Finally, her fingers left her keyboard, and she spun in her chair toward him, her expression slightly wary. "You're welcome."

He nodded toward her computer. "What are you working on?"

Her eyebrows lifted. "You *really* want to know?" She picked up a legal pad, which he knew she used as her running to-do list. Well, that and her iPad. She had some elaborate system that involved "migration," and color coding, and archiving, and he didn't know what else, but he was pretty sure it was something a little supernatural. If he believed in such things. Which he did not.

"Not really," he admitted. "But I'm sorry if Claudia's interruption today necessitated your working late."

"I'm not going to tell you what we talked about," she said, starting to turn back to her computer.

Irritation rippled through him, partially at her assumption that curiosity over her conversation with Claudia was the only reason he'd asked what she was working on, partially at the fact that she was right.

"Besides, I always work late," she said without looking back at him.

It was true. Not so long ago, they'd *all* worked late. He, Matt, and Ian had rarely left the office before eight, and none of them ever left before Kate. But things changed after Ian had met Lara and decided to become a one-woman man who preferred dinner—or sex—with his fiancée to late nights in the office. One down. Then Matt had married Sabrina. Two down.

Now it was just Kate and him in the office most nights, an occurrence that was comforting and yet caused some little fissure of unease through Kennedy, and for the life of him, he couldn't say why.

"You should at least get something to eat if you're going to be here late."

"I had a cheeseburger and fries at three with Ian and Matt, and we talked work, so you can spare me the lecture on extended lunch breaks during work hours."

Kennedy was torn between wanting to smile at the tart retort and banging his head against the door because they always seemed to come to this. Arguing.

"Kate."

"What?" *Tap tap tap.*

She didn't turn around, but he waited her out, refusing to finish his sentence until she turned.

Better, he thought once her irritated gaze finally came around to meet his. *Much better.*

By the book, he supposed Kate would be considered plain. Her hair was usually parted down the middle or pulled back in a no-nonsense headband thing. If she wore makeup, he didn't notice it. She was small—shorter than average, with slim shoulders and zero curves.

And yet he'd always liked looking at her. She was . . . interesting. Not that he'd tell *her* that. He may not have the smooth-talking charm of his friends, but even he knew not to tell a woman she was *interesting*-looking. But Kate was. Her eyes were wide and tilted down at the corners, just as her nose tilted slightly up in an oddly compelling combination. Her mouth was full and slightly sulky, at least when she looked at him . . .

Kennedy cleared his throat and looked away. *Off-limits.* Not that he was attracted to Kate. She was too damn antagonistic, too forthright,

16

too . . . *much*. Not his type at all. But even if she were, she wasn't for him. Back when he, Matt, and Ian had started at Wolfe and realized they had one hell of an assistant on their hands, they'd made a pact:

Kate Henley was off-limits on the romantic front.

The last thing they needed was for one of them to seduce her and then have it end badly, leaving them without the best executive assistant on the planet.

"*What?*" she said again, finally turning fully to face him.

"Ah . . ." Crap. He'd forgotten what he was going to say. He scrambled and tried to recover. "Sorry if Claudia's been bugging you lately."

Kate shrugged. "You already said that. She's fine." Hardly a ringing endorsement, but then this was Kate. She wasn't inclined to gushing.

"What'd she want with you, anyway?"

Kate's eyes narrowed slightly. "Maybe she just wants to be my friend."

Kennedy tensed. He couldn't say why the idea of Kate and his girlfriend becoming friends made him nervous, but it did. Which was irrational. Kate was friends with Ian's fiancée, as well as Matt's wife. Hell, Kate was going to be a bridesmaid in Ian and Lara's wedding and had been one of only twenty people present at Matt and Sabrina's surprise Vegas wedding just a few months earlier.

Not that Kennedy had plans to marry Claudia. It had been only two months.

He respected Kate a hell of a lot, even considered her a friend in a cautious, circle-around-each-other kind of way, but they'd always steered clear of each other's romantic lives. And he did not, for one second, like the idea of his assistant and girlfriend gabbing about him in the conference room.

"Well, be sure she doesn't get in the way of your work," he said, choosing his words poorly, the way he often did around Kate.

Her eyebrows lifted. "*Claudia's* not the one getting in the way of my work tonight."

"Sorry," he snapped. "I'm sure you had riveting plans."

It was a low blow. He knew it even before he saw the flicker of hurt in her eyes. She whirled around, turning her back to him.

Damn it. Kennedy was known for acting with thoughtful precision in all things. Regret was not a particularly familiar or welcome feeling for him.

Apologizing was even more unfamiliar.

"Kate—"

She opened her desk drawer and pulled out a set of headphones. She punched one end into her computer, holding the earbuds out to the side, prolonging the motion so he could see them before tucking the earpieces beneath her hair.

Conversation over.

Kennedy sighed. Fair enough. He still needed to apologize, but he'd wait until tomorrow. Probably around ten a.m., when she was at peak caffeine, lowest stress, and when she smiled the most often.

Not at him, but, well, someday.

A guy could hope.

3

Mondays were typically the most hectic, hair-pulling days at Wolfe Investments, but this week, Thursday was giving Monday a serious run for its money.

"Kate Henley," she said, picking up her fifth call in as many minutes. "Mr. Cannon's in a meeting right now. May I take a message or connect you to voice mail? Sure, one moment . . .

"Kate Henley . . . Mr. Bradley's in a meeting at the moment. May I—Oh, hi, Mrs. Stilner. I'll let him know you called.

"Kate Henley," she said as she scribbled Mary Stilner's name on her notepad. "Hey, Stacey. Thanks so much for getting back to me. Can I call you in a few? I'm drowning over here . . . Yep, the party's this Saturday. Perfect, thanks so much."

She hung up the phone, her hand hovering over the receiver for a full ten seconds, knowing that for whatever warped reason, phone calls seemed to come in bursts on days like this. When a full thirty seconds passed, Kate slowly pulled her hand away from the receiver, not wanting to jinx the fact that finally she was between bursts.

"Is it always like that?"

Kate looked up from her notepad at the interruption, her right hand never pausing in its note-taking. Then she saw the face behind the masculine voice, and her pen slowed to a halt.

The man looming above her was Kennedy but . . . not. The eyes were hazel instead of brown, the hairline slightly less square, the mouth . . . smiling?

Grinning, actually. Definitely not Kennedy.

The man extended a hand down. "I'm—"

"Jack," she said before he could introduce himself. "You must be Jack Dawson."

"Guilty. And just unlucky enough to be born a few years too early for my parents to realize I'd share a name with Leonardo DiCaprio's character dying on the *Titanic*."

"Leo's character *dies*?" Kate asked, letting her chin wobble for just a second.

Jack's smile dropped, and Kate laughed. "I'm kidding. I'm Kate Henley, and yes, I've seen the movie." She shook his hand.

"Ah, Kate . . . as in Winslet."

"Wow." She let her voice take on an awed, hushed tone. "Exactly how much mileage do you typically get out of this *Titanic* thing?"

He gave an exaggerated wince. "Too much?"

"It's really embarrassing for you," she teased lightly, even as she marveled that she'd known Kennedy for years and they'd never developed the easy rapport she'd established with his brother in five seconds.

Even if he and Kennedy hadn't shared a last name, she'd have known who he was immediately. The family resemblance was strong among all four Dawson brothers, though this was the first time she'd met Jack.

"I thought you were in London." She scrolled through her memory, remembering that he was in international business of some sort.

"Paris, most recently."

"Ah. You're back for the party?" she asked after a quick glance over her shoulder to make sure Kennedy's door was still closed.

"Yeah, although I'm also back in New York for good. Well, at least for the foreseeable future."

"Oh! I hadn't heard. Your parents must be thrilled."

"Actually . . ." He put his hands in his pockets and leaned forward, lowering his voice. "You're among the first to know. It just became final yesterday. I was hoping to tell Big Brother Extraordinaire in person. He around?"

Kate smiled. "Does he know you call him that?"

Jack lifted one eyebrow. "You've met Kennedy, right? He *insists* upon it."

"Let me double-check his calendar," she said, since Kennedy frequently added meetings without telling her, although unlike Matt, he managed to do so correctly. "Are your other brothers coming to the party as well?"

"Pretty sure. Fitz lives in the city now, and John's always back and forth between here and Boston."

Kate smiled the way she usually did upon hearing the brothers' names all at once.

Kennedy, Jack, John, and Fitzgerald. There was little doubt in Kate's mind that if Diane and Roger Dawson had had a daughter, she'd have been a Jackie.

"He doesn't have anything on the calendar," Kate said, looking back at Jack, "but he might be on the phone."

"But there's no one in there with him?"

"No. Though he hates—"

"Interruptions. I know. I had the room next door to him in our teens." Jack wiggled his eyebrows, and she laughed again. "Point me to his office," Jack said, gesturing at the multitude of closed doors behind her. "I promise to tell him you put up a hell of a fight to keep me out, but I just strong-armed past all . . . fourteen pounds of you."

"Very rude to comment on a lady's weight," she said, unable to keep a straight face as she said it.

"True. Please don't tell my mother when you see her at the party. You will be there, right?"

"Yeah, though more as a party planner than a guest," she said, then hid a wince, hoping Jack wouldn't notice the slight snip in her voice.

No luck there. His eyebrows lifted, and he rested a hip on her desk. "*Whaaaat?* You mean Claudia wasn't able to plan a party for a hundred people while also juggling four charities? Well, color me shocked."

"So you've met her," Kate said with a knowing smile.

"No." He stood again. "Haven't had the pleasure. But we spoke on the phone a couple times, and it was . . . illuminating."

"She's very nice," Kate said, because it was true. Claudia was nice, which was more than she could say about some of Kennedy's past girlfriends. They all had the type of pedigree he seemed to find irresistible—old-money bloodlines, family ties to the mayor *and* governor—but Claudia was neither cool nor snobby.

Jack *tsk*ed. "Now, Kate. Just when I was starting to like you."

"Jack!"

Kate and Jack both turned to see a grinning Matt come toward them. "What the hell, man? I didn't know you were in town."

The two men man-hugged, and Jack caught Matt up on his new status as a New York resident.

"That's great. Kennedy know?"

"Does Kennedy know what?"

"And there he is," Jack said, turning to Kennedy, who'd emerged from his office. "I was just about to start banging down doors."

"Is that your usual way of doing business?" Despite the brotherly jab, Kennedy was smiling as he hugged Jack. "What are you doing here?" Kennedy asked, pulling back.

"Mostly chatting up your girl, Kate Winslet, here," Jack said, gesturing back at her.

Kennedy's smile slipped as he looked at Kate, his dimples disappearing. Because yes, by some weird twist of fate, an irritable grump of a man had been blessed with deep, matching dimples in each cheek when he smiled. Which was seldom, which meant said dimples rarely saw the light of day.

Kate gave Kennedy a finger-waggle wave to irritate him, and his jaw tensed. *Success.*

"Actually, I'm sort of . . . moving here," Jack said.

"Here?" Kennedy's gaze swung back to his brother.

"Well, not *this* neighborhood. I'm thinking something in the Village."

"I live in the Village!" Kate said.

"Yeah?" Jack turned back to her. "Which part?"

"Sort of the border between Greenwich and West; it depends who you ask."

"I'm asking you, and be very specific," Jack said. "The closer our places, the more times we can have *Titanic* movie parties."

"Still with the *Titanic* thing? Didn't that quit working in high school?" Kennedy said.

"I don't know. Kate, did it stop working in high school?"

"Seeing as I'm feeling quite fluttery, obviously not."

Jack turned to Kennedy and shrugged as though to say, *See?*

Kennedy scowled. Not at Jack but at her.

Kate scowled back as her phone started ringing. She picked it up and proceeded to listen as Ian's sweet, longtime, and very chatty client immediately began giving Kate a traffic report on the FDR.

Kennedy nodded for Jack to follow him toward his office, and Matt followed as well.

Jack turned back to Kate at the last moment and made an awkward charades gesture, as though clinging to something while his teeth chattered.

Kate covered the mouthpiece with her hand and mouthed, *I'll never let go, Jack.*

Kennedy looked between the two of them and then shoved his brother into his office.

And even as she was barraged by yet another unending string of phone calls, Kate found she couldn't stop smiling.

4

Thursday, March 28

"So," Jack said, placing the pad of his finger on Kennedy's globe and giving it an idle spin.

Kennedy made a sound of irritation. "It's not a basketball, man."

"Oh, spoiler alert," Matt said, snapping his fingers as though just remembering something to tell Jack. "Kennedy doesn't like when people touch his stuff."

"He never did," Jack said, dropping into a chair and putting his hands behind his head. "Which one of you wants to tell me what the deal is with Kate?"

Kennedy tensed slightly, because he knew his brother. He knew that tone. "What about her?"

Jack shrugged. "She's cute. Like a little tiger cub."

"Don't be an ass," Kennedy said.

"Actually," Matt said, "I think Kate would sort of love the comparison. A predatory cat? She'd be all over that. Or not," he muttered when Kennedy gave him a *shut the fuck up* look.

"She's my assistant. Leave her alone."

"She's *our* assistant," Matt corrected. "And she's single."

Kennedy gave his friend a look of irritation. "Jesus, Cannon, don't you have somewhere to be?"

"Not really. And I'm just saying, I saw them talking. They had chemistry."

Kennedy stared hard first at Matt, then at Jack. "It's Kate. She's off-limits."

"But she's not married. Is she straight?" he asked, glancing at Matt for confirmation.

Matt nodded, and Jack spread his hands to the sides. "Well, then. Nothing off-limits about that."

"We made a pact," Kennedy said, leaning forward. "Kate's off-limits."

"Who made the pact?" Jack asked.

"Cannon, Ian, and me."

"So not me," Jack said with irritating patience. "Right?"

"Sounds right," Matt chimed in.

Five minutes ago, Kennedy had been thrilled to see his brother. Jack did most of his business overseas, so Kennedy rarely saw him outside of holidays and occasional visits. He'd been even more thrilled to hear Jack was moving back to New York, and he was glad, truly. And yet . . .

Kennedy had seen what Matt had seen. More than that, he'd heard Kate's laugh. Kate had a sense of humor, but it was more of a facetious, witty humor, not a giggling humor.

But she'd been giggling at Jack.

Of course she was. That's what Jack did. He charmed the crap out of women. Easily. John, too, though his other brother had been decidedly less easygoing since his divorce last year. Hell, even Fitz, who'd always been a straight-up geek, had come out of his awkward years with more girlfriends in a month than Kennedy had in a year.

But Fitz and John weren't here. They weren't sniffing around Kate.

"Can you just . . . not?" Kennedy said, rubbing his forehead.

"Can I not what?"

"That *thing*. Where you make every woman in your current zip code revolve around you."

"What are you worried about?" Jack said, stretching his legs out in front of him, crossing his hands over his trim stomach. "It's not like I was flirting with your girl."

Like hell you weren't.

It took Kennedy an embarrassingly long moment to realize that Jack meant Claudia. *Claudia* was his girl. Not Kate.

"Besides, you're not exactly a repellent monk," Jack was saying. "For reasons I've never been able to quite grasp, women seem to flock to your brooding Heathcliff routine just as much as they do my Leo thing."

Kennedy scratched his temple. His brother wasn't entirely wrong. Kennedy had never struggled for female attention. He was fit, not awful to look at, and had more money, quite honestly, than he knew what to do with. And while his tastes tended toward classic, bordering even on old-fashioned, to his brother's point, women had always seemed to like that, too.

Most women. Not all. Definitely not Kate, who had called him stodgy once or twice to his face. Kate, who apparently preferred Jack's easy grins and lame *Titanic* references.

Kennedy looked at Matt for help and saw his friend was watching him carefully. Then Matt turned to Jack. "Look, for what it's worth, if you mess with Kate, I'll join Kennedy here in kicking your ass."

Jack held up his hands, palms out. "I get it. I promise not to drag her to my lair or whatever the hell it is you two seem to think it is I do to women. Good?"

Matt shrugged, and Kennedy forced himself to let the issue drop, if for nothing else than his own peace of mind.

To be fair, his brother was a good guy. Yeah, Jack had a larger than usual string of broken hearts behind him, but Kennedy also knew Jack never intentionally led women on. The guy didn't have the settle-down itch, and he let women know it up front.

Plus, Kate was too smart to fall for a guy who had short-term written all over him. The woman went to visit her parents in Jersey every other weekend and had a half dozen photos of her niece and nephew on her desk. Surely, she had intentions of settling down—

Kennedy frowned a little at the thought. Kate didn't seem to date much, but then again, Kennedy wasn't entirely sure he would know if she did. Matt and Ian always seemed to be the ones who knew those details about Kate, not him.

Still, if and when she did settle down, it'd be with some high school science teacher who told corny jokes, not Jack . . . who definitely told corny jokes. *Shit*.

"Where's your third musketeer?" Jack asked, interrupting Kennedy's thoughts.

"Ian? Well, let's see, it's four o'clock on a Thursday . . . I'm going to guess he's working. Some of us do that," Kennedy said.

"Actually, I'm pretty sure he and Lara are doing it in his office," Matt said.

Jack sat up straight. "Seriously?"

Matt shrugged. "Some of us do *that*."

Jack laughed, and Kennedy shifted slightly in his chair, trying not to look—and feel—like a disapproving old man. He wasn't a prude. Far from it. He just didn't fully grasp the concept of being so overwhelmed with lust that one couldn't wait until they were at home to have sex in as civilized—or uncivilized—a manner as one pleased.

There was a quick knock at the door, and Ian opened it before Kennedy's "come in."

Jack rose to greet him, and Kennedy listened with half an ear as they discussed who owed whom what after their poker game last summer.

All three of them actually owed Kennedy, but he didn't say so. He didn't need the money. None of them did. There was a reason he, Ian, and Matt were known as the "Wolfes" of Wall Street. They had a good deal more morals than the scam artists they were named after, and their partying had never veered toward the illegal hard stuff. But over the years, they'd had their fair share of late nights, dropped too many hundred-dollar bills on God knows what.

Kennedy wasn't ashamed of it, not really. The old work-hard-play-hard adage may as well have been written in the Wolfe Investments offices. Kennedy's family was old-money wealthy, but every dime he spent was his own, earned through determination, smarts, and long hours in this very chair.

But sometimes, at least lately, the whole thing had started to feel a little hollow. Mostly, Kennedy chalked it up to the fact that Ian and Matt had settled down with women so perfect for them that it was vaguely irritating to watch.

Not that he was jealous, but—well, hell. He *was*, a little. The two of them had always been wilder than Kennedy, and yet here he was, the tamest of the trio, feeling a little left behind.

His brother and friends had moved on to discuss when they could fit in a round of golf at Matt's club out in Connecticut, when Kate marched into his office, armed with a stack of messages.

She was wearing what he thought of as her work uniform—neutral slacks and a white blouse, one button undone to reveal only a hint of skin at the base of her throat. The woman was the literal definition of buttoned-up.

Kate began handing out sheets of paper. A couple of years ago, she'd implemented what she referred to as her "hybrid" system, a combination of old-school paper messages as well as an email conveying the same message. It was her way of ensuring their *I didn't get it* excuse didn't fly when she had to deal with the aftermath of whatever message they'd forgotten or ignored.

"Dave's called three times," she said, handing a sheet of paper to Ian. "He broke his TV. Again. Needs a replacement before 'the big one,' his words."

Kennedy smiled. Dave was Ian's rough-around-the-edges foster father who, while never having raised a hand to Ian, had a bad habit of losing his temper in the middle of whatever sporting event was currently on in front of him and breaking the television with a various arsenal of projectiles. Beer bottles, a basketball, the remote. Ian replaced each and every flat-screen with an ever bigger, improved model without question. To Ian's thinking, it was a small price to pay for Dave being the only man who'd given a troublemaking orphan even a hint of stability.

Ian sighed and took the paper. "I wonder if they have subscription models for televisions. You know, where Best Buy or some company can auto-replenish every month."

"I'll look into it," Kate said.

"I was kidding."

"I'll look into it," she repeated, handing a message to Matt. "Felicia called. Apparently, your mother's refusing to let her join her book club."

"Wait, my mom isn't keen on my dad's mistress joining her book club? *That's* weird. What's this?" Matt asked as Kate handed him another piece of paper.

She tapped a finger against the top of the paper. "A different book club. Carol Madigan is Joe's sister-in-law. She lives fifteen minutes from Felicia, and they've got a book club dedicated mostly to Scottish romance novels. I think she'll love it."

"Scottish romance novels," Jack said, looking a little in awe of Kate. "That's a thing?"

"Definitely. Men in kilts? Delightful," Kate said without looking up as she handed a piece of paper to Kennedy. "Claudia called. Said to remind you not to forget to keep Saturday afternoon open."

Damn. He was drawing a blank. "Remind me?"

"Her parents are back in town from Paris."

Kennedy groaned and closed his eyes. "Any chance I can get out of it?"

"No."

His eyes popped open in surprise, because the answer came not just from Kate but from the three guys as well.

"Seriously?" Kennedy asked. "This from you clowns? Ian, you once *literally* climbed a hedge to escape a woman you'd slept with. Matt, you took a city bus to avoid someone you thought you might have slept with. And Jack, don't even get me started with you and Carly Booker—"

"That was in the eleventh grade!" his brother protested.

"Point is, don't you think two months into the relationship is a little soon for the meet-the-parents?"

"She's met yours," Kate pointed out.

"Mine live uptown, and Claudia insisted. Hers have retired to eight different houses across Europe."

Kate shrugged. "Knickerbocker Hotel, three p.m. Saturday."

"Where?"

"It's on 42nd and Broadway."

This time, Kennedy's groan was even more heartfelt. *"Midtown?"*

"Wait, now hold on," Jack said, holding his chin and narrowing his eyes in a thinking face. "I always thought that Fitz was the baby of the family, but hearing you whine like that . . ."

Kennedy shot his brother the finger.

"Lovely," Kate said. "I'll leave you boys to whatever this is." She made a circling gesture at the four of them. "I'm heading out for the day. Alison from Fourth is manning my phone till five, but I'll keep an eye on email. Don't call my cell unless there's blood."

Kennedy, Ian, and Matt exchanged surprised looks. They had no issue with Kate making her own schedule, but leaving before five—hell, before seven—was unusual.

"Hot date?" Ian asked, his tone playful.

"Well . . ." She folded her hands in front of her. "It's been brought to my attention that I don't have much of a life outside the office aside from my friendships with Lara and Sabrina, and I'm not sure that even counts, since they're crazy enough to marry my bosses."

"Who said you didn't have a life?" Jack asked.

Kennedy flinched, still regretting his careless words from the other evening. He kept meaning to apologize, but the moment never seemed quite right.

His brother saw his reaction and smirked. "Ah. All caught up."

"Anyway," Kate said primly, "I've decided to take a me day. Well, a me afternoon."

"A what now?" Matt asked.

"I'm going to The Plaza for a glass of champagne, then shopping at Bergdorf, then getting my hair done." She counted on her fingers, and Kennedy knew she had the time at each stop planned down to the minute.

"Spontaneous," Matt teased.

"Baby steps," she said lightly, though Kennedy could have sworn he noticed the slightest pause, as though Matt's teasing had struck a nerve.

"Remember," she said, pointing around the room. "Tell Allison if you need anything. Only call me if one of you kills the other, and there's blood to clean up."

"Out of curiosity, who do you think would be the offed and who would be the off*er*?" Matt asked.

"You three, dead," she said, pointing to Jack, Matt, and Ian. "Him, guilty." She pointed at Kennedy.

"Hey," he said, affronted. "Why am I the serial killer?"

She shrugged. "You're so pent-up all of the time. I figure it has to eventually come out, and when it does, it'll be in a big way." Then Kate turned on her heel and swiftly left his office.

Kennedy just stared after her.

"She has a point," Jack said. "You're very—"

"Shut up," Kennedy muttered. "Just shut up."

5

"So what are we thinking? Just a trim or . . . ?"

The way the chic platinum-haired stylist picked up a lock of Kate's hair and then let it fall limply back to Kate's shoulder said it all. She needed more than a trim, and not because her hair was particularly damaged. She didn't color it, and she didn't have the time, inclination, or know-how to properly wield a curling iron or blow-dryer to make it look better than how it was:

Blah.

Her hair was blah.

In fact . . . Kate gave herself a critical once-over in the salon mirror. *Everything* about her was blah. Blah blue sweater that was neither pastel nor bright but just sort of a medium blue that was—wait for it—blah. Same went for the black slacks, the brown eyeliner—Hold up. Kate looked closer. Nope, she'd forgotten the eyeliner today.

Her fingers itched to text Sabrina or Lara. What were girlfriends for if not moral support when undertaking a mini makeover? But she'd stubbornly left her phone in her bag. She couldn't explain why, but she needed to do this by herself, for herself. Lara and Sabrina, because they were the best of friends, armed with the best of intentions, would probably tell Kate that she was perfect just the way she was. That she didn't need the eyeliner, the haircut, or a wardrobe refresh.

But Kate already knew all of that. Of course she didn't need any of that. Of course she wasn't lesser just because she wasn't glamorous. Kate knew who she was, and she liked who she was, even if Kennedy Freaking Dawson had dismissed her as *hardly irresistible*.

Not to him, maybe. But one day Kate would meet a guy who *did* find her irresistible, just as she was.

Regardless, that wasn't why Kate was doing any of this. Today's shopping and salon escapade wasn't about men. It was about Kate and the fact that she was itching for a change. It was the same itch she'd gotten a few years earlier. She'd scratched it then by going to business school, financed by a very generous Ian.

Kate had gotten her MBA, which resulted in a title upgrade from administrative assistant to office administrator, as well as the corresponding pay increase. But more important, she'd felt like a new, changed woman.

It hadn't occurred to her that the luster of getting her MBA could ever dull, but here she was again with that same itch. And though a haircut was a poor comparison to a master's degree, her gut told her a fresh look was exactly what she needed. As a starting point, anyway.

She met the stylist's gaze in the mirror. "Can you just make it . . . better?"

Brianna grinned. "How short are you willing to go?"

"Eh, don't go crazy," Kate said. "I had a very ill-advised pixie cut once. Let's just say I do not have the bone structure to pull that off."

"Oh, I think you do," Brianna mused, lifting Kate's hair away from her face and studying her. "But don't worry, I think we can keep it long and still remove some of the weight. You also booked a color. What are you thinking there?"

"I'm thinking that I want to stay a brunette, but I'd love if my hair was something other than Hershey's-bar brown. Especially since it's not even the Hershey's Special Dark variety of chocolate," she said grumpily, glaring at her hair. "It's like the milk chocolate kind you put on s'mores, because it's too boring on its own."

Brianna patted her shoulder. "Trust me. I know exactly what you want. I'm going to go mix some color. Can I get you a magazine?"

"Yes please," Kate said. "Maybe something with a beauty section and makeup tips?"

If she was going to freshen up her look . . . might as well go all the way.

◆ ◆ ◆

"Oh my gosh, I'm so glad you called," Sabrina said, plucking a lipstick tube off the counter, winding it up to study the color, then winding it back down again when she saw it was a violent orange shade. "Nobody knows their way around this city's cosmetic counters like I do."

"You know you can buy all of this stuff online. Free shipping," Lara said, tapping her nail against a foundation bottle.

"Which normally I'd do," Kate said, giving an overwhelmed glance around the cosmetics department. "But I confess, with this stuff, I don't know where to start."

Yes, she'd ended up calling her friends after all. She'd managed just fine on the hair front. Thanks to Brianna's skill, Kate felt like a whole new woman. Somehow the stylist had managed to leave Kate with her trademark long locks, but her hair was shinier, straighter, and seemed to move *with* Kate instead of just sort of hanging there. The color, too, was exactly what she'd wanted. There was no crazy change, no too-light streaks, just a little bit of something to make Kate's natural color look richer.

But then Kate had hit up the cushy department store for stage two of her mini makeover, with the intent of splurging on high-end lipstick, because . . . how hard could that be?

Hard, apparently.

Normally, Kate walked into Sephora and picked up the same beige-pink lipstick she'd been wearing since her very first post-college interview. The brown liner that she sometimes wore, sometimes forgot, was drugstore variety and suited her just fine—when she could remember it.

Today, though, she'd wanted something different, wanted to change it up.

Turns out, too much selection was not always a good thing, and she had found herself overwhelmed by all of the options.

"Okay, what are we thinking?" Sabrina said, surveying the dozens of counters. "Something to go with the new hair, obviously."

"Which I can't get over," Lara said reverently. "How do you get it to swing like that?"

"Money," Kate said, trying not to think too long or hard on how much damage the style had cost her credit card. "And enjoy it while it lasts, because there are no guarantees I'll ever be able to get it to look this way again."

"You could always do a ponytail like I do," Lara said.

Kate and Sabrina exchanged a look.

"Sweetie," Sabrina said, tugging Lara's hair. "You realize you can pull off this cheerleader pony because you have seven times more hair than normal, right? The rest of us only wear this style to Pilates or to wash our face because *our* ponytail looks about like what you probably shed in the shower."

"Most disgusting visual ever," Lara said, and Kate nodded in agreement. "Besides, your hair's fabulous."

"Because I know what works for me," Sabrina said, touching a hand to the sleek knot of dark hair at the nape of her neck. "And I know exactly what makeup works for Kate. This way, pet."

Kate and Lara dutifully followed after Sabrina, who walked with the confident side-to-side sashay of a woman who *was* irresistible and knew it.

"So what brought this on?" Lara asked casually. Too casually.

Kate gave her friend a knowing look as Sabrina began rattling off something about warm pinks to a saleswoman at the Chanel counter. "You know that doesn't work with me."

"What?" Lara pushed her glasses up her nose.

"The *I'm just a curious little thing asking harmless questions* routine that makes you so good at your job," Kate said. Lara had recently joined the FBI's New York white-collar division and was already climbing the ranks at record speed.

Lara laughed. "Sorry. Habit. Since you're my friend and not a suspect, I'll ask straight up. Are you okay? I'm all for self-pampering and feeling gorgeous, but I've always known you to be more of a cherry ChapStick kind of gal. I've also seen you use a chip clip to tie your hair back."

"One time," Kate said, holding up her finger. "I did that one time. And I washed the clip after."

"Fair enough. So you just wanted a change?"

"Yes, exactly," Kate said, grateful her friend got it. "I promise if I find myself in some sort of deep-rooted crisis, I'll tell you, but this really, truly is just me itching to change something up, and my hair and makeup seemed like a good place to start."

"And clothes," Sabrina said, waving a tube of mascara over her shoulder without turning around. "Don't think I'm not coming along for the wardrobe part of this party!"

Kate leaned toward Lara. "I did do the right thing asking you guys to join, right?"

Lara linked arms with her and nudged her toward the counter. "Considering I'll make sure we go get a glass of wine *before* Sabrina has her new-clothes way with you, yes. Yes, you did."

6

"You going to turn that glare on me if I say happy birthday, old man?" Sabrina Cross said, approaching a glowering Kennedy.

Kennedy moved his eyes to his right without turning his head. "Probably not."

"What if I tell you that the ice sculpture is just the spitting image of you? Though I think they overdid it on the biceps . . ."

Kennedy made an exaggerated show of looking around the crowded rooftop of the Knickerbocker Hotel.

"Who are you looking for?"

"Your husband. I don't want him to see me pushing you off the roof."

Sabrina laughed and linked a slender arm with his, lifting her other hand to take a sip of her champagne. "Let's just stand here for a minute and pretend we're in a riveting conversation so that we don't have to make small talk."

"You're good at small talk."

"I am," she agreed. "*You're* not, unless it's one of your clients. Most of whom are in attendance, I noticed."

"I think half of Manhattan's in attendance," Kennedy said, not bothering to hide his annoyance.

"There's the birthday spirit," she said sarcastically.

He looked down at her dark head. "Thanks for coming."

A smile played on her lips. "Better."

She looked up, presenting Kennedy with one of the more objectively beautiful faces he'd ever seen. More important, he actually liked Sabrina and always had. She was a longtime friend of Ian's, their friendship dating back to their rougher days in Philly, before they'd reconnected in Manhattan at the top of their games—he as a BSD of Wall Street, she as New York City's most notorious and sought-after fixer, a woman who could make just about any problem go away. For a price.

But stunning as the woman was, and as much as he enjoyed her company, there'd never been even a spark of anything resembling chemistry between them. Probably because all of the chemistry in the room—any room—had been consumed by Matt and Sabrina until they'd finally given in to the inevitable and hooked up last year, giving everyone in their orbit relief from observational blue balls.

Sabrina had married Matt this past New Year's Eve, and though she had opted not to take his name (something about the Sabrina Cross brand being legendary), she'd taken Matt's heart full stop and given hers right back. It was sort of nice to see, albeit in a slightly nauseating way.

Sabrina lifted her champagne flute to get someone's attention, and a moment later, Matt joined them, carrying two Manhattans, one of which he placed in Kennedy's hand. "Thought you might need this."

"Why's that?" Kennedy said, taking a sip of the whiskey cocktail.

"Because you're lurking in the corner of the room at your own party with someone else's wife."

"Oh, but we were in *riveting* conversation," Sabrina said. "Did it not look riveting?"

"You looked like you wanted to rip my clothes off, and Kennedy looked like he wanted to throw himself backward over the ledge."

"Actually, he was going to push me over the ledge," Sabrina said.

Matt nodded. "I could see that." He gave Kennedy an assessing look. "Are you going to throw *me* off the roof if I ask where your girlfriend is?"

"Great question," Kennedy grumbled. "I should probably go find her."

"She *did* pull out all the stops," Matt said.

Understatement.

Kennedy looked around at his over-the-top surroundings, seeing a bit more clearly now that the irritation—surprise, he meant surprise—of the unexpected party had faded slightly. He supposed he should have seen it coming. Claudia had been jumpy all afternoon. He'd chalked it up to nervousness over introducing her boyfriend to her parents. Had he been paying closer attention, he'd like to think he'd have seen the signs. Maybe then he'd have been at least a little prepared and managed more than an under-the-breath "Jesus" when one hundred of his closest and not-so-close friends had shouted "Surprise!" when he and Claudia had stepped off the elevator into the St. Cloud bar.

He appreciated the effort. He did. It was just that the Dawsons usually treated birthdays with a quiet, dignified nod to the coming year. A special dinner when they were kids. A nice bottle of scotch when they'd hit drinking age. He thought everyone in his inner circle knew he liked quiet birthdays.

He didn't mind getting older, but he sure as hell didn't want to celebrate another year with ice sculptures and cocktail servers and . . .

"Are those oysters?" Kennedy asked, finally noticing the elaborate raw bar set up to his left.

"Your favorite," Ian said, clamping him on the shoulder as he and Lara joined them. "Maybe you'll die."

Kennedy ignored his friend and bent to kiss the cheek of Ian's better half.

"Happy birthday, old man," Lara said, squeezing his hand.

"Why do people keep calling me that? I think I liked you better when you were an SEC agent out to put Ian in jail. At least then you were polite to me."

"Actually, it's a good thing when she's rude to you," Ian said. "She's unfailingly polite to people she doesn't really like."

"That isn't true!" Lara protested, adjusting her glasses and glaring at Ian.

Ian pointed his Negroni—a bitter red cocktail that was his trade-mark drink of choice—in the direction of the partygoers. "Really? I think you nearly knocked over Claudia's parents just now with your eyelash fluttering."

"Okay, well, they were snobby," Lara said. "No offense, Kennedy."

"None taken." Claudia hadn't been entirely lying about the night involving him meeting her parents. The Palmers were at the party, and Lara was right—they were snobby. Granted, *his* parents could be labeled as such, too. But his parents had a cool, sort of reserved snob-bery that thawed once you got to know them. The Palmers were openly snobby. The sort of name-dropping, gossip-hungry social climbers who Kennedy hated the most.

"Oh, Kennedy." Lara tapped his arm with the base of her wineglass. "Before I forget, if you get hungry, there's a table on the far side of the room with little roast-beef slider things. Since, you know . . ." She waved at the shellfish bar.

Kennedy nodded, relieved. He hadn't eaten since breakfast, having expected an early dinner with Claudia's parents. Plus, roast beef was his favorite. Bonus if there was extra-hot horseradish sauce on the side.

"Thanks," he said. "Guess that's what I get for not mentioning to Claudia that I'm allergic to oysters."

"Oh, she knew," Sabrina replied, the slightest edge in her tone.

"No, I don't think I ever mentioned it to her," Kennedy said, feeling the need to defend his girlfriend. "It's obnoxious when people unneces-sarily announce allergies, like those people who essentially introduce themselves as gluten intolerant, as though anyone needs to know that. Just don't order the damn thing."

"Oh no, she *definitely* knew," Lara said, backing up Sabrina. "Kate told her."

"Why would Kate and Claudia—" Kennedy broke off as he put the pieces together. "*That's* why Claudia's been in the office the past couple weeks."

"Took you long enough," Matt said into his drink.

"What did you think she and Kate were doing in the conference room all of those times?" Ian asked. "We thought for sure you'd figure it out."

He should have. How had he not connected his upcoming birthday with Claudia's repeated visits to the office with that little notebook in hand?

Kennedy ran a hand through his hair. "I don't know. It wouldn't be the first time a woman's used Kate to try to get the inside track on us."

"*I* never did," Sabrina protested.

"That's because it's your job to know everything about everyone," Lara said. "I totally did."

Ian glanced down in surprise. "You did?"

"Try to get the scoop on you, your romantic status, your entire life history from Kate? Hell yeah, I did," Lara said without repentance.

"Did she spill?"

Lara shrugged. "She told me what I needed to know. Just like she told Claudia what *she* needed to know."

"Yes, and look how well Claudia listened," Matt said cheerfully, pointing at the elaborate display of shellfish.

"It's not a big deal," Kennedy said.

And it wasn't a big deal, truly. Sure, it was a little odd. Crab cakes and shrimp cocktail, he could understand. He didn't expect people to forgo all seafood just because he was allergic to shellfish. However, he saw his friends' point. The raw bar was clearly the focus of the evening's food options.

But he couldn't really bring himself to care, because . . .

"Where is she?"

Sabrina pointed. "Two o'clock. Talking with the Sams."

He followed Sabrina's gesture, then winced, not only because the sight of his newish girlfriend chatting it up with his bosses was a little unnerving but because he hadn't been talking about Claudia. And he saw from the way Matt and Ian exchanged a look that they knew it.

Kennedy knew it wasn't fair to be annoyed, and certainly not to feel hurt, that Kate wasn't here. But when he stepped off that elevator and had been barraged by the shouts of surprise, and happy birthday, and drunken *did you see his face?* proclamations, he'd scanned the room for the one person who centered him. Instinctively, he'd sought Kate out, because Kate was steady in a world that was so often ridiculous. But she hadn't been there.

Because she wasn't here.

Ian glanced down at Lara. "What time did you say Kate was getting here?"

Kennedy's gaze snapped to Ian, both irritated and relieved his friend had read his mind.

Lara tilted Ian's watch face toward her. "It should be any minute now. She said she needed to run home to change, but that shouldn't have taken this long."

"Change from what?"

"Poor thing was here at, like, ten a.m. setting everything up," Sabrina chimed in. "She couldn't very well be overseeing your girlfriend's oyster feast in cocktail attire, so she had to go home and change. We ladies don't wake up like this, you know."

"So true," Matt said. "You should see this one." He mimed a cloud around his head and mouthed, *Huge.*

Sabrina shrugged and pointed to her sleek dark hair. "It's true. The miracle of heat tools, ladies and gentlemen."

Sabrina may be one of his good friends, but he didn't give a crap about her hair. He wanted to know why the hell his assistant had wasted her Saturday setting up his birthday party.

"This isn't part of Kate's job," he said. "It's not what we pay her for. What the hell was she thinking?"

"Kennedy," Lara warned quietly, just as Matt said, "Moron," a little less quietly.

"What? I just mean—"

"Dude." Ian interrupted Kennedy sharply and jerked his head for Kennedy to turn around.

He stilled, knowing even before he turned who he'd find standing there. *Kate.* Kennedy turned to face her, ready to explain that he hadn't meant it like that. That he didn't expect—didn't *want*—her being his girlfriend's unpaid assistant . . .

The explanation died on his lips.

"Damn, girl," Sabrina said as she went to hug Kate.

Kennedy couldn't have said it better himself. Kate looked . . . different. He gave her a once-over, trying to put his finger on what had changed, but it seemed to be a little of everything. Her dress was hardly scandalous. It showed off toned shoulders and was cut diagonally, revealing plenty of her right thigh. She was still short, but the stiletto heels gave her a few inches he wasn't accustomed to, the silver shoes wrapping around trim ankles that were . . .

Kennedy swallowed and dragged his eyes back up again, careful not to let his gaze linger on her small but definitely *there* breasts.

Her hair was mostly the same, but it looked extra shiny, and instead of overwhelming her small features, it seemed to accentuate them, calling attention to the glossy, full lips, the pink cheeks, the . . . angry eyes.

There she was. That was still the same.

"Kennedy. Happy birthday." Her tone was cool, at odds with the fire in her brown eyes.

"Kate. I understand I have you to thank for the party."

"Oh gosh, no." She looked vaguely appalled. "I mean, Claudia asked for my help with the organization, because, well, I'm awesome at it. But this was all her."

Kennedy nodded. Not that he didn't appreciate Claudia's good intentions, but he was relieved, somehow, to know that Kate got him. That she understood he'd have much preferred a different type of party—or none at all.

"Can we talk about the dress?" Lara said, twirling her finger, indicating for Kate to spin. "It's fantastic! Even more fantastic than it was in the dressing room. Ian, doesn't she look fantastic?"

"Fantastic," he repeated with a wink at Kate, who blew him a kiss.

Kennedy frowned at this, too busy trying to wrap his head around this new version of Kate. "When—? What—?" He cleared his throat. "You look different."

"Nice," Matt muttered.

"She got her hair cut Thursday, remember? She left early?" Ian mimed snipping motions with his fingers.

"Right." Kennedy had forgotten the strange anomaly of Kate leaving before eight p.m., much less five p.m. And he'd been out of the office most of the day yesterday on the trading floor, and then at a few off-site meetings.

Besides, it was a hell of a lot more than a haircut. Kate was . . . *arresting*. And he couldn't look away.

"You guys going to be here for a bit?" Kate asked. "I'm going to go get a cocktail."

"I'll get it," Ian and Matt said at the same time.

Kennedy had the oddest urge to slap them. Or himself. Why did he not offer? He normally would have for any other woman. But with

Kate he was never at his best. Even less so, apparently, when he could see her thigh.

"Nope, stay here," Kate ordered, already moving away. "I want to check on a few of the vendors, make sure they didn't ignore my demands. Requests," she amended quickly. "Also, I have a private bet with myself to see exactly how long that stupid ice sculpture will last."

"Oh, thank God that wasn't your suggestion," Sabrina said with relief.

"Offensive," Kate said, waving her finger at Sabrina. "Very offensive that you'd even consider it could be mine."

Kate continued walking away, and the rest of the group began placing bets among themselves on the fate of the ice sculpture.

"What do you think?" Matt asked Kennedy. "How long until that frosty jawline of yours becomes a puddle?"

"I bet a hundred bucks the frown will be the last to go," Lara said.

"I don't think anyone would take that bet," Ian said.

"Will you excuse me a moment?" Kennedy asked, too distracted to respond to their ribbing. He walked away before any of them could reply.

The pink of Kate's dress made her easy to spot in a sea of the usual New York black. She was talking to a server carrying a tray of champagne, who nodded at something she said. Kate was on the move again before Kennedy could reach her, and he followed her across the room to a table, where she spoke to a burly man behind it wearing a chef hat and holding a carving knife.

He reached her just as the man handed her a plate with a slice of damn good-looking roast beef. "Thanks, Larry."

"My pleasure," the man said in a voice higher than Kennedy would have expected for someone built like a linebacker. "You know, this is the first time I've worked the USDA prime beef carving station at a dedicated slider bar, but it seems to be a big hit."

"Yeah, well, the birthday boy's got a thing for French dip sandwiches. This is the closest I could get while still counting it as cocktail-party-friendly finger food."

Kennedy froze. She knew his favorite food?

Kate picked up a roll, then pointed at one of the bowls of sauces. "Is that the extra-hot horseradish or regular?"

"One on the left is hot; right is regular. The little signs labeling them had a Chardonnay-related incident. Someone's getting replacement cards now."

"Perfect," Kate said, dolloping a small scoop of the sauce on the right onto her plate. "Regular for me. Who needs the assault on the senses with the hot stuff?"

"It wakes you up," Kennedy said.

Kate looked over her shoulder, not looking the least bit rattled by his presence as she sucked a bit of sauce off her thumb. "Oh. Hey. What wakes you up?"

He nodded at the dishes. "The extra-hot horseradish sauce."

"Oh, right. The devil sauce," she said, taking a napkin off the table. "Listen, Kate, I—"

"Kennedy! There you are!" He turned toward the interruption and saw Claudia coming his way, dressed in a short navy dress that showed an impressive look at her long legs. He'd thought the dress slightly overkill when he'd thought they were just going to an early dinner with her parents, but it made sense for a party at a trendy rooftop bar.

Strange that a brief glimpse at a sliver of Kate's thigh resonated with him more than the near entirety of his girlfriend's legs.

"Hi, Kate!" Claudia said with a friendly smile before turning to Kennedy. "I've been looking everywhere for you! I should have known the second we walked in, we'd both be swooped into the crowd. I feel like I've barely seen you."

She pressed her mouth to his, and Kennedy dutifully pecked back.

"You love it, right? Tell me you love the party. Kate warned me surprises weren't your thing, but *everyone* says that, and I thought, *What the hell.* You do like it, right?"

Kennedy caught the note of nervousness in her voice and smiled to reassure her. "Of course I like it. Thank you. I was actually just about to dive in to this spread." He gestured at the carving table.

Claudia glanced over. "Right! That was Kate's idea."

Kate lifted her slider in silent acknowledgment, her cheeks full of the sandwich.

"You know I don't really like red meat, but Kate said you were allergic to shellfish, and we had to feed you something, so . . . good?"

"Yeah. Really good." As he said it, he looked at Kate, who merely watched him as she chewed.

"Okay, let's go take a pic with Mom and Dad really quick, 'kay? Then you can dig in and eat all of the roast beef you want, promise. Do you think your parents would be in it?"

"You want a picture of . . . both our parents?" Kennedy asked, trying to ignore the faint warning bell in the back of his head.

"Are you kidding? They'd *love* it," said the very last person Kennedy wanted to see right now.

"Hey, Jack," he said as his brother draped an arm around his shoulders and clinked the neck of his beer bottle against Kennedy's cocktail.

"Happy birthday, big bro. Did he tell you we're all embarrassingly close in age?" Jack asked Claudia. "Kennedy is thirty-six, John's thirty-four, I'm thirty-two, and baby Fitz will be thirty next month. Our parents were *busy*, am I right?"

"Can we not?" Kennedy said, his appetite fading. "Also, let's not forget that of the four of us, *you* were the only accident."

"Happy accident," Jack said, unfazed as he took a sip of beer. "Very happy for everyone." He glanced over, then did a double take, his smile turning flirty. "Well, well. If it isn't Kate Winslet."

"You've got till midnight," she said, swallowing, then taking another bite of sandwich.

"Till what?"

"Till the *Titanic* references expire."

"Chicks dig it, Smalls."

"I'll definitely take Smalls over Winslet." She smiled at Jack, who smiled back, and Kennedy looked between the two of them, slightly aghast. *Nicknames?* No. Just no.

Claudia tugged his arm. "One picture, babe, I promise."

"Yeah, *babe*. Don't worry," Jack said as Claudia started to pull Kennedy away. "I'll keep Smalls company."

Yeah. That's exactly what I'm afraid of.

7

The dress? A hit. The new hairstyle? Pretty darn good, given that it was Kate's first time styling her hair herself without the superpowers of the salon's blow-dryer.

The shoes? A massive failure. She was no stranger to high heels, but she usually had a two-and-a-half, maybe three-inch limit, and she'd decked out all of her work stilettos with about fifteen different cushions to prevent blisters and the agonizing pain of her current situation.

Kate rested her elbows on the cement railing perched several stories above ever-bustling 42nd Street and tried to look casual as she shifted her weight from one foot to the other, giving each foot its break in turn.

A seat would have been preferable, but since this was a cocktail party instead of a seated dinner, chairs were limited, and a woman sitting alone on a chair rubbing her feet was just a little sad. At least this way she could pretend to be looking at the view.

And there was nothing sad about her evening, thank you very much. In fact, it was the best party she'd been to in a long, long time.

Kate was never a wallflower, per se, but even when she was in the middle of things, she often *felt* on the periphery. She was well aware that she wasn't the one who sparkled. She was the one who always had a bobby pin, a safety pin, a breath mint, to make sure other people sparkled.

Tonight, though, she'd felt at least a *little* sparkly. Whether it was the pink dress itself or the confidence she'd felt when she walked into the room, for the first time in her life, she'd felt like people *saw* her. And though she hadn't been able to resist keeping an eye out to make sure everything went smoothly, she did so because she wanted to, not because she had nothing else to do and no one else to talk to.

Tonight, everyone had seemed to want to talk to her, not just her circle of friends. It was . . . nice.

Kate always enjoyed her friend circle, but she was also sensitive to the fact that she was a fifth wheel. Seventh wheel, if you counted Kennedy and Claudia, though she preferred not to. She loved spending time with Lara and Sabrina. And with Matt, Ian, and Kennedy. But with all of them together, Kate couldn't help but feel apart somehow. And maybe just a tiny bit jealous.

Tonight, though, she'd felt like part of a unit, with Jack Dawson of all people.

Kate was no dummy. She knew Kennedy's brother had heartbreaker written all over him. The man was so charming it should be illegal, and she'd watched as one woman after another had gone literally breathless when he'd spoken to them.

And yet he'd stayed with her almost the entire evening, up until his father had dragged him away to talk to Something Something the Fourth, and Kate had politely begged off in the name of sore feet.

More surprisingly, Jack had seemed to stay with her all night because he wanted to, not because he needed her to fix something for him or solve a problem. He seemed to *like* her, just as she liked him. He was easy to be around. And yet . . .

A large male figure came up beside her, suited arms resting on the railing beside hers. "What's with the stork routine?"

She turned her head to look at Kennedy. "The what?"

He lifted one foot, then the other. "Stork."

"*You* try wearing these shoes."

He glanced down knowingly. "Ah. We could sit?"

Her stomach did something stupid at his use of the word *we*. "Nah, I'm good. Plus, I tried that for about two minutes, but every time someone came to talk to me, I either had to stand or crane my neck."

"You're short. Don't you always have to crane your neck?"

She let out a little laugh and dropped her head forward as she muttered, "You look nice, Kate. Thanks for being here, Kate."

"What?"

She turned slightly to face him. "Nothing. Do you need something?"

He scowled. "Why is that your assumption?"

"Because I'm your assistant."

"You're my friend."

"Am I?" she said, more to herself than him, as she turned back to the view below the balcony.

He touched her elbow briefly, and she felt a corresponding tingle in her palm. "You don't think we're friends?"

"I don't know what we are, Kennedy."

He turned toward her. Studied her. "We're different, huh?"

"You and me?" She turned slightly toward him, trying to figure out what was behind his strange mood.

He lifted his shoulders. "Me and Jack."

"Definitely," she said with a laugh.

He looked away, and she had the uncomfortable sensation that maybe she'd hurt his feelings.

"The world only needs one Jack," she replied softly.

He searched her face. "You two were pretty inseparable all night."

She didn't pretend not to know what he was talking about but kept her answer vague. "Not really."

"What's that mean?"

"I don't really know," Kate admitted. "He'd mention a restaurant we both wanted to try or an exhibit we both wanted to see, and he kept saying things like, 'We should go!' But I couldn't tell if he meant it as a date or was just being polite."

Kennedy turned and faced the railing again, his turn to study the street below. "Probably a date," he said. "Though for what it's worth, he's lying if he says he's excited about museum exhibits. They're not his thing."

"Well, maybe you could lend him your season tickets," she teased. She knew Kennedy loved his museums.

He rewarded her with a half smile that revealed his left dimple. "Never."

"Nerd."

"They're underappreciated," he said, his tone a little gruff, as though embarrassed but unable to keep from defending New York's museums.

"They are," Kate agreed, deciding to give him a break. "It kills me how often they're derided as tourist traps. So many locals take them for granted."

"But not you?" he asked skeptically.

"Well, I'm not going to start collecting globes and crap like you, but yeah . . . I do love a good museum," she said. Kate didn't have a specific passion for art, or history, or science. She just liked knowing that museums existed. She liked the feeling of stepping outside New York to a different world, whether it be Impressionist paintings, quirky modern art, or the planetarium, all without actually leaving New York. "Our secret?"

"That we're cultured?"

She laughed. "*I'm* cultured. You're pretentious."

"Prove it."

"That you're pretentious?" she asked, excited at the prospect. "Where to begin. Let's see, you always—"

He stopped her words, not with a retort or even the usual scowl but by reaching out and setting his fingers against her mouth.

They both froze, and her eyes flew to his. It wasn't a caress, but neither was it a playful shut-up kind of gesture. It was somewhere in between, his three middle fingers resting lightly over her mouth, his pinkie finger brushing against her jaw, softly, as if by accident.

He met her eyes for only a second before his gaze dropped to his fingers. He frowned slightly, as though puzzled to find himself touching her. But he couldn't be half as puzzled as she was.

Or as electrified.

Slowly, Kennedy let his hand drop, his fist clenching hard and fast, so quickly she thought she'd imagined it, before he resumed his former position, casually, as though nothing had happened at all. "I didn't mean list the ways I'm pretentious. I meant tell me the ways you're cultured."

"Ah." She tried to gather her thoughts, but she could still feel the warmth of his touch. Wanted to replay it a thousand times over. Wanted to ask her friends what the heck it had meant . . .

He'd asked her something. What was it? Right, culture.

"I used to dance."

He gave her a skeptical look.

"Ballet," she clarified, "until I was seventeen and decided I didn't want it badly enough to go all the way. I probably wasn't talented enough, either. But I still love it. I'd go more often if it wasn't so expensive."

"I didn't know that about you."

She shrugged. She doubted Matt or Ian did, either. "It's not your job to know things about me. It's mine to know things about you."

He was quiet for a moment, looking thoughtful. "What else?"

"Um . . ." She bit her lip and considered. "I love old books. I mostly just read classics on my Kindle, because my apartment's too small to keep much of anything. Someday, though, I'm going to have a collection of first editions. Or second or third editions. Whatever. But, I should be honest, I'm also really into young adult books. If it's for a teen, I love it. If it's got a vampire or an alien and a love story, I really love it. Go ahead. Judge."

He leaned toward her and spoke quietly, pointing at himself. "Spy novels."

She gasped in mock horror. "No. *You?* Who quotes Shakespeare?"

He gave another of his half smiles. Left dimple again. "What else?"

"I play chess. I played every weekend with my grandfather, and then every day when he lived with us while I was in high school."

"You guys still play?"

"No, he's passed now," she said a little wistfully. She hadn't thought about those quiet nights with a chessboard and an old soul in ages.

Kennedy was silent, then turned his head over his shoulder for a moment, scanning the slowly dwindling crowd. "You have to do anything else for the party?"

"What do you mean?" she asked, confused and a little disappointed by the change in subject. It was one of the more civil, enjoyable conversations they'd ever had.

"Paying vendors, whatever."

"Oh. No, Claudia's supposed to take care of that part, and it'll be a while yet. There're still fifty or so people. But I should probably—"

"Get your coat."

Kate blinked. "What?"

He straightened. "Your jacket."

"I don't have one."

He frowned. "It's March, not August."

"No, really? I had no idea. Is there a way to know such things?"

"Shut up. Come on."

"Come on where?"

He turned away without answering.

"Come on where?" she said louder.

Finally, she huffed, realizing he wasn't going to turn around or answer.

She followed him through the still-crowded room, just as the elevator doors opened. He held them with his arm and gestured her in.

"You're being weird," she muttered, but did as instructed, curious and feeling oddly exhilarated.

On the ground floor, he led her across the hotel lobby, but she balked a little when he headed to the exit. "We can't leave."

"Sure we can. It's my birthday."

"But your party's up there. Claudia—"

"Claudia didn't ask what I wanted to do to celebrate my birthday. If she had, you know what I would've said?" he asked, taking a step closer to her.

Kate shook her head, wide-eyed.

"I'd have said that I wanted a quiet night with someone I didn't have to talk to. Or that I could, but not party talk. Real talk."

She tried to follow. "Okay. I can see that. But you have friends upstairs, and—"

Kennedy grabbed her hand and pulled her through the revolving doors into the spring evening. The wall of midtown noise immediately enveloped them, but in a comfortable, anonymous sort of way.

"There is exactly one good thing about this part of town. You know what it is?"

"The library?" she asked.

"Okay, two things."

"Grand Central?"

"Fine. There are a few things," he said as they crossed Sixth Avenue.

"Bryant Park?" she asked as he led her onto the large square lawn that sat in the shadow of the famous New York Public Library. The park was nice and all, but she was failing to see why he'd be excited about it outside of Christmastime, when the whole thing turned into a sort of winter wonderland.

He didn't reply, instead leading her toward the southwest side to a covered area with . . .

Kate gasped at the beautiful sight of chessboards set up in the middle of the city. "How did I not know this was here?"

Kennedy led her to a small table. "Want to play?"

"Hell yes!" she said, grinning as he went to rent pieces and a board.

A few moments later, they were sitting across the table from each other, and Kate realized there was something better than a chess oasis in the middle of Manhattan.

Kennedy Dawson's *full* smile. Both dimples.

8

Kennedy felt a little absurd, enjoying himself as much as he was in this moment.

Not because he didn't love chess. But if anyone had asked before today, he'd have said that his love of chess was more about the circumstances under which he typically played. Usually he was in the comfort of his living room, in his custom-made Italian leather chair. He played with hand-carved wooden chess pieces passed down to the eldest Dawson son for four generations. His partner was typically his eccentric, elderly neighbor, Edmund, who brought excellent scotch and even better chess skills.

This evening, however, was proving him wrong. As it would turn out, Kennedy apparently preferred playing chess outside on a slightly too-cold evening, on a wobbly table in a public park, with slightly sticky pieces, including a knight whose head had been lopped off, sitting across the board from . . .

Kate Henley.

Kennedy sat back in his chair and rubbed a hand idly over his jaw as he watched his playing partner. Kate took her time deliberating each move, but he didn't mind. He kept himself occupied by studying her as she studied the board.

She wasn't used to her new haircut. He could tell by the way she kept trying to tuck a shorter piece behind her ear, then frowning when it fell into her face, as though she wasn't accustomed to it not doing as it was told. He suspected Kate didn't like it when things didn't behave the way she wanted or expected them to.

She chewed her bottom lip as her eyes darted between her rook and her queen, and he knew she was debating whether or not to take a risk or play it safe. It was the thrill of chess with a new partner, where you didn't know the other person's skill or style, didn't know whether a bold move was going to bite you in the ass.

After another minute of deliberation, she went with neither piece, instead nudging her pawn forward in a surprisingly tepid move. He didn't mind. He'd take a chess match at a wobbly table with Kate over one with Bobby Fischer any day.

Kennedy already knew his next move but took his time studying the board anyway, partially out of habit, partially to prolong the game.

"You don't feel a little guilty?" Kate asked.

He looked up. "About?"

"Ditching your own party."

"A little," he admitted. "But I figure if I can ever get away with a social gaffe, it's on my birthday."

"Oh, that reminds me, I forgot your present. And do *not* do that annoying thing where you say I didn't have to get you anything," she said, before he could do exactly that.

"All right," he said, moving his bishop, and then sitting back in his chair. "What did you get me?"

"It was between a plastic bobblehead and a fake plant for your office."

"Both things I love," he said dryly.

Kate nodded. "I thought it would be nice with all of those weird wood chunks you keep around."

"They're collectibles."

"Yeah, okay, Ross."

Kennedy frowned. "Ross?"

"Yeah," she said, starting to move her rook and then changing her mind. "You know, like from *Friends*?"

He shook his head.

"Oh, come on," she said. "You have a television. What do you watch, documentaries?"

He said nothing.

"Of course you do," she said with a laugh. "Okay, well, watch *Friends*. You'll like Ross."

He'd seen *Friends* once or twice—he was discerning, not *completely* out of touch with reality. But he had no idea who Ross was. Kennedy made a mental note to look into it and get some insight into who he was in Kate's eyes.

Kate's attention was back on the board, as she chewed her lip once more. She shivered, then gave him a brief, knowing look. "You going to lecture me again on not bringing a coat?"

Discomfort rolled down his spine.

That's who you think I am? That guy? The lecturing, sanctimonious asshole?

But had he given her reason to think otherwise? Kennedy knew he could be stodgy. Hell, he intentionally cultivated the image most of the time. He *liked* being old-school in an industry chock-full of *bros*. But there was a difference between being old-school and serious, and being an uptight prick.

Kate, apparently, put him in the latter category.

He stood and shrugged out of his suit jacket just as she moved her knight. She blinked in surprise as he came around to her side of the table and unceremoniously put his jacket around her shoulders, careful not to let his fingers brush against the bare skin there.

"Thank you," she said as he sat back in his chair.

"You don't have to sound so puzzled," he said, shoving his pawn forward.

She lifted a hand and rubbed the fabric of his lapel between her fingers thoughtfully. "Well, you have to admit, while on paper I'd describe you as a gentleman, the chivalry doesn't typically extend to me."

"That's not true," he said automatically, shifting in the uncomfortable chair.

"It's a little bit true," she said, studying the board and then moving her queen. "But it's fine. I know I drive you crazy."

"Well, that's true," he admitted.

She laughed at that—a genuine, unfiltered laugh—and Kennedy found himself smiling back.

"Why?"

"Why do I drive you crazy?" she asked, looking up.

He stiffened slightly at the question. It felt too direct, somehow, demanding thought in a direction he wasn't ready to go. "Why do you go out of your way to push my buttons?"

A small smile flirted with her lips, and she didn't meet his eyes. "I don't mean to. Or at least, I didn't, at the beginning . . ."

"And?" he prompted when she fell silent. "What happened?"

Kate let out a little huff and met his gaze once more. "*You* happened. Whatever this thing between us is, *you* started it."

"Real mature, Kate."

Her eyes narrowed just slightly. "Is that your problem with me? That I'm not worldly like your other women?"

"What?" He blinked, genuinely confused. "First of all, I don't have a problem with you. Second, I don't date worldly women. What does that even mean?"

"It's fine," she said, her eyes dropping back to the board. "I realize I'm hardly irresistible."

Kennedy frowned, sensing from her tone he was missing something important, but he had no clue what it was.

Before he could ask, she pointed to the board. "You going to make your move or what?"

It was Kennedy's turn to narrow his eyes. "Don't order me around the way you do everyone else."

"Trust me, I've *never* thought I could order you around," she snapped back. "You're more stubborn than Ian and Matt combined."

"Right, and you're so easygoing and agreeable," he muttered, moving a piece forward at random, then wincing when he realized he'd just set up his knight to be taken.

Luckily, their argument seemed to have distracted Kate from the game, too. She was glaring at him, a little line between her dark eyebrows. "Why her?"

"What?" Kennedy resisted the urge to rub his forehead. He didn't enjoy complicated conversations, and this was turning into one of them. And yet, he didn't want to walk away, either. It had always been that way with Kate. She demanded so damn much from everyone around her, and as someone who liked everything in order, *his* way, all of that stubborn energy made him wary. And yet he was never quite able to walk away, either.

"Why Claudia?" she specified.

"Why not Claudia?" he replied automatically.

Kate's eyebrows lifted. "Wow. Romantic."

"You know what I mean," he said, feeling oddly self-conscious, looking down, studying the chessboard for his next move rather than facing her prying gaze.

"No, I don't really," Kate said with her usual forthrightness. "When I find The One, he will have a reason better than 'why not' for being with me."

He smiled a little at her unshakable confidence. *When* she found the guy, he *would* have a better reason. Then a mental image of Kate and Jack laughing together flashed in his mind, and Kennedy's smile dropped.

"What's wrong with Claudia?" he asked. To his surprise, it came out as a genuine question, and he realized he actually did want Kate's opinion. And God knew she had one. She had an opinion on everything.

"Nothing. She's a genuinely nice person. But you hardly seem besotted with her."

He let out a startled laugh. "I don't know that I've ever been *besotted* with anyone."

"Well, that's your problem, then." She took his knight, though he barely noticed.

"Have you?" he blurted out. It was suddenly vitally important to Kennedy that he know every detail about what sort of man could woo the no-nonsense Kate.

Kate smiled, a smile both secretive and a little sad. "Once."

Kennedy swallowed the sour taste in his mouth. He moved a pawn, then looked up. "What happened?"

She shrugged indifferently but didn't meet his eyes. "It wasn't mutual, so I moved on."

"To whom?"

"What?" She glanced up.

"You said you moved on. Who'd you move on to? When was this?"

"Oh." She looked uncharacteristically flustered. "I just meant I moved on from him. Not necessarily to someone else, specifically."

"But you've dated," he said, not really sure how he'd gotten himself into this conversation but not quite wanting to turn back, either.

"Yes. I've dated." Her tone was clipped and just a bit defensive.

"When was your last relationship? What was your longest?"

"None of your freaking business."

"Says the woman who helped my girlfriend plan my birthday party."

"All part of the job," she said smoothly, moving one of her pawns to counter his last move.

Kennedy felt a stab of something that felt suspiciously like hurt at the fact that she'd helped plan his birthday party only out of duty.

"Maybe Jack will be the next guy?" he said, keeping his voice indifferent as he moved his queen on the board.

"Maybe." She immediately moved her queen in a hasty move that told him she'd lost her focus on the game. Just as he had.

Kennedy looked at her. "He's not the right guy for you."

Her laugh was genuine and a little startled. *"Really."*

Kennedy picked up one of the white pawns he'd captured early on and rolled it between his palms as he sat back in the uncomfortable chair, studying her. With her hair falling over one eye, her eyes dark and smoky and a little mad, and his jacket accentuating her tininess, she didn't look like Kate, his no-nonsense assistant. He saw only a woman. An angry woman.

"Maybe I'm wrong," he admitted, struck by an uncomfortable reminder that perhaps he didn't know this woman nearly as well as he'd like to. "What is it you want out of a relationship?"

To his relief, instead of answering defensively, she seemed to consider his question seriously. "Probably the opposite of what you want."

"Perhaps."

She bit her lip. "You can't make fun if I tell you."

"I won't."

She met his eyes. "I want someone who's all in."

All in? "You mean . . . loyal?" he asked, trying to understand.

"No," she said with a laugh. "I mean, yes, of course loyal, but also someone who's not afraid to fall wildly, crazily in love with me."

Kennedy was beginning to see her point about their having opposite visions. He didn't do wild. Or crazy.

"I want the struck-by-lightning kind of love," she said, her eyes bright and cheeks pink as she seemed to warm to the topic. "You know, where you lock eyes with someone, and both of you just know."

They locked eyes as she said it, and he was oddly disappointed when she looked away immediately. "You mean like love at first sight?" he said, the words sounding more stilted and incredulous than he intended.

Kate smiled and shrugged. "It can happen."

"Infatuation at first sight, maybe," Kennedy said. "But that's not the lasting kind of steady love needed to make a relationship work."

"Wrong," she insisted. "My parents met when they were nineteen, and they both knew they were it for each other from the very first moment. They got married a year later, and they've been crazy in love ever since."

"And that's what you want? Crazy in love?"

"I do," Kate said with quiet confidence. "I don't want to have to convince someone to fall in love with me. I want a guy who just *knows* I'm The One and goes all in."

"Sounds . . . exhausting." He regretted his words as he watched her smile dim, saw her shut down.

"Like I said," Kate replied, her tone a little stiff, "I think we have different visions."

To say the least. Kennedy wasn't one of those cynics who didn't believe in love, but he knew that love wasn't magic. You didn't just look at someone and know, as though you were fated for each other. It was work. You had to learn each other's nuances, assess compatibility.

He didn't know how he and Kate could both thrive so well on organization and order, and yet approach their personal lives so differently. When Kennedy pictured his future wife, it was someone who had the same practical approach to marriage as he did. Someone who understood that the most successful relationships weren't about passion and butterflies but hard work and like-mindedness.

He was pulled from his thoughts as Kate gave a start, then pulled his iPhone from the pocket of the suit jacket she was still wearing. "You're buzzing." She handed over the phone, screen up, Claudia's name impossible to miss.

He stared at the screen a moment, then looked up. "I should probably get this."

"Definitely," Kate agreed.

He continued to stare at the screen and then, surprising himself with the impulse, used his thumb to silence the buzzing before setting the phone facedown on the table and moving his piece. "Let's finish our game."

Kate shrugged, turning her attention back to the board. "Can I ask something?" She didn't look up as she said it.

"Hmm?"

"If your brother asks, will you give him my phone number?"

Kennedy tensed. "You don't want me to do that."

Her gaze flew up to his. "Excuse me?"

"I just mean . . ." He started to backpedal, knowing that telling any woman what she wanted was a bad move. Telling a woman like Kate was suicidal.

"What did you mean?" Her voice was quiet, and the vulnerability there caught him off guard.

Kennedy chose his words carefully, reminding himself that he was her friend. "Jack's not your all-in, crazy-in-love guy."

"Ah," she said lightly. "Because I'm not that kind of woman, right? The irresistible type?"

"Not what I said."

"But it's what you meant," she said, her tone clipped as she made her move on the chessboard. Then she stood, the sleeves of his jacket falling well beyond the tips of her fingers. "We should get back to the party."

Kennedy scowled. "You can't leave in the middle of a chess game."

"Oh, did I forget to mention?" she asked casually, pulling her hair out from the neck of the jacket and letting it fall, dark and heavy, against the lapel, then pointing down at the board. "Checkmate."

Kennedy looked at the pieces, his disbelief shifting quickly to shock as he realized that his king was out of moves. He gave a thoughtful look at the woman he'd known—or thought he'd known—for years.

And wondered just what else he'd underestimated about her.

9

"Damn it," Kennedy muttered under his breath, tapping his six iron in irritation against the toe of his golf shoe. "Where's the drink cart? I need a beer."

"Yeah, I'm sure that'll help," Ian said, shielding his eyes from the sun and looking in the direction of Kennedy's ball to the far right. "Hell of a slice."

"Actually, sometimes a drink really does help with this game," Jarod Lanham said from behind the wheel of the golf cart he was sharing with Matt. "Gets you out of your head a bit."

"I don't think Kennedy's ever been *out of his head* in his life," Matt said.

"Sure he has. He's had sex, right?"

"Even then, I'm not so sure if he really loses himself," Ian said. "I wouldn't be surprised if there were diagrams in his nightstand with all of the various erogenous zones labeled."

"You fools realize I can hear you, right?" Kennedy asked.

Kennedy had gladly accepted the invitation to join his friends and Jarod for a golf getaway in Florida for the weekend. He'd have said yes regardless, but even having grown up around money, he couldn't deny that Jarod Lanham bumped the definition of luxury up to a whole other level.

For starters, the man was a billionaire with a capital *B*. Kennedy knew plenty of seven- and eight-figure guys. But meeting an eleven-figure guy face-to-face was rare, even on Wall Street. Even more impressive, Jarod wasn't some old fossil who'd amassed his fortune over the course of seven decades. At thirty-eight, he was only two years older than Kennedy. It would be annoying, if Kennedy didn't like the guy. Which he did.

Despite the private jet, the elite golf membership, and God knew how many private villas he had in about eight countries, the man was surprisingly down-to-earth.

Jarod also was an exceptional golfer, and yesterday, Kennedy's game had been on point. He'd beaten Matt and Ian and come within a respectable four shots of Jarod. Today was a different story.

"Stupid sport," Kennedy muttered.

"That it is," Jarod said, taking a sip of the expensive bottled water from the cart. "One day you're on top of your game, then one little thing gets out of alignment, and it all goes to hell."

"Is it your back, old man?" asked Matt, who, at twenty-nine, liked to pretend he had the youthful vigor of a college kid while the rest of them hobbled around on walkers.

"Oh, the body's rarely the problem," Jarod told Matt. He tapped his temple. "It's up here. A work stress gets in your head, a woman . . ." He spread his fingers wide and made a bomb noise.

Kennedy rolled his eyes and walked around to the back of the cart he and Ian were sharing, dropping his club into his bag. "Whose shot?"

"Mine," Ian said, pointing at a ball fifty or so yards up on the fairway. Then he looked back. "No rush, though. No one's behind us. Plenty of time."

"Absolutely. We've got all day to discuss what's got you flubbing every other shot," Jarod agreed, grinning at Kennedy.

"Could be that you guys won't shut up," Kennedy supplied.

"Could be that Avetna crashed on Friday," Matt suggested.

"Nah, we'd all be screwed on that one," Ian said, referring to the stock that had plummeted unexpectedly a few days earlier, causing a mini shock wave on the NYSE floor.

"So a woman, then," Jarod said to Kennedy. "I hear your woman had an ice sculpture made in your likeness for your birthday party. Sorry I was out of town and missed it."

"It was *extremely* majestic," Matt said.

"That's what's on your mind, Dawson? PTSD from your party?" Ian asked.

"I don't have anything on my mind!" Kennedy looked around. He *really* needed that drink cart.

"Not even the fact that your brother and our assistant are dating?"

Kennedy's gaze swung back around to Matt, who was innocently studying a tee. "They're not dating."

"Not what I heard," Ian said.

Jarod pretended to settle into the leather seat of the golf cart. "*Now* we're getting somewhere."

"What did you hear?" Kennedy said, laser-focused on Ian.

Ian's light-blue eyes flicked to Matt before coming back to Kennedy. "Just that Jack and Kate went out to dinner last week. Twice."

"Lara told you that?"

"Kate did."

Kennedy felt a surge of frustration that Kate had mentioned to Ian she was going out with Jack, but not him. Though, Kennedy had suspected what was going on. After the party, Jack had asked him for her number, and as Kate had requested, Kennedy had handed it over. Reluctantly.

He'd reminded himself that it wasn't his business who Kate dated. Jack may have been the bane of his existence when they were teens, but they were close now. He was a good guy. A serial dater, sure, but no more than Kennedy or any of the other guys used to be.

"You guys get in a fight?" Matt asked.

"My brother and I are fine."

"Not you and Jack, you and Kate. You two have been more impatient with each other than usual the past week."

"Ever since you disappeared together at your party," Ian added.

"We didn't disappear. We just went to play chess. It wasn't a big deal."

"You've never asked me to play chess," Matt said.

"Do you play?"

"Yes, and I'm excellent."

"Which means you're a heinous opponent."

"He is," Jarod agreed. "He acts like it's a mathlete competition."

"Which I always won."

"Hey, you know what you should do?" Jarod said, turning to Matt excitedly as though he just had a great idea. "Record yourself talking about your mathletics, then play it for Sabrina. See if she still chooses you."

"She will," Matt said smugly. "You lost, man, fair and square."

"I didn't fully put myself in the game," Jarod said. "And is that any way to talk to your fairy godmother?"

Kennedy couldn't help but smirk at Jarod's self-appointed nickname. Late last year, Jarod had shown a brief interest in Sabrina, realized that she was entirely hung up on Matt, and switched allegiances, getting all up in their business to bring them together.

"The point is," Matt said, looking back toward Kennedy, "we need to help Kennedy come to grips with Jack and Kate's relationship so his golf game can get back on track."

"Two dates is not a relationship. And if it were, I wouldn't care. I'm happy for them."

"And?" Ian prompted when Kennedy said nothing more.

"And what?" Kennedy grabbed a bottle of water.

"I know this will upset your carefully built walls, but we know you, man. What's on your mind?"

Kennedy exhaled and looked around at the vast amount of green, realizing, though it galled him to do so, that maybe he did need to talk it out.

"What do you guys think about Claudia?"

"She's nice," Ian said automatically.

Nice. There was that word again, the same one Kate had used the night of the party.

"Never met her," Jarod said, holding up his hands when Kennedy looked his way.

Kennedy shifted his gaze to Matt, who gave an indifferent shrug. "Yeah, she's nice."

Damn it. He knew they meant it. Just as Kate had meant it. Because Claudia *was* nice. And beautiful. Smart. Generous. So why the hell did the people closest to him sound so bored when her name was mentioned?

Worse, why did Kennedy feel bored?

"Are things getting serious between you guys?" Jarod asked.

"It's only been a couple months," Kennedy said automatically.

"So?" All three of the guys asked it at the same time.

Kennedy gave them an incredulous look. "*So* people do not get serious after two months."

"I did," Ian said matter-of-factly.

Matt nodded in agreement. "I think I knew Sabrina was it for me the second I met her. It just took me a couple years to figure it out, a couple more to convince her . . ."

"*I* convinced her," Jarod said.

"Shut up, man," Matt said.

"Guys." Ian nodded at Kennedy. "Focus."

"Right," Matt said. "Okay, so you and Claudia are just casual for now, and yet you look awfully serious."

"That's just my face," Kennedy said.

Ian laughed. "True. But you do seem extra pensive. And not just about your golf game."

Kennedy squinted up at the sky, not quite sure how to explain himself. Not even sure why he wanted to explain himself. He was hardly prone to talking about what was on his mind, and he definitely wasn't inclined to share *feelings*. But something had been brewing deep inside him lately, and he figured if he didn't get it out with these guys, he never would. "You guys ever think it's weird that both of you are getting married before me?" He didn't include Jarod, but he knew the other man well enough to know he wouldn't mind being left out—he was new to their group.

"I guess," Matt said. "I mean, I never gave much thought to *any* of us Wolfes getting married, but I guess if I had, I would've assumed you'd be the first one to the altar."

Me too.

Kennedy hadn't spent the past decade planning his wedding, but he also had never been one of those guys who squawked about being a bachelor for life. He always figured he'd find a nice woman, settle down, have kids.

And yeah, he sort of thought it'd have happened by now.

"So is anyone else confused why Kennedy's got marriage on the brain but also is insisting he and his girlfriend aren't serious?" Matt asked.

"No," Jarod said. "He's thirty-seven now—"

"Thirty-six," Kennedy ground out.

"I'm just saying, it makes sense. You're not getting any younger—"

"Jesus." Kennedy turned back to the golf cart and pointed at Ian to follow suit. "Get in. We're done here."

"You know I'm right," Jarod said, calling over his shoulder as he and Matt drove off.

Once they were alone, Ian turned to Kennedy, his voice atypically serious. "You're not having some sort of midlife crisis because of your birthday and the fact that Matt and I are married and almost married, are you?"

"No, that's not it," Kennedy said, meaning it. He was happy for his friends, and he wasn't foolish enough to rush out and find the first wife available out of competition or fear of getting older.

"So what is it?"

Kennedy put his hands on the wheel of the golf cart but didn't take it out of "Park." "Kate and I sort of got into it the other night at my birthday party."

"Kate?" Ian asked, sounding puzzled by the mention of their assistant's name when they'd been talking about Claudia. "And what do you mean *got into it*?"

Kennedy rubbed his forehead. "You know how we always say the wrong thing to each other?"

Ian nodded. "You're too much alike."

Kennedy gave him a surprised look. "We're nothing alike."

"Neither one of you can stand for things to be out of order, and yet you can't seem to get the other person in order. Alike."

"Well, maybe," Kennedy said, unable to deny that both he and Kate thrived on organization. "But when it comes to relationships, we're apparently opposites."

"Relationships?" Ian's voice was startled and a little wary. "When were you guys talking about that?"

"At my birthday party. You know she believes in love at first sight?"

"And?"

"And," Kennedy snapped, annoyed that Ian wasn't sharing his concern, "I'm worried she'll get her heart broken when she realizes that love at first sight doesn't exist, especially with my brother."

"How do you know?"

"Seriously? You're taking her side on this?"

Ian held up his hands. "I'm not taking anyone's side. I'm just saying that Kate and Jack seemed to really hit it off. It could be something. And besides, what does it matter if she has a different vision of relationships than you? You've got Claudia. She has Jack."

His stomach clenched. "I thought you said it was only two dates."

Ian studied him. "Okay, I'm going to say this while you don't have a golf club in your hands . . . You're acting jealous, man."

"I am not," Kennedy said automatically.

"Okay," Ian agreed just a little too readily before gesturing at the fairway in front of them. "Then can we play golf now, or . . . ?"

Kennedy nodded in agreement and drove the golf cart forward to Ian's ball, which his friend proceeded to land nicely on the green.

Kennedy's game, on the other hand, continued to deteriorate.

He refused to let himself think about why.

10

"We should have brunch in every day," Sabrina said, sitting back in her chair and rubbing her stomach. "So much better than a restaurant."

"Well, the food came from a restaurant," Lara said, adding a bit more orange juice to her mimosa. "Lest either of you was assuming I could whip up bananas Foster French toast or whatever magic is happening with that quiche."

"Cheese. Cheese is what's happening with that quiche," Kate said.

"Oh great. My wedding dress likes cheese almost as much as it likes this bread," Lara said sarcastically, dragging a last bite of French toast through a puddle of syrup.

"It's the sugar that'll get you," Sabrina said absently.

Lara glared at her.

"*Could* get you. *Would* get you if you were a different body type, without your wondrous metabolism." Sabrina looked at Kate. "Help."

Kate grinned. "Nope. I think that was one of the few times I've ever seen you verbally flounder. It was sort of glorious."

"Totally glorious," Lara agreed gleefully.

Sabrina, in addition to being one of the most beautiful women Kate had ever seen, seemed to radiate chic, effortless confidence. It had been intimidating at first. Even though Kate considered herself fairly secure in her own life and choices, it was hard not to feel like a wannabe in Sabrina's presence.

But the more she'd gotten to know Sabrina, the more she'd seen beyond the rough edges and the cool polish to a woman who was warm and vibrant and giving. She'd won Kate over, first by being a fiercely loyal friend to Ian, who she'd known since childhood, and then later as Matt's soul mate.

Of course, it had taken Matt and Sabrina a while to realize their soul-mate status, but Kate had known from the beginning. You couldn't be in the same room with them and not feel the electricity.

"You know, I'm not worried," Lara said after she finished chewing the French toast and pushed her empty plate away. "It won't matter if my wedding dress is snug, because I have two of the most competent women on the planet as bridesmaids."

"Well, that's true," Kate said. "You know, you'll be my tenth wedding?"

"Tenth?" Sabrina asked. "As in you've done the bridesmaid thing ten times?"

Kate nodded. "And maid of honor twice."

"Overachieve much, Miss Congeniality?"

"It's not like that," Kate said. "I mean, yeah, I love my cousins and college girlfriends, but I'm pretty sure some of them included me for the reason you just implied. Competence. I'm *super* handy in a crisis."

"That you are, but you *know* that's not why I asked you, right?" Lara said, studying Kate.

"Of course," she said automatically. Kate hadn't known Lara as long as she had Sabrina, and as a former SEC agent and current badass FBI agent, she was an unexpected addition to their group. But although she'd been wary of Lara when the other woman had been assigned to investigate Ian for insider trading, Lara made it pretty difficult to dislike her. With her big blue eyes, black-rimmed glasses, and her trademark blonde ponytail, she looked like the girl next door and acted like it, too. She was as kind as she was ambitious, funny as she was smart.

No doubt about it, her guys had picked good ones. Well, two of her guys had. Jury was still out on Claudia.

"Okay, so when do we get details?" Lara asked Kate.

"On what?" Kate helped herself to more champagne.

"Kennedy's billionaire brother!"

Kate's champagne flute froze halfway to her mouth as she stared at Sabrina. "Jack is not a billionaire. Is he?" If anyone would know, it would be Sabrina.

Sabrina lifted a shoulder, her white silk blouse shimmying at the gesture. "If he's not officially, he's close."

"How is that even possible?" Lara asked. "He's in his early thirties."

"So? Jarod's late thirties, and he's part of the billionaire club."

Kate fanned herself at the name. Jarod Lanham was *hot*. Unlike so many of the guys who worked downtown and freaked out at the first sight of gray hair, discreetly paying hundreds every other week to take care of it, Jarod had embraced the gray, resulting in a Clooney-worthy silver-fox vibe.

"I guess I don't know for sure about Jack," Sabrina admitted. "But he does a ton of business overseas, and that's a whole other world of power and money."

"Okay, it's official, he's never coming over to my place," Kate said.

Sabrina and Lara stared at her.

"What? I'm not inviting a billionaire, or an *almost* billionaire, to my studio apartment."

"We adore your apartment, as do you," Lara pointed out. "But we're far more intrigued by the fact that you were even *thinking* of inviting Jack over to your apartment."

"Those must have been a couple of awesome dates," Sabrina said. "Are you thinking third date is sexy time?"

"No," Kate admitted. "The apartment thing was hypothetical."

"So no third date?"

"Well, he asked . . ."

Lara reached over and excitedly patted the table beside Sabrina. "Our girl's snagged a billionaire!"

Sabrina put her hand over Lara's to still it, watching Kate. "Have you snagged him?"

Kate sighed. "It's only been a week, but he does seem weirdly interested."

"Why *weirdly*?"

"Because . . ." Kate gestured down at herself. "Look at what I'm working with."

"Kate," Sabrina said in a warning tone.

"No, I mean it. I realize I'm not like, garbage disposal goo to look at, but this guy can literally have anyone. Anyone! Did you know his last girlfriend was an actress? A big one."

"Who?" Lara demanded.

"I said I wouldn't tell. Apparently they had this super-hot fling. But the point is, how can I compete with that? I'm too plain."

"You're down-to-earth, and maybe that's exactly what attracts him to you, aside from your great hair, big Bambi eyes, and how adorably tiny you are."

"Purse size," Sabrina chimed in.

Kate rolled her eyes. "Yes, I'm sure that's what every hot rich guy wants. A purse-size girlfriend."

"Look, babe, forget all of that. The real question is, do you like him?"

Kate inhaled, held her breath, and let it out slowly. It was something she'd given a good amount of thought to lately, because while there was no doubt in her mind that she liked Jack Dawson, she was also acutely aware that something was missing. They'd had that first flirtatious moment, with some sort of chemistry there, and yet . . . she didn't know. She didn't know why she wasn't head over heels for him, and it was driving her crazy.

"I do like him . . ."

"But?" Sabrina nudged when Kate trailed off.

When Kate didn't reply, Lara asked softly, "But . . . Kennedy?"

"What's Kennedy have to do with this?" Kate said automatically.

Lara turned away and looked at Sabrina. "Flip for it?"

"Nope, I've got this. You get more champagne. We're going to need it."

"For what?" Kate demanded as Lara went to the fridge and came back with another bottle.

But Sabrina didn't answer. Instead, she waited until all of their glasses were full of another mimosa before turning to Kate. "Okay, babe, we're way past due for this. Are you in love with him?"

The question hit Kate like a punch in the gut. Had it been anyone else besides Lara and Sabrina, she would have played dumb. She'd have pretended to assume Sabrina was asking if she was in love with Jack. But she knew she wasn't, and Kate wouldn't lie to her closest friends. What's more, she realized Sabrina was right. This conversation was past due.

And she needed to talk about it.

"Not anymore," Kate answered simply. "But yes, *once* I was one hundred percent crazy, all-the-way in love with him."

"Oh," Lara said on a breath, sounding a little bit awed and a little bit sad. "When was this?"

Kate gave a small smile and sipped her drink. "My very first day at Wolfe. It was the Tuesday after Memorial Day. I remember it felt like the first day of school. The office manager at the time gave me a hurried tour of the building and showed me to my desk, which was in the middle of the bull pen."

"Wait, how'd we get to baseball?" Sabrina asked.

"Not that kind of bull pen . . . It's like a clump of desks where the all of the junior brokers sit. The Sams think it breeds healthy competition to put them all in the same area instead of separate offices, to see who wants it most. The bull pen is arranged into clusters of desks of four—one assistant to three brokers."

Lara nodded to indicate she understood, and Kate continued with her pathetic story. Because in hindsight, it was *really* pathetic.

"Ian and Matt introduced themselves immediately," Kate said. "They were like cute little puppy versions of the guys we know now. Smart and charming. Not quite *desperate* for people to like them, just sort of *determined* that everyone would."

Sabrina laughed. "A puppy is the best comparison for those two back then. They humped just about anything in front of them, like boy dogs who haven't figured out what to do with their nuts."

"Where was Kennedy in all of this?" Lara pressed.

Kate tried to ignore the way her heart still did a weird little flip, just at the memory of that day. "He was on the phone when I got to my desk. I saw his profile, could hear his voice, and yet I was totally unprepared for it."

"It?"

She bit her lip and tried to think of how to explain what had happened next. "You know that moment in cheesy movies, where the nerdy girl first lays eyes on the hot guy, and the whole thing switches to slow motion, and the music changes? It was humiliatingly *exactly* like that. He stood, extended his hand to introduce himself, and the second our eyes locked, I just . . . knew."

"Knew what?" Sabrina asked with a frown.

Lara flicked her arm in reproach. "Oh, come on. Love at first sight, literally. It's romantic as heck."

"It's really not," Kate said. "It was so silly. Even back then, I knew it. I was twenty-two years old, fresh out of college, and my shirt had an honest-to-God bow on it. A big one. And then there was Kennedy. He was twenty-nine, broad-shouldered, serious, and just so *manly* compared to the college boyfriend I'd broken up with."

Sabrina fanned herself. "Damn. I am so getting it now."

"So what happened?" Lara asked, resting her chin on her hand and looking like a preteen at a slumber party, wanting to hear more about the popular boy.

Kate shrugged. "Nothing, really. I poured all of my energy into trying not to get flustered and breathless every time he spoke to me. He didn't make it easy. Did you know he took his grandmother to church every Sunday until she passed away last year? Or that he'll wait forever to hold a door for a woman. Or that he used to fake not getting along with his brothers so Ian would agree to come home with him at the holidays to act as a buffer."

"Because he knew Ian's only option was a foster father who thinks Top Ramen counts as Christmas dinner," Lara said softly.

Kate nodded. "And once, he overheard me on the phone with my dad, who was super bummed because the fishing lodge in North Carolina he and his childhood friends went to every year had been shut down. The next morning, Kennedy sent me an email with the confirmation code for a vacation rental on Lake Norman. He'd rented a six-bedroom house right on the lake for my dad and four men he'd never even met. He barely accepted my gratitude and wouldn't take any of the money I tried to pay him back with." Kate threw her hands up in the air. "How was I *not* supposed to be in love with him?"

Lara nodded thoughtfully. "You know, if Kennedy did that for your dad, maybe he—"

"Felt the same way?" Kate made an elimination buzzer noise. "Wrong."

"You don't know that," Sabrina chimed in. "Maybe he was too afraid to say anything, just like you were."

Kate withheld the flinch, hating that she'd let herself hold on to that same foolish dream for as long as she had, and instead took a deep breath to tell her friends the rest of the story—the part that *really* hurt.

"So you know how the guys have that pact? The one where they can't date me?" Kate said.

Lara stared at her. "Wait. *You* know about the pact?"

"Yup," she muttered. "I was there when they made it. I mean, they don't know I was there," she rushed to explain. "They thought I'd left for the day, but I'd forgotten my umbrella, so I came back, and they were in Kennedy's office."

"You heard the whole thing?" Sabrina asked with a wince.

"No," Kate said softly. "Just enough."

"Oh, sweetie." Lara touched her hand. "What'd those morons say?"

"Just the one moron," Kate replied. "They were sort of arguing, and Kennedy said, 'The little thing's hardly irresistible, but better safe than sorry in case any of us gets drunk and stupid.'"

Her friends were silent for a moment, and then Sabrina shook her head. "He is so lucky he's not here right now."

"Seriously," Lara said in heated agreement.

"Yeah, well." Kate shrugged. "It's actually a good thing, because my childish infatuation with Kennedy needed to die, and that little nugget delivered a swift and fatal blow. Which is a good thing," she repeated, in case they'd missed it the first time. "Outwardly, nothing changed. He was still all broody and hot; I was still the capable, businesslike assistant. Only, from then on, I wasn't harboring any romantic delusions about him one day professing his love for me."

"Don't kill me for asking," Sabrina said, "but are you positive you're really, truly over him? Because sometimes you seem a little . . . aware."

Kate took a gulp of her mimosa. "I may not be in love with him anymore, but my body hasn't quite gotten the message that we no longer want him."

"Ah," Lara said. "So the physical thing is still there."

Kate scrunched down in her chair. "Unfortunately. But it's getting better."

"Because of Jack?"

"Maybe? I'm not going to lie. It wasn't like it was that first meeting with Kennedy, where I felt it tip to toe. But Jack's the opposite of

Kennedy. Kennedy's never seemed to notice that I'm a woman, while Jack . . ."

"Is very aware that you're a woman?" Sabrina wiggled her eyebrows.

Kate exhaled, too embarrassed to tell her friends that she and Jack hadn't exactly gotten to the physical part of dating. She sensed that Jack was more than interested but was waiting for her to give the green light, and she just . . . wasn't there yet.

"We're happy for you," Lara said, seeming to sense Kate's discomfort and giving her an out. "We just hope . . ." She trailed off and looked to Sabrina.

"What?" Kate asked warily, glancing between the two of them.

Sabrina picked up where Lara left off. "We just hope that eventually, whether it be Jack or someone you haven't met yet, the person you end up with gives you butterflies. That it's something *more* than 'nice.' You deserve that."

"I do deserve that," Kate agreed emphatically, feeling a rush of gratitude that she'd found friends like these women. She raised her glass in a toast. "Here's to hoping that the next time it happens, it's for someone who feels them back. Because this unrequited-love thing is absolute garbage."

11

"Our first double date!" Claudia said, wrapping both her arms around Kennedy's and squeezing. "This will be so fun. Though I have to say, I totally thought it would be with Ian and Lara or Matt and Sabrina. Still, I guess Jack and Kate make a cute couple, right?"

Kennedy grunted as the taxi crawled through traffic toward the West Village Italian restaurant where they were having dinner with his brother and his assistant. Two people he never imagined being in the same orbit, much less together as a couple.

A couple he'd have to sit across the table from for the next two hours or so.

"This is us," Claudia said, glancing out the window and leaning forward to get the cabbie's attention. "Right side, please, at the light."

A moment later, Kennedy opened the front door of the restaurant for her, then followed her in to a wall of noise, trying not to wince. He hated places that were packed to the gills even at six thirty on a Thursday. There was a reason he avoided the night scene in the city. He liked to be able to hear himself speak without shouting. He liked to be able to hear himself *think*.

"There they are!" Claudia said, lifting her hand and waving.

Kennedy followed her to the table, wondering for the hundredth time how the hell he'd gotten himself into this. Why, when Claudia had insisted that the four of them get together, he hadn't come up with an excuse. Any excuse.

Kennedy had opted for a normal suit, since it made up about 80 percent of his wardrobe, though he regretted it when he saw Jack, who managed to look both polished and relaxed in a light-gray sweater and dark-gray slacks. Of course he did. That was Jack's thing, managing to look both perfectly at ease and perfectly in control, no matter where he was or what he was wearing.

Kate was wearing a dress. Not as fancy as the one she'd worn to his birthday party, but this one was also pink, with a gray belt around her small waist that perfectly coordinated with Jack's attire.

Great. They were matching outfits now.

Claudia hugged Jack, then did the same with Kate. "You're so little," Claudia said, bending down to the smaller woman. "I could just scoop you up and put you in my purse!"

"Do it. I think I could be quite happy in Chanel," Kate replied with a smile.

Claudia laughed and moved to sit down. Kennedy pulled out the chair for her, nodding a greeting at his brother. He glanced at Kate, but she was ignoring him, instead complimenting Claudia on the restaurant choice.

"I've definitely got my eye on the mushroom ravioli with truffle cream sauce," Kate was saying.

"Oh gosh, I would be, too, if I did carbs," Claudia said.

"I love carbs," Kate said with a contented sigh. "I could never give them up."

"The other night I watched her put a potato on top of a piece of bread," Jack said, smiling down at Kate, who gave him a mock glare beneath the hair that had fallen across her forehead.

Kennedy picked up the menu to keep from asking if the sexy Jessica Rabbit hair was annoying her yet. Where were the headbands she used to wear? The ones that signaled practical Kate not *date Jack Dawson* Kate.

"They were very good potatoes and good bread. It was a time-saving measure," Kate said, shrugging.

"Oooh, cauliflower risotto," Claudia said, her attention on the menu. "When I was with Dior, the girls ate that constantly. You'd be surprised how much it tastes like real rice."

"Call me crazy, but if I wanted rice, I'd eat rice," Jack said. "And if I wanted cauliflower . . . I'd die."

"You don't like cauliflower?" Kate asked, turning toward him.

"He doesn't like vegetables," Kennedy said without looking up from the wine list.

"I didn't like vegetables when I was twelve," Jack clarified. "Mom hasn't caught me sneaking broccoli into the potted plants in at least a year and a half now."

The women laughed, and Kennedy rolled his eyes. He was thankful when the server came by to take orders for some much-needed alcohol.

They started with a round of cocktails, and when the server left, Claudia put her menu aside and leaned forward with a smile. "I'm so glad we did this. I've been telling Kennedy forever that we need some couple friends."

"They're not a couple," Kennedy said automatically. "It's only been a week."

Kate tilted her head in a gesture that was meant to look innocent and confused, but he knew it was a warning. *Knock it off.*

He ignored it.

Jack glanced down at Kate. "Did you not tell him, sweetheart? About the engagement?"

"Nope," she said in a loud whisper. "Not about the baby, either."

"Hilarious," Kennedy muttered.

Claudia swatted his arm. "Be nice."

"Oh, he can't help it," Jack said. "It's written into his older-brother DNA to be Highly Disapproving."

"Just like it's written into yours to be Highly Annoying?"

"When's your birthday, Jack?" Claudia asked, clearly trying to steer the conversation to friendlier territory.

"November twenty-sixth. You can imagine my hardship over the years, having to share so much with Thanksgiving." He put a thumb between his eyebrows, as though trying to ward off bad memories.

Kate played along, rubbing his arm. "Poor baby."

Kennedy ground his teeth.

"What about you, Kate? Wait, no, don't tell me. You're a . . . Virgo?"

"Her birthday's in July," Kennedy said before Kate could reply. He had no idea whether that made her a Virgo or Ram, a Waffle, or whatever. He didn't give a crap about astrology. He didn't even know why he'd answered for her, except it seemed important, somehow, to remind everyone that of the three of them at the table, he was the one who'd known Kate the longest.

Though, that wasn't particularly fair. Truth be told, until the night of his birthday party, he hadn't realized how unnerving it was that she seemed to know the smallest details about him, and yet he hadn't known she liked museums. The ballet. Chess.

Hadn't known that she believed in love at first sight.

Kennedy didn't like surprises and had made it a point ever since to gather whatever details he could about her. It was just smart to stay on a level playing field.

To stay one step ahead of his brother in all things Kate Henley.

"July twentieth," Kate was telling Claudia. "A Cancer, I think?"

"Yeah, Cancer," Claudia said thoughtfully as their waiter placed cocktails in front of them. "Surprising."

"How's that?" Jack asked. "I don't know anything about the signs."

Because it's all crap, Kennedy thought, taking a sip of his drink. It had some froufrou name, but it was basically a slightly bitter Manhattan. He didn't really care. It had whiskey.

"Well, Kate's got Virgo written all over her," Claudia explained. "Virgos are extremely capable with *amazing* attention to detail. Which is what makes Kate such a great assistant."

Kennedy inwardly flinched. Claudia didn't mean it as a slight. Kennedy knew enough about his girlfriend to know that she was never unkind. Just oblivious.

"Kate actually went to business school," Kennedy said.

"You did?" Jack looked over at Kate, but she ignored him, staring right at Kennedy.

"What's that have to do with the conversation?" Kate asked, her voice testy.

"I just meant that you're not only capable as an assistant," Kennedy said, taken aback by the fire in her eyes. "You can do anything you want to do." *I was defending you.*

Kate's smile was tight. "I don't think Claudia meant assistant as an insult."

"I didn't," Claudia said quickly.

"Okay, so what's my sign?" Jack asked Claudia in an effort to get the conversation back on track. "End of November makes me a—"

"There's nothing wrong with being an assistant," Kate said, interrupting Jack.

"I didn't say there was," Kennedy said, meeting her angry gaze levelly. He meant it. He couldn't begin to do what Kate did on a daily basis. He didn't know anyone who could.

Slowly she dragged her brown eyes from Kennedy back to Jack. "I got my MBA in business administration a couple years ago. Ian actually paid my tuition. He heard me say I wanted to continue my education, and next thing I knew, I was enrolled at Columbia. I wish he'd let me pay him back, but . . ." She shrugged. "I'm grateful."

Kate was taking a sip of her drink and wasn't looking at Kennedy after she said it, but his brother was. Jack's eyes narrowed slightly, and Kennedy pointedly ignored his brother's prying gaze. He'd managed to keep his secret for this long; he wasn't about to give himself away now. It had been hard enough to get Ian to cooperate. Kennedy didn't want to have to drag Jack in on the lie, too.

Not to mention, his brother would want to know why. *Why* had Kennedy paid for Kate's MBA? *Why* had he asked Ian to take the credit for it?

Kennedy didn't want those questions, because he wasn't entirely sure of the answers. He'd always told himself it was because Ian and Kate's relationship had been easier than his and Kate's relationship and that she'd accept tuition payment from Ian, not from him.

Lately, however, he wasn't as sure. He knew only that he really didn't want her to know the truth. That Kennedy had been the one who'd paid for her degree. That he'd do it again in a heartbeat and keep it just as secret.

Claudia and Kate's conversation had shifted course to a movie starring Ryan Something-or-other, who Claudia thought was hot and Kate deemed overrated.

Kennedy finally chanced a look at his brother, braced for mocking but getting only thoughtfulness.

The server reappeared. "You guys ready to order?"

Kennedy had barely looked at the menu, but he nodded. Anything to speed the evening along. Kate ordered her mushroom truffle ravioli. Claudia got a salad. Jack ordered the duck and a bottle of wine for the table, and Kennedy opted for the bone-in rib eye.

"You two have any fun plans this weekend?" Claudia asked. "Kennedy and I are going to a black-tie thing at the Guggenheim on Saturday, and I know the coordinator. I could get two extra tickets."

"Actually, we do have plans," Jack said. "I scored tickets to the opera. Kate's never been."

Because she prefers the ballet.

"I've always heard it's a NYC must," Kate said, "but I've never had anyone to go with."

Kate said it casually, matter-of-factly, and he genuinely doubted she expected or wanted sympathy, but her words caused a strange pang in his chest all the same. The woman had always seemed so confident and complete in herself—so utterly independent—it had never occurred to him that same reliance might have a side effect of loneliness.

Though it should have. Somehow, *he* managed to be lonely, even while in a relationship. Even, if he were fully honest, while he was among his friends.

"Oh, you'll love it!" Claudia said. "Won't she love it, Kennedy?" she asked, nudging him.

It took him a second to come back to the conversation. "Maybe. Opera's sort of a love or hate thing."

"Kennedy's in the love category," Jack said. "You know he used to listen to Bach, even in eighth grade?"

"Bach's *symphonies*. An entirely different genre than the opera."

Jack unsubtly delivered a "dork" behind a fake cough, and Claudia and Kate laughed.

"I think it's adorable," Claudia said, tucking her arm in Kennedy's and resting her cheek against his shoulder.

"Definitely," Kate said over the rim of her martini. "*Adorable* is definitely a word we all use for Kennedy."

"What word would you use?" he asked Kate, since her sarcasm was clear.

"*Adorable* works," she said sweetly.

He held her gaze. "Come on, Kate. Let's hear it."

"Kennedy." The warning in his brother's voice was clear, but Kennedy ignored it.

"So, Claudia, how are things going with that new charity you were trying to start up?" Kate asked.

"What word?" Kennedy snapped, refusing to be thwarted.

"Oh my God," Kate said, shooting him an angry gaze. "Would you drop it?"

"Yes, do," Claudia murmured quietly, rubbing her hand over his arm in a way that did absolutely nothing to soothe him. Especially not when Jack's arm dropped around Kate's chair. Casually.

That was the thing. There was no deliberate possessiveness in Jack's gesture—the motion seemed spontaneous, as though it were second nature for his brother to be draped all over his assistant . . .

The truth hit Kennedy hard. And uncomfortably.

Surely he wasn't . . . *jealous*?

No. Absurd. He was just protective. He knew that Jack traded out women with casual ease, and Kate had some grand vision of whatever it was her parents had.

He gave Claudia a forced smile of reassurance that he'd drop the topic, and the rest of the meal passed . . . tolerably. He was forced to rethink his opinion on the restaurant. It was small and crowded, yes, but the steak rivaled anything he'd had at any of the top steakhouses, and the wine Jack had selected was excellent. And yet, even as he forced himself to relax, to participate in the lively conversation around him, he couldn't stop dwelling . . .

What word would Kate use to describe him? Not *adorable*. He got that. He didn't particularly want to be seen as adorable by anyone. But it suddenly seemed vital to know how Kate saw him. Who knew, someday he could be her brother-in-law . . .

The steak that he'd just enjoyed suddenly wasn't sitting so well, and he pushed his plate away.

"Dessert?" Kate asked as one of the bussers began clearing the table.

"No," Kennedy said curtly, his stomach still churning at the thought of having Kate at family dinners. As his sister.

"Definitely not," Claudia agreed. "I'm stuffed."

"From the lettuce?" Jack asked curiously.

"It expands in your stomach," Claudia said matter-of-factly.

"Okay," Jack said easily before turning to Kate. "Wanna grab some ice cream on the way home?"

"Make it gelato, and you've got a deal."

He lifted his hand for a high five, which she returned with a grin.

Kennedy tipped back the remainder of his wine in one large swallow.

"This was *so* fun," Claudia said a few minutes later as the four of them stepped out onto the sidewalk outside the restaurant. "We should definitely do it again soon."

"Absolutely," Jack agreed, helping Kate into her coat. "We'll at least see you next weekend, right?"

"Ah . . ." Claudia frowned in confusion.

Shit. "My parents' anniversary party," Kennedy said, hoping to save her embarrassment. "You can still come?"

"Oh! Sure. Yes. I'm so sorry, I must have totally spaced on it."

She met his eyes just for a moment, her gaze questioning. She hadn't forgotten. He hadn't invited her, not that he'd intentionally intended not to. He just hadn't gotten around to it . . .

Out of the corner of his eye, he saw Jack lean down and murmur something in Kate's ear that made her laugh.

"Saturday at five. Please come," he said to Claudia, even as guilt gnawed at the realization he was asking her for all of the wrong reasons.

12

Kate's gaze flicked to her cell phone that was faceup on her desk, even as her fingers kept typing out an email to Jarod Lanham's assistant, arranging a time next week for Matt to swing by Jarod's office.

Her phone had been lighting up for the past five minutes with a string of messages from Lara, each and every one a gentle inquisition about last night's double date. She was surprised her friend had managed to wait this long. Sabrina had barely made it to eight a.m. before starting her interrogation.

How'd it go?

Was it weird?

Did Claudia bring her own green smoothie?

Was Kennedy a dick?

Is Jack a good kisser?

Kate had yet to reply to the messages, at least not via text. In her head, though . . .

Yes, last night was weird as heck, sitting next to the guy I'm dating, across from my boss.

No, Claudia didn't bring her own smoothie, though it was a close call. Kate was all for eating healthy and completely respected anyone's right to choose a salad, but she'd have preferred a little less *talking* about the carb-free life and the magic of giving up gluten. It had almost ruined her ravioli.

Almost.

Kate would take her pasta over the shiny hair Claudia had promised any day. Besides, Kate's hair was already shiny. Shinier than Claudia's, if she did say so herself. *Gluten for the win, thank you very much.*

As for whether Kennedy was a dick . . . *Yes, obviously.*

And Jack being a good kisser . . .

Her phone flashed again, and Kate glanced down, then did a double take when she realized Lara was apparently reading her mind from across town.

Did he kiss you?

She sent the email to Jarod's assistant, then picked up her phone, catching up on Lara's messages. They were more or less the same as Sabrina's, phrased just slightly softer.

Kate started a group message to both women. Sorry, busy day, just now catching up on texts.

That much was true. It was seven thirty p.m. She was still at the office and had another half hour or so of work to do, unless she wanted to work over the weekend. Which she didn't.

Just a couple of weeks ago, she would have. It wasn't like she had anything else to do. Now she had plans for brunch, the opera, potentially a nightcap after the opera . . .

She tapped the corner of her iPhone case absently against her palm.

Was she going too fast? She'd just met Jack, and she'd seen him, what, five times in the past week or so?

And yet, about that kissing thing . . . They hadn't. At least not the way her friends were thinking. She'd wanted to, or at least *wanted* to want to. And last night, after dinner with Claudia and Kennedy, the moment had been there, as Jack walked her home in the cool spring air, debating whose gelato was better, his chocolate or her pistachio. (For the record, they'd decided the right answer was better together and made their own swirl of sorts.)

But when they'd gotten to her apartment building, and he'd turned to face her, she'd felt only apprehension, followed by relief when he'd dipped his head, not to kiss her mouth but to brush a lingering kiss against her cheek.

She slumped down in her chair. What was *wrong* with her? A rich, attractive, charming guy was clearly into her. They got along. They laughed. And yet at night, when she closed her eyes and thought of Jack, his features always morphed, just a little. His smile became a little more reluctant, his eyes a little less gold, his jaw a touch more stubborn, the eyebrows thicker . . .

"Kate."

Her eyes snapped open, and she realized she was doing it again—thinking of *him*.

"Hey." She sat up straight and cleared her throat as she looked at a scowling Kennedy. "What do you need?"

"Why do you assume I need something?"

"Because you're standing in front of your assistant's desk, giving her a death glare?"

"I thought you were asleep."

"Well, in that case, thank you for the *very* gentle wake-up," she said sarcastically, setting her phone facedown on the desk so he couldn't see any incoming texts from her friends. "If you don't need anything, I have some stuff to finish up . . ."

"You almost done?"

"No," she said. "Why? If you need me to do something—"

"I don't." Then he stormed off toward his office.

She rolled her eyes. *Good talk.*

Twenty minutes later, the security guard called her desk phone. "Hey, Kate, it's Kevin."

"Hey, Kev." She was on a first-name basis with all of the guys downstairs. For that matter, she knew just about everyone in the building. It was what made her good at her job, and being good at her job was what made her *love* her job. She tucked the phone under her ear so she could keep typing. "What's up?"

"Just sent a food delivery up your way."

"Really?"

"Shit. Did you not order something? It was one of the normal guys from Kerrigan's. They said it was for Wolfe, so I just figured at this hour on a Friday night, it was you."

Kate glanced over her shoulder at Kennedy's office door. "Nope, but if it was Kerrigan's, I know exactly who it's for."

She knew what it was, too. Roast beef sandwich, extra jus, extra horseradish, and a mixed green salad instead of Kerrigan's amazing fries, which, as far as Kate was concerned, was a crime against humanity.

She hung up with Kevin, and a minute later, a delivery guy came through the door carrying a bag with Kerrigan's logo. No cheap plastic bag and Styrofoam for this joint. The bag was paper, the handles black and sturdy, and she was pretty sure the disposable containers were better quality than the plates in her cupboards at home.

"Hey, Joey," she said, greeting the familiar deliveryman as she pulled the envelope out of her desk drawer where she kept some cash. Usually she ordered food online and used credit cards, of which she had four— one for each of the guys, plus her own for more general office needs. It kept her expense accounting easier. But she kept cash on hand for when one of the guys got hangry, went rogue, and ordered his own food.

"I've got it." Kennedy emerged from his office, pulling out his wallet, and handing Joey some cash.

Joey fumbled for change, but Kennedy held up a hand. "Keep it."

"Ah, thanks." Joey flicked a confused look at Kate, likely because the bill in his hand was a hundred. Kate shrugged and gave him a little *enjoy the tip* smile.

"That was generous," she said when Joey was out of earshot.

"Hmm?"

She nodded toward the delivery guy. "You do realize you gave him a hundred-dollar bill, right?"

He held up the bag. "I got two sandwiches."

"Your poor arteries," she said, putting the money envelope back in her drawer.

"And yours. Come on."

She looked up as he headed into his office. "What?"

"One of these is for you. You want it or not?"

She did. She so did. She hadn't eaten since one, and though she kept a few PowerBars and snacks in the kitchen for late nights, a Kerrigan's sandwich was way better.

And yet . . .

Kate followed Kennedy to his office and stopped in the doorway. "What's the catch?"

He was already removing the containers from the bag, placing them on his desk. "No catch."

"But . . ."

He looked up. "What's wrong?"

"Nothing. Just that in the many years we've worked together, you've never once suggested we eat together." She walked into his office and accepted the packet of plastic silverware that he held out. "Is this because I'm dating your brother? Is that why you're being nice to me?"

He winced. "Are you dating my brother?"

She tilted her head. "*Shooooot.* Was that not you at the *double date* last night? I could have sworn it was."

Kennedy merely rolled his eyes and went back to unpacking the food. "How was the gelato?"

"Good," she answered cautiously as she accepted the container he handed her and sat down.

"Pistachio?"

She looked up. "How'd you know I like pistachio?"

Instead of answering, he sat across from her behind his desk and met her gaze. "I owe you an apology for last night."

That caught her by surprise. Kennedy Dawson wasn't the apologizing type.

"I was a jerk."

She laughed and picked up her sandwich. "Kennedy, I hate to be the bearer of bad news, but you're often a jerk."

He gave her a sharp look. "Is that your word?"

"What word?"

"Your word to describe me. It's not *adorable*, obviously. Is it *jerk*?"

She paused midchew, then resumed, even as she dropped her sandwich and pointed at him. "Aha! That explains it."

"Explains what?"

"This," she said, gesturing at the food on the desk. "Your buying me dinner and then suggesting we eat together when you've never done that before."

"Maybe I'm just a nice guy," he said with a twinkle in his eyes she wasn't accustomed to seeing.

"Oh please," she said with a laugh. "Save it for someone who hasn't spent, like, ten thousand hours with you."

He gave a quick grin, as though her response pleased him. "You want a water?"

She rolled her eyes. "Nice subject change. But yes, please."

He went to the small fridge in the corner of his office. She'd had one installed in all of the guys' offices last year. Her official stance was that it was so they could give drinks to their clients on hot summer days without having to wait for her to bring something in from the kitchen. Really, though, she figured the refrigerators were a better use of *her* time. The guys themselves weren't the problem, but their clients were divas. Beyond making sure she got ice-cold Fiji to Ian's clients and room-temp Sanpellegrino to Kennedy's, plus remembering that Matt's clients liked electrolyte water, always from a glass never a bottle . . .

Well, let's just say the fridges saved the company time and the cost of anger management classes for Kate.

"Still or sparkling?" Kennedy asked.

"Doesn't matter," Kate said, pulling the lid off a container of sauce and sniffing it.

"It's spicy mayo," he said, setting two bottles of water on the desk. "It comes with the fries."

She tentatively dipped a fry in, assessed that it was more mayo than spice, and dunked her next fry more enthusiastically. "So what's the deal here? Why are you being so nice? Bringing me fries and smiling?"

"I smile."

"Nope. Not at me. Whoa, where'd you get that?" she asked, noting the wine bottle in his hand. "I thought you only kept scotch in here. And bourbon. The brown liquors."

"Bigsby Black brought this in today. He just got back from Napa, and this is apparently some absurdly overpriced Cabernet."

"I love that name, Bigsby Black. Don't you wish you had a name like that? You know, instead of sharing the name of a president?"

"Did I wish that my first name wasn't a last name when I was a kid? Sure. Sometimes. Did I ever wish my name was Bigsby? Never."

"I used to wish I had a more glamorous name than Katherine."

"Katharine Hepburn was glamorous."

"I guess. But I used to think that if my name was Regina, or Giselle, or Theodora, I'd be a little less plain." She felt like an idiot as soon as the words were out. The last thing she wanted to do was remind him, of all people, how unglamorous she was. Not that he needed reminding.

"Plain," he said thoughtfully, pulling the cork out of the bottle. "Not the word I'd use to describe you."

Kate bit her tongue to keep from saying *bullshit*. "What word would you use?" *Certainly not* irresistible.

He gave her a *gotcha* wiggle of his eyebrows, and she shook her head, realizing she walked right into his trap.

"I'll tell you mine . . . ," he said with a playful taunt as he retrieved two wineglasses from the sideboard.

"Nice try, but no thank you," she said, taking another bite of her sandwich as he poured them each a glass of wine and sat down.

She lifted her glass, started to take a sip, then held it out to him. "To firsts."

"First what?"

"First dinners."

But it was more than just the first dinner they'd had just the two of them. Something was different. He was easier tonight somehow. Yeah, he was probably just buttering her up. Kennedy hated not knowing things, and even something as simple as her not letting him know what one word she'd use to describe him had probably kept him up all night.

The same way she'd be up tonight, wondering what word he'd use for her, but she wasn't about to be the first to cave.

"It's not the first dinner we've had together. We had dinner last night."

"Duh," she said. "I meant the first dinner with nobody else around."

He sat back. "I guess you're right. Seems odd."

She shrugged and dunked another fry. "Not really. We established the night of your party that we're sort of on different wavelengths about certain things."

"Unlike you and Jack."

"Does it weird you out? He and I together?"

"Of course not."

She cast aside the momentary flicker of disappointment she felt at his quick response but kept pushing, her gut telling her that something was going on with him. "Really? Because you were sort of on edge last night."

He stabbed irritably at his salad. "Fine. It was a little weird. I don't really see you two together."

"I *knew* it." She sat up straighter. "What do you have against us dating? First you didn't want to give him my phone number, and now—"

"Calm down—don't get so defensive. I just mean that you guys are different."

"How?"

"Jack's always been sort of easygoing and carefree."

"And I'm what, uptight and careful?"

"No," he said with a slight smile. "That's me."

Kate blinked. "That's very . . . self-aware."

"So which one of those was your word for me? *Uptight* or *careful*?"

She laughed. "Oh my God, are you ever going to give up?"

"Never. Quitting's not my strong suit." The way he said it, with a slight smile on his lips, had Kate wondering if she'd missed something.

"For real, though, you don't see Jack and me together?"

He swirled his wine, watched the dark-red liquid swish. "What's it matter to you what I think of your relationship?"

Touché. She looked back at her plate.

"So," he said after they'd both taken another bite. "The opera tomorrow."

Kate shrugged. Truth be told, she was more curious than she was excited. And a little nervous. She let out one of her internal sighs.

"Why nervous?"

"Oh crap." She wiped her mouth. "I said that out loud?"

"You did. And then you did that thing where you sigh but don't think anyone notices."

She blinked. "You know about that?"

He shrugged, as though to say, *Obviously.*

She glared at the traitorous wine. "But I've only had two sips."

"Maybe you just don't like self-censoring."

"Well, that's true," she said around a fry.

"So why nervous?"

She sighed, a real one this time, since he was onto her secret ones. "I don't think I should say."

"Why not?"

She looked at him, then away. "Because he's your brother."

"Ah," he said lightly. "Romance stuff."

"Yeah," she said a little awkwardly. In all of her imaginings over the years of what dinner with Kennedy would be like, she hadn't thought they'd be discussing another man. Certainly not his brother.

"Well, I'm your best bet for advice," he said, holding out his hands.

"Um, no offense, but you don't exactly give off *Dear Abby* vibes."

"I don't know who Abby is, but I've known Jack his entire life, and you're not exactly a stranger."

"Just because you know when my birthday is and that I like pistachio doesn't mean you know me."

He sat forward, his face strangely urgent. "I know you like the ballet over the opera. I know you're wickedly, dangerously sneaky at chess. Yes, those are recently learned details, but I've known for a hell of a long time that you're the most astute person I've ever met, that you never miss a single detail, and that you wouldn't be nervous without good reason. So spit it out."

Kate's breath caught in her throat. She wasn't accustomed to speeches from this taciturn man, who always chose his words carefully.

She wasn't accustomed to him looking so impassioned. Especially while looking at her.

Trying to hide her discomposure, she reached for her bottle of water. It seemed a safer choice than wine at the moment. "Maybe *nervous* wasn't the right word," she amended. "It's just . . . Why do I always forget that dating is hard?"

"Is it?"

"Well, maybe not for you." She waved her hand in his direction. "Not if your primary relationship goal is to be bored."

His jaw tensed. "I never said my primary goal was to be bored."

"No, I guess not. But you have to admit, as far as relationships go, you play it safe."

"Meaning what?"

"Meaning you don't date often, and when you do, it's with women who go with the flow and let you call the shots."

"Are you calling me a control freak?"

She grinned. "Pretty much."

He smiled back. "You're not much better in that department."

"No," she admitted. "Guess it's a good thing we're not together, then."

She waited, but he didn't confirm her assessment. "You're changing the subject. Why are you anxious about the opera tomorrow?"

"God, you're relentless," she muttered, grabbing her glass of wine. "Fine. But remember, you asked for it." She took a deep breath. "So it's been a while since I've dated. Been even longer since I've made it past a first date."

"Okay . . ."

"I'm kind of rusty at the whole, you know, physical part."

Kennedy flinched. "Yeah, I did not want to know that."

"I told you!"

"You did." He picked up his sandwich, then put it down without taking a bite. "Why?"

"Why what?" she asked cautiously, surprised that he wanted to continue the conversation.

"Why are you rusty?"

"Well, I don't know if you've noticed, but this"—she gestured at herself—"does not exactly set the menfolk on fire."

"Jack seems plenty interested."

"Did he tell you he was?" She sat up a little straighter.

Kennedy shook his head. "Yeah, we're not doing that."

She slumped down again with another real sigh. "I should have known you'd be no help."

"I'm not entirely sure what you need help with."

"Just . . . be a pal and reassure me that guys don't mind if first kisses are awkward. That it's not a deal breaker."

Kennedy went completely still. "You and Jack haven't kissed yet? Haven't you been on a few dates?"

She threw up her hands. "You're making it so much worse!"

"Sorry, sorry." He took a bite of his sandwich and shook his head. "Poor Jack."

She threw a fry at him, which he batted away before it left a grease stain on his suit. "Quite the temper, Miss Henley."

"Yeah, I do have one of those," she said. "I keep it locked up around the office."

"Really?" He looked pointedly at the fry on the ground.

"I mean, during the workday. Whatever." She dunked her sandwich into the jus. It was a little cold now but still delicious. "Did you know that this was Sabrina and Matt's first fake-relationship meal? Roast beef sandwiches?"

"Why would I know that? How do *you* know that?"

She shrugged. "I know everything."

They ate in silence for a moment. Then Kennedy wiped his mouth and looked at her. "It won't be awkward."

"What won't?"

He shifted in his chair, looking as uncomfortable as she'd ever seen him. "The first kiss."

"It might be. It's been a while." She refused to blush as she said it. There was no shame in the fact that it had been a long dry spell for her.

"What do you do, bite the guy?"

She laughed in surprise. She liked this joking version of Kennedy. "Yes. Definitely. Biting is my signature move."

"Look, just don't . . ." He blew out a breath. "I can't believe I'm having this conversation with my assistant. About my little brother."

Trust me, it's even weirder for me.

And yet she didn't particularly want to stop. It should be weird, and on some level, it was. But somehow . . . it also wasn't. Perhaps their six years of silently circling each other had built a better foundation of friendship than either of them realized. "What were you going to say?"

He swirled his wine again. Took a sip. "Don't overthink it."

"*That's* your advice? Don't overthink it? From the guy who analyzes *everything*?"

"I do not."

She gave him a look.

"I'll grant that I tend to deliberate my words and actions, but even I know that there are some things better left to impulse and instinct."

"Like sex."

The hand absently swirling his wine stilled. "How'd you go from kissing to sex?"

"Well, I don't know that I will, but I guess I'll find out tomorrow night, won't I?" She said it lightly, telling herself she was just trying to make him uncomfortable, the way she often delighted in doing. But even as she said it, she wondered if maybe she didn't have another motive at work.

Wondered if maybe it was a knee-jerk desire to make him jealous, the way she'd been jealous every day for *years* knowing he went home with other women without ever seeing *her*.

That she said it didn't surprise her. He was right: self-censorship had never been her strong suit. It was part of the reason she'd always been so prickly around the guy—a desperate need to keep him at a distance, to keep from blurting out her real feelings.

What *did* surprise her was the look on Kennedy's face. She thought she knew all of his faces, but this one was new. Stormy, brooding, and yes . . .

Maybe a little bit jealous.

13

Kennedy tried his best not to glare at the curvy blonde sitting in Kate's chair as he passed by her desk, but by the time he got to Ian's office on the other side of the floor, his glare was fully developed.

"Where's Kate?"

Ian glanced up in surprise from his computer. "Good morning. You're looking sunny as always."

"What the hell do we pay her for if she can't make it into the office by ten a.m. on a Monday morning?"

Ian slowly pulled his hands away from his keyboard, his light-blue eyes studying Kennedy carefully. "Kate has a doctor's appointment this morning. She put it on the calendar a month ago and sent a reminder email last week."

Oh.

"Well, I didn't hear from her all weekend," Kennedy grumbled.

Ian looked genuinely confused. "Did you expect to?"

It was a fair question. Though Kate was a regular part of their social circle, none of them generally saw or heard from her after hours unless there was some sort of group gathering. She didn't give them updates on what she did with her free time, and they didn't with her.

But that had been *before*. Before she'd started dating his brother. Before he'd started thinking about her kissing his brother. Before he hadn't been able to stop thinking about her, period.

"What's up with you?" Ian asked as Kennedy prowled around his office.

"Nothing."

"All right," Ian said with an easy shrug, turning back to his computer.

"She's driving me crazy," Kennedy blurted out.

Ian's hands slowly moved away from his keyboard once more. "I assume we're not talking about Claudia."

"Shit," Kennedy muttered under his breath, running a hand through his hair.

Hearing her name spoken by his friend forced Kennedy to deal with an emotion he hadn't felt in a long time—the second such emotion in a week. Because if hearing Kate's name brought up an all-consuming surge of jealousy, especially as it pertained to his brother, hearing Claudia's name brought up a corollary emotion: guilt.

"Trouble in tepid paradise?"

"No. Not really," Kennedy replied.

Things with Claudia were . . . fine. And *that* was the problem. Everything he'd thought he always wanted—a stable, unobtrusive relationship—felt boring as hell. He wasn't into it. Wasn't into her, and she deserved better. It was past time to end things there, and though he felt like an ass for thinking it, even *that* felt like an inconvenience.

"Do you think we should force Jack to be part of our pact?" Kennedy asked, glancing over his shoulder at Ian.

"What pact?"

"The one where we agreed not to get romantically involved with Kate."

Ian stared at him. "I can't tell if you're joking or not."

Kennedy resumed his pacing. "It would make sense. If he breaks Kate's heart, it'll be just as much our problem as if one of us did it."

"For the love of God, would you sit down?" Ian said. "You're making me dizzy."

Kennedy sat, but his foot bounced impatiently. This sort of restless energy wasn't like him, and it was irritating as hell.

Ian dragged his hands over his face. "I don't even know where to start with this."

"With what?"

Ian's hands dropped back to his desk, his fingers pounding out a quick rhythm on the surface as he seemed to be considering whether or not to speak.

"Okay, here we go." Ian sat forward slightly. "The pact. *No*, we can't force your brother, who's been out of the country for the past handful of years and doesn't work here, to agree not to fall for Kate."

Kennedy's stomach lurched at that. Surely Jack wasn't *falling* for her. Or her for him. Surely it was just . . . casual. Temporary.

"Second," Ian continued, "you keep calling it *our* pact. I guess technically it is, but Dawson, man . . . really, it's *your* pact."

"What are you talking about?"

Ian shrugged. "The pact was your idea. Matt and I went along with it, because we'd had too much of the whiskey the Sams gave us for Christmas and didn't have any reason *not* to go along with it. But the truth is, Matt and I have never needed a pact not to hit on Kate. Not that she's not great," he rushed to explain. "It just wouldn't have occurred to us. Kate's always been like a sister, from the very beginning."

"That's . . ." Kennedy shook his head. "Wait, so this whole time you guys have been thinking it's *my* pact? Like, *I'm* the one who can't keep my hands to myself without some childish oath?"

"I mean, I haven't lost sleep thinking about it. But yeah, I guess I figured you had your reasons for creating it."

. "I don't—" Kennedy stopped midsentence, trying to sort his thoughts. *Had* he had his reasons?

He thought back to that night in his office all of those years ago, when they'd made the pact. Yeah, he'd been the one to bring it up, but he assumed that was just because he was the most rational—and the least hornball—of their trio. He'd figured he hadn't been the only one who thought just a little too often about Kate's wide brown eyes or been strangely beguiled by her effortless competence. The only one who'd needed to tell himself that he wasn't interested, in the hopes that he'd stop thinking about what it would be like to undo those prim buttons . . .

His head fell forward. "Oh fuck."

"Thought so," Ian said sympathetically. "But for what it's worth, it worked, right? You've steered clear of her."

"Of course." Kennedy sat back and stretched out his legs. "As have you."

Ian smiled. "I always wondered if that was part of it—if that pact was not only to remind yourself but to make sure you didn't have to watch Matt or me make a move."

"You make it sound like I've been obsessed with the woman. I'm not Matt, panting after Sabrina."

"No," Ian said slowly. "That was a different thing altogether. And yet . . ."

"And yet what?"

Ian held up his hands. "And yet here we are in my office, talking about Kate and that pact when we should be working. Help me understand why."

Kennedy glared at him in response.

"Or not," Ian said. "But if you're not going to explain what's got you all worked up, at least let me get back to—"

"I can't stop thinking about her," Kennedy blurted out. "I can't stop thinking about Kate. There. Is that what you wanted to hear?"

Ian blew out a long breath. "Not really, no."

"Because of Claudia? I'm breaking up with her."

"Because of a lot of reasons," Ian replied. "Look, the pact may have been your idea, but it wasn't a bad one. I mean, it's Kate. We can't go messing with her."

"You think I don't know that?" Kennedy said, standing up and pacing again. "You think I want . . . whatever this is?"

"All right. So what are you going to do about it?"

"I don't know. Get over it."

"I think you have to. Your window closed."

"I never even had a window," Kennedy groused. Ian looked away quickly, and Kennedy halted his pacing at the telling gesture. "Did I?"

Ian started to pick up his desk phone, but Kennedy reached out and slammed it down. "Hell no. Who are you calling?"

"Matt. I always envisioned having backup for this moment."

"What moment? What am I missing?"

Ian looked at him steadily, then shook his head. "You sure I can't bring Matt in here for moral support?"

"Ian, did I have a goddamn window?"

His friend must have heard the silent plea beneath the outburst. "All right. Fine. Yes. Kate's had a thing for you."

Kennedy swallowed. He swallowed again. It didn't help. His mouth was completely dry.

"She's been, like, halfway in love with you for years. You really didn't know?"

Kennedy shook his head. *No.* Hell no, he didn't know. "She told you that?"

"Well, no," Ian admitted. "I don't know that she's told anyone. Maybe the girls. But it's obvious, man. She looks at you for too long."

"Because she's glaring at me."

"And why do you think that is?" Ian asked. "It's because she likes you, probably against her better judgment—no, *definitely* against her better judgment—and you made a pact never to date her."

Hope flared, even as Kennedy shook his head. "No. That doesn't even make sense. Kate's a straight shooter. She would have told me."

"She'd have told a guy she works for, who's been nothing but cold to her, that she's in love with him?" Ian asked doubtfully. "She's forthright, not a fool."

"I haven't been cold." But . . . he had. He kept Kate at arm's length in every way he possibly could, telling himself it was because she seemed averse to him, but what if they'd just been circling each other?

Needing time to think, Kennedy walked to the door.

"What are you going to do?" Ian asked.

"I don't know. At the very least, I need to let Claudia find someone who's not thinking about another woman constantly."

"And what about that other woman?" Ian said.

Kennedy sighed as his hand found the doorknob. "You said my window with Kate closed. When?"

Ian took his time responding. "I don't know. A long time ago. Early on, her breath would catch every time you walked by, no matter how hard she tried to hide it. And then it just . . . stopped. I thought maybe the window might have opened again with the MBA thing, but for reasons I still don't understand, you put that all on me."

"I didn't want her to know."

"Why the hell not?" Ian said, exasperated.

"Because what if she'd said no?" Kennedy shouted before he could think to filter the words. "What if she'd said no and rejected it?" *Rejected me?*

"Why would she have done that?" Ian asked, his voice quiet.

Kennedy shrugged. It sounded irrational now that it was out there, but there was no more dodging the fact that he cared about Kate. Had maybe cared about Kate for a very long time and was terrified about what that meant.

Still, Kennedy forced himself to look Ian straight in the eye and ask the question he didn't want the answer to. "Does she still?"

"Still what?"

"Care about me," Kennedy said, forcing the vulnerable words out.

"Sure," Ian said carefully. "She cares about all of us."

"Don't," Kennedy said sharply. "I mean . . . does she . . . ?"

"No, dude," Ian said, his tone kind as he delivered the blow. "She's moved on. And I'm pretty sure she's got a thing for your brother."

14

Kate had just shoved a mouthful of turkey club in her mouth when the flowers arrived.

Her morning gyno appointment had put her behind on nearly everything, and it was close to two by the time she managed to find a moment to shovel in lunch at her desk.

Cheeks still full, she waved thanks at the delivery guy. She dug around in the enormous bouquet of yellow roses for the card. Working for three dudes, flowers weren't a particularly common delivery around here. Usually the guys received booze, gourmet gift baskets of pears, or meat-of-the-month-club type stuff. But every now and then some vendor sent an obscene flower display with the hope of getting noticed and remembered the next time Wolfe was in the market for new software or office decor.

She found the card and pulled it out, muttering a curse as a thorn grazed the side of her thumb. Kate stopped chewing for a moment when she saw the name on the card. *Kate Winslet.*

She swallowed, then smiled, already knowing who the flowers were from.

Jack.

She was both pleased and . . . a little surprised.

She hadn't really known what to think after their date Saturday. The dinner? Excellent. The opera? Fabulous. Maybe not something she was dying to do again, but she'd thrilled in the novelty of it, even if that particular art form wasn't her passion.

The kiss, though—yes, she'd kissed Jack Dawson—had been fine. That's it. Just . . . fine.

She pulled the card out of the envelope.

Dinner this weekend?

Huh.

She flicked the card thoughtfully, trying to figure out how she felt about the fact that Jack was still interested, though she could have sworn he'd found their first kiss a little *meh* as well.

Kate reached for her cell phone, intending to ask Lara and Sabrina for their opinion on her next move, when she saw Kennedy headed her way. He looked as though he wanted to continue to his office, but at the last minute he detoured to her desk, his eyes on the bouquet.

"Hey!" she said. "How was your lunch with Claudia?"

"I've had better." He nodded at the flowers. "What's the story there?"

She hesitated only a moment before handing him the card. Instead of taking it, he snagged her wrist.

"You're bleeding."

"Oh. Yeah. Hazard of roses." She smiled, but he didn't smile back, his eyes on the thin line of red running along her thumb.

He looked up. "You got a Band-Aid?"

"There's a first aid box in the kitchen, but it's fine. A Band-Aid will annoy me." She forced herself to take steady breaths, hoping that he wouldn't notice the way her body seemed to come alive at his touch.

He looked back at her hand, finally registering the card it was holding. His gaze darkened slightly, and she knew he knew who it was from.

Kennedy's fingers moved, as though to release her, then they lingered, the pad of his thumb resting against the delicate skin of her inner wrist.

Her breath caught, and she watched his face for any sign that he registered her pulse was moving far too fast.

"So the opera was a success."

"I liked it."

"Liked, not loved?"

"Well, it was no ballet," she said with a smile.

"Ah yes. The appeal of a first love."

"Nothing like it."

Their gazes locked and held, and Kate became uncomfortably aware that they were in the middle of the office, with her boss basically holding her hand. Only he wasn't just her boss, he was also her sort-of-boyfriend's brother. To say nothing of the fact that he had Claudia . . .

Kate tried to jerk her hand away. His fingers tightened for just a moment as though reluctant to let her go. Then he released her, his hand falling to his side.

"So lunch was no good, huh? Where'd you go? I'll cross it off my list."

"I forget the name. Some French bistro. Claudia picked it."

Kate studied him. It wasn't like Kennedy to forget the name of anything.

"Bad food?"

"No, the food was fine."

"Okay, but you said you'd had better . . ."

He scratched his forehead and looked tired. "Let's just say I prefer meals where I'm not delivering the *it's not you, it's me* speech."

Her eyes went wide. "You and Claudia broke up?"

He shrugged.

"What happened? When the four of us had dinner, you seemed . . ."

His eyebrows lifted. "Yes? How did we seem?"

"I don't know. Content, I guess. Well suited."

He narrowed his gaze. "Is there a jab in there somewhere?"

"No," she snapped, irritated. "I said you were content. Isn't that all you want out of life?"

He stepped forward. "No, Kate. That's not all I want out of life."

"Well, whatever," she said, feeing slightly breathless at the intensity on his face. "I'm sorry to hear it didn't work out with Claudia. Was she upset?"

"More surprised, I think," he said, staring absently down at the flowers.

"Well, it does seem like it came up suddenly. What changed?"

His gaze flicked to hers just as her desk phone rang. She let it ring once, twice, giving him a chance to answer. When he didn't, she picked up the receiver. "Wolfe Investments, this is Kate."

It was Sylvia Reid, one of Matt's more high-maintenance clients, who couldn't—or didn't want to—grasp the fact that Matt was currently in a meeting with someone else. By the time Kate wrapped up the phone call, all but signing away her firstborn on the promise that *yes*, Matt would call her back as soon as possible, Kennedy had walked away, his office door closed.

Fine. It was just as well. He was in a weird mood, and she wasn't at all sure she had the emotional energy to deal with it. And then the phone started ringing off the hook, and she literally didn't have time to deal with it.

An hour or so later, Sabrina came sauntering into the office, all long legs, five-inch heels, and a tight-fitting gray dress that would have been forgettable on Kate but showed off Sabrina's feminine figure to perfection.

Sabrina carried two Starbucks cups and handed one to Kate, which she took in surprise. "Isn't this for Matt?"

"He can get his own. Plus, I've spent enough time in this office to know you need it more," Sabrina said, running a finger along one of the yellow rosebuds. "Pretty. Yours?"

"Yeah, Jack sent them." Kate took a sip of the coffee. It was an iced caramel macchiato and beyond delicious.

"Hmm," Sabrina said thoughtfully, rubbing a petal between her fingers.

"What hmm?"

Sabrina took a sip of her coffee. "How was the opera?"

"I liked it. I mean, I'll be honest, some of the arias, or whatever, got a little monotonous—"

"I'll rephrase," Sabrina interrupted. "How was the opera with Jack? How was the date itself?"

"It was nice."

"Yeah," Sabrina said a little sadly. "I thought so."

"What? I said it was nice!"

"Okay, but let's pause for a second and imagine Jack in *his* office right now."

Kate merely looked at her.

Sabrina snapped her fingers in Kate's face. "Close your eyes! Picture it."

Kate rolled her eyes first, but then did as her friend ordered, closing her eyes and trying to imagine Jack at this very instant. It took her a second to call his face to mind. She realized she hadn't given much thought to Jack unless he was in the same room.

"Now," Sabrina said, "imagine one of his coworkers stops by his desk and asks about his weekend. 'How was your date?' And Jack says, 'It was nice.'"

Kate winced as she saw the point her friend was making.

A *nice* date was barely a date at all. Not one that mattered. *Nice* sounded tired. Apathetic. Even worse, it sounded like something Kennedy would say about one of *his* dates.

Which reminded her . . .

"Kennedy and Claudia broke up," Kate blurted out as she opened her eyes.

Sabrina's eyebrows went up. "Interesting."

"Would you quit with that," Kate hissed, looking around to make sure nobody could hear. "Quit acting like some sort of cryptic love Obi-Wan, and spit out whatever you're thinking."

"All right." Sabrina leaned closer, lowering her voice as she pointed at the flowers. "Have you at any point ever told Jack that yellow is your favorite color or that yellow roses are your favorite flower?"

"No. I don't think we've ever talked about flowers."

Sabrina let out the tiniest sigh. "I figured as much. Yellow roses signify friendship, babe. Generally speaking, they are not the romantic choice. Which I wouldn't even be telling you, because I wouldn't want to hurt your feelings. But then I asked about the opera, and you told me about stupid arias, not about Jack himself, not about the kiss—"

"How did you know we kissed?"

Sabrina grinned around her green straw. "I didn't. Now I do. Just like how I know it was *blah*."

"Okay, seriously. The know-it-all thing is really annoying."

"Tell me I'm wrong about any of it," Sabrina said.

Kate picked up a pad of Post-it Notes and ran her thumb across it, fanning the pages as she looked at the flowers and considered Sabrina's assessment. "Okay, fine." She tossed the pad aside. "I *do* know that yellow roses usually are intended to signify friendship. I've practically made a career out of ordering flowers on behalf of the guys. Thank-you flowers, celebration flowers, sympathy flowers, romantic flowers . . . But I hardly think that Jack or any of the guys see yellow roses and are like, 'Oh look, friendship flowers.'"

Sabrina frowned. "Wait, back up. Who have you sent romantic flowers for? If you say Matt, I want a name. I want this woman's name, her address—"

"Would you focus?" Kate snapped her fingers in Sabrina's face. "You've got your guy. I'm trying to find mine."

"I think the problem is you already have."

119

"I thought you were *just* trying to tell me that Jack only sees me as a friend."

"I wasn't talking about Jack," Sabrina said with a meaningful glance toward Kennedy's office.

Kate stilled. "No."

"And yet you told me that Kennedy and Claudia broke up *before* you told me that you and Jack kissed. Interesting which development you seem to care about more."

Kate sipped her drink. "I hate you."

"I love you, too," Sabrina said. Her tone was playful, but Kate knew her friend well enough to see the concern in Sabrina's blue eyes.

"I'm fine," Kate said softly. "I'm over him, remember?"

"I remember you *said* that."

"Because it's true. I'm not going to waste my time loving a guy who'll never love me back, Sabrina. I'm holding out for the guy who doesn't treat relationships the way he does his stock portfolio, all cautious and analytical. I want the guy who looks at me and knows how great I am. The guy who jumps all in with both feet."

"Uh-huh. Just like *you're* jumping all in?"

"Meaning what?" Kate crossed her arms.

Sabrina gestured at Kate with her Starbucks cup. "Just a couple weeks ago, you were a new woman with the hair and the makeup and the wardrobe. You're still rocking it, by the way. The new hair is on point, that pink lipstick is amazing, and that blouse is killer."

"I sense a *but*."

"But . . . despite your sassy new look and your *all-in* talk, to say nothing of the fact that you are the boldest, most confident woman I know, all I see is someone who's scared to death of facing that." Sabrina punctuated her challenge by pointing at Kennedy's door.

"I told you—"

"You're over him. I heard. But you said it yourself, your loins didn't get the message."

Kate's nose wrinkled. "Can we not use that word?"

"Okay. Genitals?"

"Eeew."

"My point is, you may not be smitten with the guy anymore, Kate, but you still want him."

"So?"

Sabrina leaned down. "So do something about it."

"Like what?"

"Seduce him."

Kate laughed, horrified by the thought. "Um, no. I wouldn't even know where to start. And he'd probably laugh."

"We're talking about Kennedy. He's not really a jolly kind of guy."

"That is *so* reassuring."

"Sorry. I just think that maybe if you two had some hot animal sex, you could finally be totally free to move on. Heart *and* body," Sabrina said, pointing at Kate's crotch.

"Don't be creepy," Kate muttered, even as she looked at Kennedy's closed door, hating that Sabrina might be a tiny bit right. Not necessarily about the loins and all of that. Kate liked to think she could control her baser instincts.

But it stung a little to realize just how much she'd been holding back when it came to Kennedy Dawson—first by trying to disguise her amorous feelings, then by trying to disguise her hurt feelings, now by trying to manufacture all the reasons he was wrong for her.

Kate picked up her cell.

"Who are you calling?"

"Jack," she muttered.

"You're going to see him again?"

Kate nodded as the phone started to ring.

"But I thought we agreed those were friendship roses," Sabrina whispered.

"Exactly. Which is why I need to see him. Whether he meant it or not, he sent the right flowers, because apparently friendship is all I have to offer."

"For how long?"

Kate jabbed a finger in the general direction of Kennedy's office. "Until I figure out how to deal with *that*."

15

"Do you want to talk about it?"

Kennedy pulled back from the railing where he'd been staring absently at the murky water of the East River. "Hey, Dad."

Roger Dawson joined his son at the railing, his ever-present scotch in one hand.

"Great party," Kennedy said, taking a sip of his cocktail.

"Yeah, your mother always did put together a nice event."

Nice event was an understatement. Kennedy's parents had decided to celebrate forty years of marriage on a luxury yacht, chartered for the evening for two hundred of their "closest friends and family." With a caviar buffet, live jazz band, and black-tie dress code, it made Kennedy's birthday party a few weeks earlier feel like a backyard barbecue in comparison.

He felt a little flicker of guilt. The birthday party made him think of Claudia, which in turn made him realize this was the first time the woman had even crossed his mind since they'd broken things off earlier in the week.

"So you want to talk about it?" his dad asked again.

"Talk about what?"

"You tell me."

"Oh good," Kennedy said sarcastically, tossing back the last sip of his drink. "*This* game."

His father smiled, not bothering to pretend that he didn't know exactly what Kennedy was talking about. Roger had left his sons' earliest years to his wife and an ever-present nanny, but by the time Kennedy and his brothers were in high school, their dad had stepped forward a bit, played more of a role, and this had been one of his favorite strategies. Whenever there'd been something on one of their minds, whether it be school, girls, friends, or sports, he'd had the same approach: he'd ask if his son wanted to talk about it. And then wait. And wait. And wait.

It worked. Every damn time, Kennedy and his brothers were *sure* they hadn't wanted to talk about it, right up until the moment it all came spilling out. But Kennedy wasn't fifteen any longer, and he knew that talking about problems didn't necessarily solve them.

He stayed quiet, and his father changed tack. "No Claudia tonight?"

"We broke up." Kennedy reached to his left to put his empty glass on a table.

His dad nodded. "Yeah."

Kennedy let out a laugh. "You could at least pretend to be surprised."

Roger shrugged. "It was nice of her to throw you that birthday party."

"But?"

"Well . . ." His dad took a drink. "The party seemed a bit more about her than you."

"Probably. I'm not sure either of us was in the relationship for the right reasons."

"Why were you in it?"

Kennedy looked over his shoulder at the hundreds of people laughing and drinking on the yacht deck. "You know this is your party, right? You don't have to play dad right now."

"You never *play* dad. You *are* dad. And right now, this father wants to know what's got his oldest son brooding alone."

"I'm always brooding." *Always alone, too.*

It was a weird thought. He wasn't always alone, not technically. He had a great family, loyal friends. He dated when he felt like it. But whether it was from the reality of another birthday or the fact that his two closest friends and youngest brother had found women who seemed to make up their other half, Kennedy was increasingly aware that he wasn't part of a couple. And while he'd never minded solitude, this was different.

"You said you were in the relationship with Claudia for the wrong reason. What was it? The companionship?"

Kennedy gave a wry smile, because his father may as well have read his mind. "Maybe. More so, I think, that Claudia seemed like the type of woman I always thought I'd end up with."

"She was beautiful," Roger granted.

"Yes. But it was more than that," Kennedy said, glancing at the water. "Mom set us up. The Palmers live in Europe now, but Claudia grew up just a few blocks north of us. They went to our church, though a different service. She knows all of the same people we do."

"And that's what you wanted? Someone from our social circle?"

"I don't know. It seemed right on paper."

"But didn't feel right?"

Kennedy shook his head.

His father casually turned around, leaning his elbows on the railing as he faced the crowd. "This got anything to do with Jack?"

Kennedy gave his father a sharp look. "What about Jack?"

"You tell me. You're always quiet, yes, but you've been even more reticent than usual since your brother moved back from Europe. Since he took up with your girl."

"Kate's not my girl," Kennedy said, turning around so he, too, could lean back against the railing, crossing his arms over his chest.

"She sure cleans up nice, though. I always liked her."

Kennedy forced himself to follow his father's gaze, and though he thought he was braced for it, the sight of Kate and Jack together still packed a wallop in the vicinity of his throat.

Again with the pink.

What was with Kate lately? It was as though she'd gone out and bought a whole arsenal of pink dresses just for Jack, and also to torture Kennedy. He didn't even like pink. Well, that's not true. He'd never given a thought one way or the other to the color . . . until now.

The pink dress she'd worn at his birthday party had been flirty and feminine. The one on their double date had been fun and casual. But this . . .

Kennedy's gaze drifted over her, and he swallowed. The front of the rose-colored dress was demure, tying at her neck and then skimming over her frame with only a hint at the slight curves below, all of the way down to silver sandals.

When he'd first walked in and seen her, he thought he could manage the evening without staring. Maybe. But when she'd turned around and he'd seen the back, he was a goner. She'd pulled her hair up into a simple knot at the back of her head, no doubt styled intentionally to show off the large bow tied behind her elegant neck, showing off her slender back. All of it.

Kate said something to Jack, who bent his much taller frame to hers, his hand coming around to rest lightly on the smooth skin that had been demanding Kennedy's attention all night. Skin that was not his to touch. That had never been his. But could have been . . .

He turned back abruptly toward the water, away from his brother and Kate, as well as his own thoughts. Or tried to, anyway.

As usual, Kennedy's father missed nothing. "Does she know?"

Kennedy didn't play dumb. "No."

"Does Jack?"

Kennedy shook his head. "I didn't even know until a few days ago."

"Hmm." His father took a drink. "What's your plan?"

"What do you mean, what's my plan? She's my assistant. He's my brother. I get over it."

Roger continued to study Jack and Kate. "You think she's the one for him?"

Kennedy gave a fleeting glance over his shoulder, then back out at the river. "I don't know."

"Yes, you do."

Kennedy's fingers clenched around the iron railing. "Well, what do you want me to do, Dad? Go storm over there and tell him that I don't see it? That he's not able to give her what she wants?"

"How do you know what she wants?"

"She told me. She wants love at first sight, someone who doesn't hold back, who's willing to go all in," he said, recalling their conversation that night over the chessboard.

His father said nothing for a minute, then looked back at Kennedy. "You remember that summer when you were about nine or so, and we rented that house in Nantucket with the pool?"

"Sure."

"It was all you boys wanted to do, swim in that pool. Not Fitz, he was too young, but the other three of you spent all damn day in that thing."

"So?" Kennedy knew there was some sort of fatherly lesson coming, but he didn't have a clue what it was.

"It says a lot about someone, the way they approach a new pool for the first time. Your mother and I laughed about it, watching you boys that first day. Jack went cannonballing into the deep end."

"Of course he did," Kennedy said with a slight smile.

"John sat on the top step, book still in hand, because he'd wanted to finish his chapter before going swimming. But you and Jack didn't want to wait."

"Because it was never one chapter; it was always the whole book." Kennedy himself had always enjoyed reading, but his younger brother John was bookish on a whole other level.

"And you," his father said, continuing with his swimming parable. "You walked the perimeter of the pool. Checked the number painted on the side to see how deep it was. Gave the diving board a careful test to make sure it was sound. Dipped a foot in to test the temperature. I'm sure if you knew how, you'd have checked the chlorine levels, too."

"Because people pee in pools. Jack probably did."

"You were always the cautious one, and your mother and I fully expected you to go into the pool via the shallow end, taking your time."

"I get it," Kennedy said a little irritably. "Jack's the spontaneous one, John's head is more in the book world than the real world, and I'm the overly cautious one."

"But you didn't wade into the shallow end," Roger continued, as though Kennedy hadn't spoken. "After making sure it was okay to do so, you dove into the deep end without a second's hesitation. And you stayed in that pool well after Jack and John got bored and left."

His father fell silent, and Kennedy glanced over. "Okay, I give up. The moral of the story is . . ."

"You do go all in, son. You go all in bigger than anyone I know. It just takes you a while to figure out your plan of approach, dot your *i*'s, do your due diligence first." Roger Dawson clapped his son on the shoulder. "Talk to your brother. It won't do either of you any favors to keep your mouth shut if it eats you up. It won't do Kate any favors, either."

Kennedy said nothing.

"At least think about it," his father said, patting him on the shoulder. "Life goes by so quickly. Don't waste a minute of it."

Kennedy knew it was the coward's way out, but he waited until his brother was alone before making his move.

"Hey," Jack said, grinning when he saw Kennedy. "Where the hell you been? I haven't seen you since we first got in."

"I've been making the rounds," Kennedy lied. "So much for this being a small get-together."

"Classic over-the-top Mom party, right?" Jack said, snagging a stuffed mushroom off a passing tray. "Hey, sorry to hear about Claudia. She seemed nice."

"She was. Just not . . . You know."

"Yeah, I know. Unfortunately."

Jack's sardonic tone gave Kennedy pause. "Do you?"

"Yup." Jack popped the mushroom in his mouth. "Got the old *let's be friends* talk from your girl Kate."

"What?" Even as hope flared, he cared enough about his brother to be bothered. "She dumped you at our parents' anniversary party?"

"Nah." Jack picked up his glass of champagne from a table. "We had 'the talk' earlier this week. Decided we were better as friends and all of that."

"Who decided?"

"She brought it up first." Jack lifted a shoulder. "But I'd have done it if she hadn't. Sucks, though. She's one of the good ones, but the physical chemistry was off. It was a little too much like kissing my sister."

"You kissed her?" Kennedy's question came out short, angry.

Jack had lifted his hand to wave at someone across the deck, but his gaze snapped to Kennedy's, and his hand lowered. "Whoa."

"What?"

Jack studied him for a moment, then sighed and shook his head. "You're an idiot."

"You get dumped by an amazing woman, and *I'm* the idiot?"

Jack didn't rise to the bait, just gave Kennedy an irritated look. "I had my suspicions, but you had Claudia, and . . . Damn it, Kennedy. You should have told me she was off-limits."

"I did," Kennedy ground out. "I very distinctly remember telling you that Kate was off-limits, that we had a pact—"

"Forget the stupid pact. I meant, you failed to mention that she was off-limits because she's *yours*."

"She's not a possession, Jack."

"I'm aware, *Kennedy*. But don't pretend not to know what I mean. You like her."

"Of course I like her."

"You know what I mean. You *want* her. Nothing to do with friendship. Or work." Jack stated it as a fact.

And *hell*. Hearing it out loud . . .

"No. I don't know. It's complicated."

"See, that's always been your problem. You act like you want everything to be simple and straightforward, but you spend so much effort trying to simplify every damn thing that you end up with a situation that's a hundred times more complex than if you'd just gone with the flow."

"All right, Aristotle, calm down," Kennedy snapped, grabbing Jack's champagne and taking a large swallow, since it was the closest drink around. "If you two are broken up, why is she here with you?"

Jack shrugged. "Like I said, we're friends. I asked if she still wanted to come, and she said sure."

"Where is she?"

"Restroom," Jack said. "Apparently there's a long line. Boats aren't exactly known for bountiful facilities."

"Maybe that's why she dumped you," Kennedy said. "You use words like *bountiful*."

His brother threw up a good-natured middle finger and grabbed his champagne back. "Go get your girl."

"She's not . . ." The automatic denial died on Kennedy's lips. Maybe she was. At the very least, his dad was right. He owed it to himself and to her to find out.

Kennedy started pushing through the crowd even before he'd fully registered his intent to move.

"Hey, Kennedy."

He turned back to his brother, who lifted his glass in a toast. "Keep it simple."

Yeah, right.

He didn't know what he felt for Kate. But it was anything but simple.

16

Kate waited in line for the ladies' room for a solid fifteen minutes before she decided to cheat the bathroom system.

She assuaged her guilt by reminding herself that she and the owner of the yacht charter went way back. In fact, Kate was the one who'd put Kennedy's mom in touch with the company for this party. *Surely* that earned her the right to break a few rules. Like, say, using the restroom in one of the exclusive suites.

Strictly speaking, the suites were off-limits during big cocktail parties, but she'd coordinated enough boat parties during her tenure at Wolfe to know that the company kept a few of the rooms unlocked in case any of the guests needed a private place to deal with seasickness.

Or in Kate's case, a *really* full bladder.

Someone forgot to stock hand towels in the tiny bathroom, so Kate settled for shaking her hands vigorously as she stepped into the suite attached to the bathroom. It was small but nicely appointed, equipped for overnight stays with two small beds that could be pressed together as one, as well as a built-in couch in the corner and a small wet bar. She was tempted to sit for a moment and get a reprieve from the wealthy but increasingly tipsy partygoers . . .

Kate's hands froze midshake as she realized she wasn't alone. "What are you doing in here?"

Kennedy didn't move from where he leaned against the wall in the small windowless room. "Asks the woman who barged through a door marked PRIVATE."

"How'd you find me?"

"I didn't see you in line at the main ladies' room, so I asked one of the staff members, who remembered seeing 'someone in a pink dress' duck in here."

"Well, congrats, you found me. Can we get back?" She pointed to the closed door he was blocking.

"To your date?"

His light emphasis on the word *date* gave her pause. "You talked to Jack."

"I did. Pretty sexy dress to wear for someone who's just a friend."

"Save it," she snapped, marching forward. "We're not in the office, so you can't tell me what to do or what to wear."

"When have I ever told you what to do or what to wear in the office?" he said, uncrossing his arms and straightening. "Even if I wanted to, you wouldn't have listened."

"Well, why would I? You're technically my boss, but not my only one. You're not my boyfriend. We're barely even friends, so—"

"Again with that? You're not sure we're even friends?" His words were low, quiet, but she fell back a step in surprise because he looked . . . hurt.

She tried to calm her racing heart, not entirely sure why she was so worked up. "We are, I guess. It's just . . . You know. We've never been easy together."

"Let me guess. That's my fault."

"I don't know, Kennedy," she said with a small sigh. "It's probably a little of both of us."

He stepped forward. "Jack told me I have a tendency to make things more complex than I need to, so that's on me. But what about you? Why haven't you let us be easy?"

Her eyes locked on his face. He was as intense as ever, his trademark scowl firmly in place, but there was something else at work as well. Something she'd never seen, and she thought for sure she'd seen it all. The thought that there were facets of his personality she hadn't yet discovered was both daunting and thrilling.

Kate swallowed. "I don't know why."

"I think you do." His eyes were blazing with emotion. "What word?"

She shook her head. "Did I just black out and miss part of our conversation? What are you talking about?"

"The word you'd use to describe me. From that night at dinner."

She let out an exasperated, frustrated laugh. "Not that again. Just—"

"What word!" he shouted.

She froze in shock at the emotion she heard in his voice. It was more than frustration; he sounded nearly . . . desperate.

The two of them stood there, with nothing but the sound of their breathing, his every bit as heavy as hers. Kate refused to look at him as her heart beat one confused, frantic beat after another, her gaze locked on the door that would end whatever this was.

This wasn't the Kennedy she knew. He didn't look at her like this. He didn't shout.

And yet here they were.

Kennedy's head turned slightly toward her, and though she told herself he was too tall for her to feel the heat of his breath on her cheek, she swore she felt it. Or perhaps that was just the heat of his gaze . . .

"What. Word." His voice was quiet again, and his hand reached for her.

Knowing she wouldn't be able to handle his touch, she reared backward. *"Blind!"* she shouted, moving away from him. "You want to know what word I'd use to describe you, Kennedy Dawson? You're completely *blind*. You can't see what's right in front of you, and you never could. You're so damn controlled and completely oblivious to . . . to . . ." Her brain caught up to her mouth, and she stopped herself just in time.

But he didn't let her off the hook, his gaze dark and unreadable. "What am I oblivious to?"

"Nothing." She licked her lips nervously.

"Don't chicken out now, Kate," he said, moving steadily toward her.

"Please," she whispered. "Don't."

Kennedy froze.

"I just . . ." She pointed awkwardly around him toward the door. "Can we just go back to the party?"

His eyes dimmed slightly, the heat fading as he watched her closely, as though studying every feature, trying to read her. "Just . . . one more question."

"What?" Her voice didn't wobble, but it was a close call, and she fixed her eyes once more on her escape route, torn between the safety beyond and the thrill of whatever was happening in this room.

"When you kissed Jack . . ."

Her eyes flew back to his.

"Was it awkward like you feared?"

"No," she answered immediately.

His eyes narrowed. "No? Why'd you break up with him, then?"

"Kennedy."

"Kate."

She forced herself to meet his eyes, remembering her conversation with Sabrina. She realized that her friend was right—that she'd never really be able to move on with Jack or anyone until she got this man out of her system.

"It wasn't awkward," she said quietly, watching his face. "But it wasn't special. And I'm holding out for special."

She meant it as a challenge and saw from his too-quick blink that he knew as soon as he heard it.

She held his gaze. Waited.

And waited.

And waited.

Then she saw the moment he decided to turn down her challenge and stepped away from her.

Her heart crumpled. "I've got to go," she said, brushing past him.

"Kate."

She ignored him. Thank goodness it was a small space, because she was across the room in seconds, feeling the heavy weight of her hair finally pulling free of its tidy knot. But she didn't pause to fix it, didn't pause at all as she fumbled with the stupid ship doorknob, wrenching it open—

It slammed shut again before she could leave the room.

"Would you just give me a goddamn minute?" he growled behind her. "This is new to me. I'm trying to think—"

She whipped around to face him. "That's your problem, Kennedy," she snapped, trying to shove his big hand away from the door so she could get out. "You're all thought, no action—"

She gasped as Kennedy reached out, his fingers tangling roughly in her hair, tugging back so her face tilted up to his.

Then his mouth took hers.

17

Kennedy's kiss was hard and unapologetic. Kate could taste the frustration on his lips, feel it in the glorious tug of his hand in her hair.

It matched her own frustration—years' worth—and she relished it.

Her hands found his lapel, fingers gripping hard as she opened her mouth to the rough demand of his. He went still, but only for a split second before he slid his free arm around her, pulling her much smaller frame against his. Kate gasped at the contact, and Kennedy took full advantage, his lips nudging hers apart to deepen the kiss.

Her tongue touched his tentatively, then more confidently as he let out a slight groan, pulling her closer.

Kate went to her toes, her arms winding around his neck as she gave in completely. Kennedy bent down to her height, his hands sliding around her hips to her butt, and lifted her. They tumbled to the small couch, Kennedy rolling her beneath him as he ran kisses over her throat and along her jaw before capturing her face once more.

Kate hovered somewhere between disbelief and joy that this was happening, that this man she'd needed for what felt like her entire life finally needed her back.

"This dress has been killing me all night," he said, nuzzling her throat once more.

"I didn't know you saw it," she said, gasping as his hand slipped beneath her to palm the bare skin of her back.

"Oh, I saw," he said, nibbling his way to her shoulder. "I saw every damn thing. Every time you laughed with him, with anyone. You never laugh that way with me."

"You're not that funny."

He nipped her exposed shoulder, just hard enough to make her gasp out a laugh, and her fingers sank into his thick hair, pulling his mouth back to hers. Kennedy kissed her but kept his weight on his elbows, clearly trying not to crush her. But she wanted to be crushed. She wanted all of it.

Her hands slipped beneath his tux jacket, her fingers spreading wide against his warm, firm back as she tried to pull him down. *More.*

He let out a slight laugh. "Kate—"

Her hips tilted up to his, half-instinctive, half-intentional. He groaned, and she did it again, this time definitely intentional, rubbing against the unmistakable hardness.

"Jesus." His mouth slammed down on hers again, and this time he gave himself all of the way over, his body hard and heavy on hers, his erection nudging at the *V* of her thighs.

Kate was hot everywhere, every effort to assuage the ache between her legs only causing a *bigger* ache. It didn't help that Kennedy kept his hands firmly in gentleman's territory, skimming over her hips, her waist, along her arms, but making no effort to untie the halter of her dress or sneak beneath her skirt.

Her eyes opened as he nuzzled her jawline, doubt creeping in. She was dying for him, and he seemed perfectly content in first-base territory.

She glanced down as she realized he'd stopped kissing her, and she saw him looking over the length of her body, his hand skimming along her waist.

"Kennedy?"

The look on his face eased her doubt slightly. It was tortured and needing and everything she was feeling.

He swallowed dryly. "We've got to stop. We've got to stop now, or I won't stop at all, and you deserve better than to go from a first kiss to—"

She wrapped her fingers around his wrist and brought his hand to her breast, holding her breath in hopes he wouldn't be disappointed. To say she was small was an understatement.

But Kennedy's body tensed, and he squeezed his eyes shut. He moved his hand slightly, and they both groaned when his thumb rasped over her nipple, hard and yearning beneath the pink satin of her gown.

Kate had known her past sexual experiences were kind of *meh*, but the fact that Kennedy Dawson's touch over her clothes made her hotter than *anything* she'd experienced in the past made her realize how much trouble she was really in.

He kissed her again, his hand palming over her, his fingers toying with the nipple of one breast before sliding over to tease the other, back and forth until she was thrashing on the couch, her dress inching ever higher on her thighs, Kennedy's hand occasionally drifting down, closer and closer to bare skin—

"Jesus Christ!" The oath sounded a half second after the door burst open, slamming against the wall.

Kennedy sprang back, moving off her before Kate even realized they'd been interrupted.

"Dude, lock the door."

Still dazed, Kate sat up partially, to glance toward the now-open doorway, then flopped back down again with a groan.

"Get out!" Kennedy snarled.

His youngest brother did the opposite, stepping all of the way into the room, but at least he closed the door.

"Mom and Dad were worried about you. I'll tell them they were right to worry, because I'm pretty sure Jack's going to kill you."

"No, he's not," Kate said with a sigh, adjusting her dress as best she could, and then pushing up into a sitting position. "Hi, Fitz."

She liked Fitz, and he liked her, but his expression was cool as he gazed at her now. "Kate."

"Don't look at her like that. She's not with Jack," Kennedy snapped.

"Oh, come on—"

"I'm not," Kate rushed to say. "I mean, I am, but just as friends . . ."

She broke off as she realized she didn't really have much ground to stand on. True, she and Jack weren't dating, and she hadn't cheated on him. But she had come here with him, and just last week he'd kissed her—

"Oh God." Kate covered her face with her hands.

Kennedy's hand rested briefly on her shoulder. "Don't do that. Jack will be fine. He knows."

She dropped her hands and looked up at him. "Knows what?"

"Yeah, knows what?"

"Shut up, Fitz. Better yet, leave," Kennedy said, not bothering to glance at his younger, albeit taller, brother.

"What does Jack know?" Kate demanded, more forcefully this time.

Kennedy looked away briefly, then seemed to force himself to look back at her. "I told him I was looking for you."

"Oh, well, I'm sure he'll be relieved to know that you found her on her back, with her dress jacked up to her—"

"*Fitz.*" Kennedy gave his brother his full attention now, his tone leaving no room for argument.

Kate expected Fitz to push, but the brothers had a silent standoff, Fitz's blue eyes studying Kennedy for a long moment before moving to Kate. Then he shook his head and left.

"What was that?" Kate asked. She and her sister had their own kind of silent communication, but this was a whole other level of mind reading.

"Brother talk."

"Oh yeah?" she asked lightly. "What did you say?"

Kennedy looked away. "Fitz knows."

"Well, that's great," she said a little testily. "Jack knows, and now Fitz knows. Sure would be great if *Kate* knew."

She expected Kennedy to move away, to change the subject, but instead he stepped forward, looking breathtakingly desirable with his hair a mess, his tie askew.

"That you're mine," he said quietly, reaching out and gently touching a knuckle to the corner of her mouth. "They know that you're mine now."

18

Kennedy knocked on Ian's open door. "Got a sec?"

Ian glanced up. "I'm having déjà vu. Wasn't it exactly one week ago you came storming into my office with that exact look on your face, brooding about your brother and Kate?"

"You free or not?" Kennedy said, wanting to get this over with before he lost his nerve. He'd been running this conversation over and over in his head for about twenty-four hours now.

Time to get it done.

"Yeah, sure," Ian said, waving him in.

Kennedy nodded at Ian's desk phone as he sat. "Can you see if Matt's free?" He was hoping he'd get lucky and have to say this only once.

Ian picked up his phone and punched the button for Matt's extension. "Got a minute? Kennedy's in here looking sulky and weird . . . Yeah, more than usual . . . I know. But yes, it is possible."

Kennedy rolled his eyes, and a minute later, Matt came into Ian's office.

"Close the door," Kennedy said.

"Yes, sir," Matt muttered, shutting it and then sitting beside Kennedy. He studied him a moment, then looked at Ian. "Damn, you were right. Extra pensive."

"Should we get Kate in here, too?" Ian asked.

Kennedy forced himself not to react to her name. He knew why Ian asked—Kate was as much a part of their team as the three of them. But the thing was, he was here to talk about Kate.

"She's not here," Matt said.

Ian glanced at his watch. "Really?"

"Nope. Hasn't come in yet. I thought she was just in the restroom, but I've gone by her desk, like, five times, and her computer's not even on. And the phone's still set to the weekend voice mail."

Kennedy frowned at this. She hadn't been at her desk when he'd gotten in or walked by, but he assumed he was just missing her while she was in the kitchen or away from her desk.

She wasn't here?

"Huh. Okay, well, she's allowed to be an hour late for once in her life," Ian said. "Kennedy, what's up?"

Kennedy had never been one to ease in to things, and he knew it wouldn't get any easier the longer he waited, so he laid it out for them. Bluntly. "I broke the pact."

"What pact?" Matt asked distractedly, typing something on his phone.

Ian caught on quicker. "Cannon."

Matt looked at Ian, then at Kennedy. "Oh." He straightened, his thumb locking his phone as he gave the conversation his full attention. "*That* pact."

Kennedy looked between his two friends, looking for anger or disgust, but he saw only curiosity and maybe a flicker of concern.

"What happened?"

Good question. What had happened on Saturday night? One moment he'd been trying to assess if she had any lingering feelings for Jack, not sure he could survive it if she did. The next moment his mouth had been on hers, his body above hers . . .

"I don't know," Kennedy said in response to Ian's question, leaning forward so both elbows were on his knees, trying to gather his thoughts. "She was at my parents' anniversary party this weekend."

"As your date?"

Kennedy looked up. "As Jack's date."

"Damn," Matt breathed.

"They were there just as friends. They'd broken up earlier that week, but it was still . . ." He stared at his hands. "Not well done of me."

"The hookup or you cuckolding your brother?"

"I didn't . . ." Kennedy shook his head. "Jack was fine with it."

It was true. Even if Fitz hadn't lorded over the situation like some sort of nun, escorting Kate home so that Kennedy could "come clean" to Jack, he would have told his brother what happened.

Not only had Jack not been upset, he hadn't even seemed surprised.

"He was fine with it," Kennedy repeated before looking at his friends. "And I need to know if you guys are as well."

"Why? We've never dated Kate."

"I know. But the pact . . ."

"Fuck that weird pact," Matt said. "I mean, whatever, I never minded it, but that was your deal from the very beginning."

Ian looked smugly at Kennedy. "Told you."

"Yeah, you did. Still, we made a deal, and I broke it. That's not right."

"I don't even know if I want to know this," Matt said. "But did you break it all of the way? Or just . . . bend it? Actually, no. Don't tell me."

"Yeah, don't," Ian agreed. "Though, I've got to ask . . . What's the plan here?"

"I don't have a plan."

Ian frowned. "You always have a plan."

"Yeah, well, not with her," Kennedy said, sitting back in frustration. "It just happened."

"Do you want it to happen again?"

Yes. Again and again, this time not on a hard, cramped couch on a boat. This time without his youngest brother's interruption. When it happened again, she wouldn't be his brother's date, and he wouldn't stop until he found out if the skin of her thighs was as sweet as the taste of her shoulders, if she made those little noises when he—

Kennedy shifted in his chair, and Ian made a knowing face. "Oh God. I regret asking."

"Wait, are you guys dating now?" Matt asked.

"No. We're . . . I don't know," he said irritably. "I kissed her, Fitz interrupted us, and then she went home so I could talk with Jack. But she didn't return my texts or calls yesterday."

"Shit," Ian muttered. "And now she's a no-show this morning. Maybe you were right to set up that damn pact. But this doesn't seem like her."

"Agreed," Matt said. "Kate's hardly one to run from something. Unless you were weird," he said, glancing at Kennedy.

"I wasn't weird," he snapped. "We were two consenting adults who . . . consented. I don't regret what happened, only that I didn't tell you guys first. A pact's a pact, even if I was the only one who ever intended to honor it."

"No," Ian corrected. "You're the only one who *needed* it. It's like I told you the other day, she's like a sister to me. I didn't need some weird bro agreement not to touch her."

"Same," Matt said. "I always just figured you were a rules guy, and without setting up that rule for yourself, you'd have been all over our assistant, thus risking . . . Well, hell. Risking her not showing up to work."

Ian reached for his cell. "That's it. I'm calling her."

"Already on it," Matt said, his cell phone to his ear.

"Put it on speakerphone," Kennedy demanded.

Matt ignored him, then slapped at Kennedy's hand when he tried to take the phone. "Knock it off. Maybe she doesn't want to hear from you."

Matt said it jokingly, but the words clawed at Kennedy all the same. Was his friend right? Was Kate avoiding him?

The other guys were right. It didn't seem like her. He could see her taking yesterday to think things over. Hell, he'd needed a beat to sort things through himself, and he still wasn't completely there. He had no idea what was next for them or how to make any of this work. He didn't know how to reconcile that they wanted different things out of a relationship—that he would never be the wild, passionate lover she wanted, and she would never be the uncomplicated woman he wanted.

And yet, he did want her. He wanted her more than he'd ever wanted anything.

"Voice mail," Matt said with a frown.

"That's it," Kennedy said decisively, standing.

"That's it?" Ian repeated. "What is this, a Nicolas Cage movie? What are you going to do, go scale her building? Sit down, Dawson. Let's make a plan."

Kennedy ignored him and headed to the door.

"Hold up," Matt said. "What are you going to do?"

"I'm going to her place to check on her."

"That's an HR nightmare, dude. A boss can't go storming over to his assistant's apartment because she's late."

"I'm not going as her boss," Kennedy said. "I'm going as her friend."
He suspected they all knew that he was really going as a hell of a lot
more than that.

◆　◆　◆

Kennedy had been to Kate's apartment in the Village only once, right
after she'd moved in a couple of years ago and thrown a housewarming
party. And even then, he'd been only on the rooftop deck.

Privately, he thought they should pay her more if the best she could
do was a small studio atop a SoulCycle building, but from what he'd
been able to tell, she loved the place.

And he had to admit, as he climbed the stairs to the fourth
floor, it wasn't without its charms. The hallway was tiny, there was
definitely no air-conditioning, and there was a baby stroller outside
one of the doors, through which he could hear baby screams. But it
was clean and smelled vaguely like cookies, and almost everyone had
a welcome mat.

He stopped outside door 402, and if he wasn't so worried about
her avoiding him, he might have smiled at her doormat, that said
Welcome. Price of Entry: and then a wine bottle.

Next time. Next time, he'd bring wine. And there *would* be a next
time. He'd make sure of it.

Kennedy lifted his hand and knocked, feeling a little nervous in a
way he hadn't since senior year when he'd asked Regina Morris to prom,
even though he wasn't entirely sure she hadn't been interested in the far
more popular Pat Delaney.

She'd said yes to Kennedy. Then spent most of the dance trying to
make Pat jealous.

In hindsight, Kennedy realized it was a double win for him. He'd
gotten the cute date, and he'd been right about her and Pat.

But right now, he wanted to be right about Kate. Right in thinking that they'd just barely scratched the surface of the chemistry between them.

No answer. The knot of dread that he'd been trying to ward off all morning doubled in size.

He pulled out his cell phone to call her, even as he lifted his hand to knock again—

The door opened, and Kennedy started to close his eyes in relief, only to freeze when he saw her face, red and streaked with tears.

"Kate. What's—"

Acting on unfamiliar instinct, Kennedy stopped talking, sensing that words weren't what she needed. He stepped into her apartment, shutting the door with one hand and reaching for her with the other. She came easily, her face pressed to his chest, her arms wrapping around his waist as she let out a sob.

His throat knotted as he slid one hand to the back of her head, the other wrapping around her, trying to absorb her shaking.

For long moments he just held her, absorbing her pain as best he could, even as he bit back demands to know what was wrong so he could fix it.

"Sorry," she said around a hiccup. "I keep thinking I'm all out of tears, but they just keep coming."

He bent his head lower, his lips brushing the side of her head. "What's wrong? What can I do?"

"Nothing," she whispered. "Just hold me a little bit longer."

He did. He held her a lot longer, through another round of tears, until finally, all cried out, she eased back and looked up at him with heartbroken eyes. "I've got to go."

He brushed a tear from her cheek. "I know better than to tell you what to do, but respectfully, you don't seem to be in any condition to go anywhere."

"I'm not," she said, wiping away more tears. "But I have to get home."

"Home? To your parents?"

Her face crumpled again, but she regained enough composure to speak through her tears. "I got a call from my sister. My dad had a heart attack."

"Kate." He tried to pull her in, but she resisted.

"He didn't make it, Kennedy. My dad died this morning."

PART TWO

PART TWO

19

Friday, May 10
Three-ish weeks later

"Okay, it's decision time," Kate said, holding up two DVD cases. "Do we go old-school with your favorite or new-school with my favorite? Because while I'll grant you that *Sleepless in Seattle* gets high points for originality, the banter in *You've Got Mail* is pretty top-notch."

Kate's mother looked up from her reading chair, studied Kate for a moment, then slowly placed a bookmark in her novel and set it aside. She patted the ottoman. "Sweetie. Sit."

Uh-oh. She knew that tone. Anytime her mom made *Sweetie* its own sentence, Kate rarely liked what followed.

Sweetie. I know you wanted a dog for Christmas, but this goldfish needed a home!

Sweetie. You could always just go to the prom with your friends.

Sweetie. Your sister did a load of laundry and accidentally put a red sock in with your favorite white blouse . . .

Maybe this was it. Maybe her mom was finally going to have a breakdown and tell her that she just didn't know how to go on anymore without her partner. Kate was ready for it. She'd been living with her mom for the past two and a half weeks and had read every book on grief there was.

"What's up?" Kate asked with a forced smile, setting the DVD cases on the end table next to her mother's tea before sitting on the ugly mustard-colored ottoman.

Her mom reached out and tucked a strand of Kate's hair behind her ear, her smile a little small. "I've been so grateful for you these past few weeks. I don't know what I would have done without you."

Kate reached up and squeezed her mom's hand, her eyes watering a little. The day of her dad's death, Kate had come up to be with her mom and sister and hadn't left. Mostly because she hadn't wanted her mom to be alone in the house she'd shared with Kate's father for the majority of her life. But the truth was Kate had needed to be here for her own sake as well.

She'd known, of course, that her parents wouldn't live forever. That eventually she'd have to say goodbye. She just thought she had so much more time. That her dad would be there to walk her down the aisle someday. To meet Kate's children.

To be there when she needed him.

Kate blinked rapidly to keep the tears from falling. The nights were for crying. The days were for being strong for her mom.

She forced a smile. "I'm here as long as you need me. The guys found someone to cover for me at work, and Lara and Sabrina cleaned out the fridge in my apartment so I don't go home to spoiled milk and moldy cheese."

Eileen smiled. "You have good friends."

Kate nodded in agreement. They hadn't come to the funeral, because there hadn't been a funeral. For as long as Kate could remember, Archie Henley had good-naturedly griped about funerals, saying they were depressing as heck. And he didn't buy into what he called "that celebration-of-life nonsense."

Celebrate me when I'm alive. Let me have a long-overdue nap when I'm gone.

The Henleys had honored Archie's wishes. No funeral. And Kate was secretly glad for it. She was aware and appreciative of the love and support she knew was just a text or phone call away, but she needed space and time. From work. From New York.

Even from whatever was happening with her and Kennedy, because Kate wasn't sure she could survive two emotional roller coasters.

The details of the day her dad died were a blur, but Kate remembered breaking down in Kennedy's arms. Remembered him packing a bag while she lay curled on her couch. She remembered him hiring a town car to drive her to her parents'—to her *mother's*—holding her hand all the way. By the time they'd arrived, her mom and sister were home from the hospital, and friends and extended family had already heard the news, stopping by with the intention of helping but clueless as to how to do so as they wrestled with their own grief.

Kennedy had taken Kate up to her parents' bedroom, where her mom sat unmoving and uncomprehending on the bed, Kate's sister looking as shell-shocked as Kate had felt. Hours later—Kate had no idea how many—she'd gone back downstairs. Kennedy was gone, as was, thankfully, everyone else.

Days later, Kate's aunt had told her that a "serious man in a blue suit" had kindly but firmly ushered out everyone in the house with instructions to come back in a day or two. Somehow, Kennedy had known what Kate and her family needed, which was solitude and time, and he'd made it happen. If she had to guess, she'd bet that it had also been him who'd taken charge at Wolfe, finding a temporary replacement for her, as well as getting in touch with Lara and Sabrina to make sure her mail was collected and her plants watered.

She kept meaning to thank him. To thank all of them, but her mom needed her more. Her place was here in Jersey, close to her father's memory.

"Kate, I think you need to go home."

Kate blinked and stared at her mom, who seemed to have aged a hundred years in the past few weeks, and yet . . .

Kate looked closer, looking beyond the grief, the slightly red-rimmed eyes, and saw something else she couldn't quite identify.

"I am home," Kate said.

Her mom smiled and took Kate's hand in hers. "Of course you will always have a home here—my door will always be open."

My door. Not *our* door. This was her mother's house now, not her father's.

Everything had changed. The home that had once seemed to burst with joyous chaos was almost unbearably quiet. Her parents had had the noisy, messy kind of love that never let you doubt it was real because you could *feel* it. It had been in the unembarrassed kisses in the kitchen, the bear hugs, the little gifts they'd get for each other. Even the way they'd argued about who'd had the car keys last, if Mom had snuck vegetables into the spaghetti sauce, whether Harrison Ford's most iconic performance was Han Solo or Indiana Jones—it had been full of passion. Kate had always thought she wanted that for herself. Her parents were the very definition of all in—they'd given everything to one another.

But she was seeing another side of that now—the dark side.

Because when you gave everything to someone else, and then it was taken away, what were you left with?

"If this is home, why do I feel like you're kicking me out?"

"You know your father would be so pleased that you kept me company those first couple days. I don't know that I'd have had the strength to get up without knowing you would be there to have those first sips of coffee with."

"And yet still with the *kicking me out* part . . . ?" Kate said with a smile.

"Your dad would be pleased to know you were by my side those first few days," Eileen repeated. "And *appalled* to know you're still here."

Kate's mouth dropped open. "Mom!"

"I'm sorry, sweetheart. I love you, I love your company, but it's been almost three weeks."

"He was my dad. Your husband. I think we're allowed for the mourning process to last longer than three weeks."

"The mourning process, yes. The avoidance process, no."

Kate tugged her hand away from her mom's, feeling defensive. "Meaning what?"

"We've both been avoiding getting back to our real lives, because we know life is irrevocably changed, but it's not going to get any easier the longer we wait. It's time for me to start figuring out what my life will look like without my partner. And long-term, that's not my daughter living in her childhood bedroom. I don't want that for you, and neither would Dad."

"But—"

"You can of course take a couple more days if you need." Her mom reached out and retrieved Kate's hand once more. "Take a week. I never want you to feel unwelcome, but I wouldn't be doing a good job as your mother if I didn't nudge you out of the nest."

Kate smiled. "You know, I've been thinking that I would eventually need to have this talk with you, to gently tell you that your life will still go on, just differently. But it sounds like you're wiser than I am."

"Age does that to women." Eileen smiled. "Not that I'm saying any of this will be easy. I'm not going to pretend I don't feel completely shattered inside, but I loved that man and everything we built far too much to dishonor it by becoming a hermit who can't even get her roots done."

"You're right. Dad would hate knowing you let those grays show. I mean, surely he still believed you're a natural brunette?"

Eileen swatted her shoulder. "Darn straight he did. Now about you . . ."

"Also a natural brunette. No grays . . . yet."

Her mom was watching her closely and clearly knew she was dodging. "Kate."

"What?"

"Are you okay?"

"Yeah. Well, no. I mean, I miss Dad. I still can't believe he's not here. That's normal, though."

"It is," Eileen said slowly. "Have you spoken to that man you were seeing?"

"Jack? No, we broke up."

"Oh." Her mother's disappointment was clear. "I so hoped that when you returned to the city, you'd have someone to lean on."

Kate patted her mom's arm. "It's like you said: I have really great friends."

"Not what I meant, and you know it."

Kate *did* know it. She knew that her mother was hoping she'd have a man to return to, a romantic partner to help her through the grieving process. A month ago, Kate might have had that same thought.

But that was before Kate had had her naive vision of the perfect type of relationship turned upside down. It stung a little to realize that all of this time, it had been Kennedy who'd had the right approach to relationships after all. Caution was better. Holding back was better.

Love at first sight didn't guarantee you happily ever after. She knew that now. Just like she knew now that giving all of yourself to another person was foolish.

Because when they left, they'd take everything with them.

20

Her first day back at work, Kate arrived at 7:59 a.m. and not a minute before. A far cry from her default of beating the guys into the office so she could get a head start on email and the necessary calendar updates that cropped up in the wee hours of the morning as various Wall Street big shots closed down bars and realized their chances of making it to a nine a.m. meeting were slim.

Not today, though. She had too much self-respect to be late, but she'd done some thinking over the past three weeks and had had a realization of sorts. It was time for a change. Not just her hair and makeup, though that had been a step in the right direction.

Instinct told her she needed to lean even further in to her gut belief that it was time to change things up, starting with the job front. Not that she wanted a new job. She loved her job, truly. But it was demanding as heck and not *just* because she managed three guys. Ever since she'd gotten her business degree and been promoted to office administrator, she'd become the go-to resource for all of the other admins—the one who trained the newbies, who mentored the juniors, who handled the crises. She loved that part of the job and took pride in not just doing her job well but showing others how to do theirs well, too.

But she'd also just seen how short life could be, and as much as she loved coming to work every day, she didn't want her entire life to be work. She didn't want to wake up one day and realize she'd spent the prime of her life behind a desk.

Something had to give.

Kate stepped off the elevator, braced for the overwhelming sense that she wasn't ready, but instead she felt a layer of calm seem to settle over her at the familiarity of the Wolfe offices. She headed toward the kitchen to put her lunch in the fridge, then to her desk, where . . .

"Oh." She skidded to a halt. "Hello."

The boy—and yes, that really was the best word—stood up so fast, the wheeled chair shot backward, and she was pretty sure he'd been tempted to salute but caught himself just in time. His blond hair was thick and just a little bit curly, his eyes enormous and green. He had the lanky awkwardness of a colt and the perfect smile of someone with an excellent orthodontist.

"You must be the new guy," she said with a smile. She knew her temporary replacement would be here today so they could transition, but she'd expected him to be a *nine a.m. and not a minute before* kind of guy. Instead, he'd beat her in.

"You must be Miss Henley."

"Good God, did you just *bow*?" she asked good-naturedly, going to her desk and setting her bag in its usual spot.

The kid winced. "Sorry. I've just heard a lot about you. I'm sort of in awe."

"Good things, I hope," she murmured, her gaze skimming over her desk, relieved to see it was every bit as tidy as when she'd left. "Christian, right?"

He extended a hand. "Christian Loubin."

She blinked. "As in . . . ?"

"Yeah. I know. It's close to the designer. My dad had no idea; my mom definitely did. He finally caught on and gave her a pair of Christian Louboutins for my first birthday."

"What'd *you* get?"

"My first taste of chocolate. I maintain I got the better end of the deal."

"Totally," Kate agreed, frowning when she saw him picking up his mug and bag. "What are you doing?"

"You're back now. I thought . . ."

"What, that I'd make you sit on the floor? Stay. Actually . . ." She pointed at the computer. "Since you're already logged in, let's write an email to Tim in facilities and see about getting another desk up here."

"Up . . . here? A second desk, just for the day?"

She crossed her arms and leaned against the desk. "Do you like it here?"

He nodded as he pulled his chair back in and brought up a new message. "I do. It's fast-paced, but I love that. And I thought it'd be overwhelming to support three directors, and it can be, but they're fair."

"Yeah, they're great."

They also liked Christian. She'd texted with Ian and Matt over the weekend, and though they'd made it very clear they couldn't wait to have her back, they'd also reassured her that the new guy had held down the fort quite well.

"Who's your favorite?"

His already wide eyes went even bigger, and she laughed. "Kidding. We don't know each other well enough for that."

"Who's *your* favorite?" he asked, surprising her.

"Oh, you know," she said with a wave of her hand. "They're like my brothers, which means I love them and hate them with equal intensity depending on the time of day." She didn't add that for one of the guys, the sentiment was only half-true. She had loved and hated Kennedy with intensity over the years, but she could safely say that he had never, *ever* felt like a brother.

Especially not now.

"You know what time he gets in?" Kate asked.

"Which one?"

Kate froze, then smiled to recover. "Sorry. All of them."

Christian clicked open the calendar. "Average day for all of them. Should be any minute." He looked over at her, then looked away. "Hey, I know we just met, but I'm sorry to hear about your loss."

Kate forced a smile. *Loss* was such an insignificant word, but she appreciated the sentiment. "Thank you." Desperate to change the subject, lest the tears start coming before her day even began, Kate leaned down to look at the screen. "Is there any time they're all available today?"

"Let's see . . . They've all got a gap at eleven."

"Perfect. Can you put me on their calendars?"

"Sure thing. Whose office?"

"Matt's. It's the biggest."

"Really?" Christian said as he typed. "I actually thought Kennedy's had the most space."

It did. But it was also Kennedy's turf. And if Kate had any hope of surviving this day without a breakdown, she needed to keep as much emotional distance from Kennedy Dawson as possible.

"Have I mentioned it's good to have you back?" Ian said, scooping Kate up off the floor, her flats dangling at about his shins.

"About ten times," she said, patting his head. "Now put me down."

"Or what?"

She kicked his shin in response, and he grunted, setting her back on her feet. "Fair enough."

"I'm damn glad you're back, too, but I have to give the new kid credit," Matt said around a mouthful of potato chips that were apparently his prelunch. "He managed to keep my calendar in order. No easy task."

"Understatement," Kate said, glancing at her phone for the time. "Is Kennedy joining or what?"

"Or what? I'm thirty seconds early."

She ordered herself not to tense up at the sound of his voice, and though she was pretty sure she succeeded, there was nothing she could do about her quickened heartbeat or slightly sweaty palms.

Kate forced herself to paste on the same bright smile she'd given the other guys. "Hey! Long time no see!"

His eyebrows went up. *Really?*

Kate looked away from his silent challenge.

"Good to have you back," Kennedy replied.

Kate risked another glance his way. She'd been expecting sarcasm—or more likely irritation—at the fact that she hadn't returned a single one of his texts. Instead, his tone was casual but genuine. Not quite indifferent, but he also hardly looked like a man who'd been losing sleep over her radio silence.

Had he even noticed?

"So what's up?" Matt said, gesturing for Kate to sit in one of his two guest chairs. She did, mostly because Ian and Kennedy towered above her whether she was sitting or standing. Might as well be comfortable.

"So, Christian," she said. "You guys said he's been great."

"Sure," Matt said with a quick glance over at Ian, then Kennedy.

"Good. Facilities is coming up this afternoon to install a new desk for him."

"Uh. What?"

"There's plenty of room," she said. "The space is meant to fit desks for three people."

"I don't think the space is the question," Ian said slowly. "And I'll preface this by saying we'll support whatever you want, whatever you need, but do you plan on Christian sticking around for longer than a day or two of transition?"

Kate had expected this to be harder, but with the moment upon her, she felt more confident than ever that she was making the right decision. Still, she chose her words carefully. "You know I love working here. For all of you. It's been the biggest part of my life for so long, and I wouldn't change a single thing about the past few years."

"But?" Matt asked.

"But," she continued, increasingly aware that Kennedy hadn't said a word since she started talking but not brave enough to glance his way. "It's a lot. Working for all three of you. Three schedules, three sets of clients, three inboxes, three sets of demands. Plus being the point person for many of the other admins."

"It's too much," Ian said quietly. Not a question. "It would be for anyone."

Kate glanced at him in relief. "It's more than I want right now. I can't stress how much I've loved it, but losing Dad . . ." She looked down at her hands and swallowed the lump in her throat. "Life is so short. You think you have time to do all of the things, and then—"

"What sorts of things?" Kennedy asked, speaking up for the first time.

"What?" She glanced at him and found him watching her with an unreadable mask.

"You want to work less so you have more time to do other things. I was just curious what sorts of things."

"Oh. Right. I don't really know," she said, tearing her gaze away. "I've just realized that for the past six years, I've had sort of a single-minded focus on work."

And you, she thought, deliberately not glancing at Kennedy.

But how did you tell someone—even friends—that you'd realized it was time to stop caring so much about a few things and instead wanted to care a little about a lot of things? That way, if fate rolled the dice to take one of those things away from you, it wouldn't hurt so damn badly.

"I think maybe it's time to develop some hobbies," she added. "Or, I don't know, work out. Yoga? Barre?"

"What the hell is barre?" Matt asked.

"A ballet-based workout," Ian explained. "They have classes, lots of stretching and balance. You get toned as shit."

All three of them stared at him.

Ian shrugged. "Lara does it. It's made her ass absolutely—" He cleared his throat. "Anyway."

"Gross," Kate said. "But yeah, I'd forgotten Lara did barre. Maybe I'll tag along to her next class."

"Okay, I'm loving this plan," Matt said, sitting forward and folding his hands on his desk. "Just tell us what you need from us. You want to cut back? Part-time? Hire Christian as your assistant and have you delegate?"

"I thought about both of those, and they *could* work, but everything around here happens so fast. By the time I figured out what to delegate to Christian and got an extra few minutes to fill him in on the details, it'd probably already be too late. What makes me so good at my job—and yes, I know I am, thank you very much—is that I know everything that's going on in every area of your lives. I'm good at managing your calendars, because I know when your individual clients are going through a divorce or when one of you is hungover.

I'm good with reservations, because I know that if I booked you at Keens on Tuesday, I shouldn't send you to Wolfgang's on Wednesday. Too much steak."

"No such thing," Kennedy said.

"Well, whatever. The point is, I can't be a *partial* assistant for all three of you." She took a breath and held it just for a second. "I need to be a full assistant to two of you."

Nobody spoke for a full thirty seconds.

Ian finally broke the silence. "Wait. Are you *firing* one of us?"

She nodded. "I am."

"Who?" Matt demanded.

"It shouldn't matter," she pointed out. "You guys all said Christian is great."

"He is. But he's no you."

"That's nice," she said, reaching out and patting Matt's hand. "But buttering me up won't make a difference."

"Why not?"

"Because *I'm* not going to decide. You guys are."

Ian nodded approvingly. "Classic Monica move."

"What?" Kennedy asked.

"From *Friends*. Monica didn't want to choose between Phoebe or Rachel as her maid of honor, so she had them decide."

"Kennedy's never watched it," Kate said.

"I have, too. Just not as much as Ian, apparently. And by the way, Ian, I distinctly remember a time when you didn't know what barre was and didn't know Penelope and Rachel by name."

"Phoebe," Matt corrected.

"You too? Is this what marriage does to a man?" Kennedy asked.

"Well, I'm sure you'll never know," Kate said sweetly. "I'm sure you and your placid wife will only watch documentaries."

"Hey, you like documentaries."

"I do. I also like *Friends*."

"Forget *Friends*," Matt said. "This situation is more like *Sophie's Choice*. You can't seriously expect one of us to give you up?"

"It's not easy for me, either," Kate said softly, looking at all three of them, careful not to let her gaze linger on Kennedy. "And know that however it works out, I'll still be in all three of your lives. We'll still all be friends. One of you will just go to Christian when you need a dinner reservation or new ink for your overpriced pen, and so on."

"All right. We can handle this," Ian said. "We'll do it randomly. Coin toss."

"That works," Matt said. "You got a coin?"

"No. Get one out of your desk."

"You think I keep coins in my desk?" Matt asked incredulously. "Do I also go to the saloon and get weirdly possessive of my horse?"

"Whatever. Kennedy?"

"I literally can't remember the last time I touched a coin."

"Don't look at me," Kate said, holding up her hands. "I may not be in the millionaire club with you guys, but I don't use cash that often, and when I do, it's a keep-the-change situation."

"Fine. Rock, paper, scissors," Ian said, already bringing his hands into position. "Loser gets Christian."

"That's a two-person game. What about the guy who doesn't play?" Matt asked.

"Guess he wins by default, just by staying out of the ring." Ian paused. "Something I did not think through before I did this," he said, glancing down at his hands.

"I'll do it," Kennedy said.

Ian turned toward Kennedy with his rock, paper, scissors stance still armed and ready. "Brave man. I'm sort of a pro at this. Best out of three?"

"No. I mean, I'll take Christian."

Ian's fist ceased its amped-up *let's do this* pounding against his palm, but other than that, he didn't move. Or speak. Neither did Matt.

Kate stared straight ahead, trying not to feel stung and failing miserably, because it hurt. Truth be told, she had been pretty sure it'd come down to a coin toss or some sort of game of chance. Not necessarily because she thought she was that great of an assistant but because she'd been pretty sure none of them would have wanted to hurt her feelings by willingly choosing Christian over her.

She'd been wrong.

"All right, then," she said, slapping her palms against her thighs and scooting toward the edge of her chair. "Guess that's that. Matt and Ian, you guys are still stuck with me."

"Happy to be," Ian said, putting a hand on her shoulder. It lingered just a little longer than necessary, and Kate recognized it for what it was. A show of sympathy. Comfort.

He knows, Kate realized. He knew about her kissing Kennedy on the boat. For a half second she felt embarrassed, but she forced herself to shove it aside. Ian was her friend. He wouldn't judge.

And besides, it didn't matter. Kate didn't feel that way anymore. *Wouldn't.*

If nothing else, this was proof that their getting involved was a thoroughly awful idea. If it hurt this badly when Kennedy chose another assistant, how would it feel when he chose another woman?

Kate stood. "Do one of you want to initiate the conversation with HR or should I? We'll need to start the process of making Christian an official offer as an employee. I'm assuming he's a temp now?"

"I think so?" Matt said, glancing at the other guys, who shrugged.

"I'll take care of it," she said, grateful to have something to do.

She headed toward the door, not expecting Kennedy to say a damn word. And she was right. She was already through the doorway when she heard Ian's low rumble. "I hope you know what the hell you're doing, man."

Kate walked away without hearing Kennedy's response, telling herself with each step that she didn't care just how easily he'd tossed her aside.

21

If there were a limit on how much time one could, or should, spend on Pinterest looking at penis paraphernalia, Kate hadn't reached it yet. People were just so dang creative!

Lara had been pretty adamant about not wanting a traditional bachelorette party but had been coaxed into what Sabrina had called a "slutty slumber party" next weekend with the three of them and Lara's friend Gabby. Sabrina was in charge of entertainment, Kate in charge of food.

She took a sip of her wine and scribbled *bologna* onto her shopping list. Not exactly her or Lara's favorite food, but if they weren't allowed to have a stripper, Kate was making damn sure they'd have phallic-shaped food.

She clicked on the next picture and nearly spit out her wine. "Oh, I've got to try this," she muttered to herself.

Kate went to the kitchen, dug around for wooden skewers she had from a barbecue last summer, and found grapes in the fridge.

Less than a minute later, she held up her creation. "Perfect."

The old-school phone by her front door rang, and she jumped. The awful thing rang only when someone was at the front door downstairs, and that happened only when it was a wrong number. That was the thing about having super-well-off friends—it almost always made more sense to meet at one of their places.

"Hello?"

Silence greeted her. Kate hung up with a shrug. Someone had probably figured out their mistake and—

The knock at the door made her jump for the second time, and she made a mental note that maybe she should invite people over more often, so she didn't react like a total recluse when someone did stop by.

She checked her peephole, expecting Sabrina or Lara or a lost pizza guy, and saw . . .

Kennedy.

Even as her hand reached for the doorknob, she hesitated. The only other time she'd seen Kennedy Dawson standing on the other side of her door had been the morning she'd learned her dad died.

Kate opened the door, noting first that he was dressed in a dark-gray suit, even though it was early on a Saturday evening. He was carrying a garment bag in one hand, a bottle of champagne in the other. *Fancy* champagne, the kind that came in a box, not the Prosecco that was her go-to.

Kate was suddenly uncomfortably aware that her staying-in ensemble of choice was not exactly hostess material. It was unseasonably hot for mid-May, so she was wearing ancient (and rather tiny) shorts and a tank top that she'd gotten at . . . Old Navy? H&M?

Couture, it was not.

"Um, hi?" she said.

He nodded. "Hello."

She waited for more, but he said nothing. Kate rolled her eyes. "You can't show up at your employee's apartment on a weekend, unannounced, dressed like that, and simply say, 'Hello.'"

"Dressed like what?" he asked, glancing down at his suit.

"Please tell me you own jeans." It was an honest question. She couldn't remember ever seeing him in jeans.

"Probably. Maybe. I'm not sure. Can I come in?"

"Sure," she said, her curiosity getting the best of her. "What's with the bag?"

He looked down at the black garment bag, then back at her. "It's for you. But seeing you in those, I'm having second thoughts."

Kate blinked rapidly. "You . . . brought me clothes? And what do you mean, 'seeing me in those'? Seeing me in what?"

"Tiny tank top. Even smaller shorts."

"It's the weekend," she snapped, braced for a fight. "Believe it or not, I don't just prance around my apartment in a fancy dress."

"Yeah, well, you might not like this, then," he said, handing her the garment bag.

She took it reflexively, and he turned and went to the kitchen, setting the champagne on the counter and opening her cupboards.

She glanced at the bag, then at the man pulling two champagne flutes from her kitchen cabinet. They were the stemless kind, and cheap, but he didn't seem to mind as he pulled the bottle of champagne out of the box.

"Kennedy."

"Yes?"

"What the heck are you doing?"

His gaze flicked up, and he looked like a damn movie star, all thick hair, mysterious gaze, and expensive wine. His hands stilled. "Would you care for something other than Taittinger?"

"Would I care for—No, I mean, what are you doing here? At my apartment, dressed all fancy, bringing me . . ." She glanced at the dress bag. "Whatever this is."

"Do you have alternate plans? I got a tip that your night was free."

"What tip? Who—" She gasped. "That *traitor*." Earlier in the afternoon, she'd been texting with Sabrina about the bachelorette party ideas, sarcastically mentioning that she had big evening plans of cheap white wine and browsing penises on Pinterest.

The champagne cork gave an authoritative pop, and though she wanted to berate his high-handedness, she wanted the champagne even more. To say nothing of her curiosity. Because no matter how much she might tell herself that she'd decided not to do this—that whatever happened between them on the boat had been a fluke best not repeated—she couldn't deny that having Kennedy show up bearing gifts as though he owned the place had once been among her very top fantasies.

He walked toward her and handed her a glass.

Kate hesitated, then accepted it. "Kennedy, I mean it. Tell me what's going on."

He clinked his glass to hers, holding her gaze as he took a sip. "Open the bag."

Curiosity took over, and after taking a quick sip of the champagne—then another, because, delicious—she handed the glass back to him, freeing up her hand to unzip the bag.

The zipper had made it only a few inches down when she sucked in her breath. The fabric was stunning, a color so vibrant it didn't look real.

"It's like a Shirley Temple," she said as she scooped the hem of the dress out of the bag with one hand. "Not quite red, not quite pink."

"Perfect, so I bought you grenadine," he said drolly.

She looked over, not sure if she was more surprised he knew what gave the girlish Shirley Temple drink its color or that he'd bought her the dress. Both were completely at odds with the man she knew. Or thought she knew.

"You . . . got this for me? Why?"

"I wanted to make sure you had something to wear tonight. In case all of your other dresses were at the dry cleaner."

"Yeah, that's what I do," she said. "I take my collection of three dresses, that I wear almost never, to be dry-cleaned all at the same time. Wait." Her sarcasm scattered. "What do you mean, wear tonight?"

Kennedy handed back her champagne, then reached into his pocket and pulled out two tickets, holding them up for her to see.

She read the ticket, read it again, then looked up at him in confusion. "The ballet?"

"They just opened *A Midsummer Night's Dream*," he said, putting the tickets back in his pocket. "And I made dinner reservations for after, since we won't have enough time to eat before curtain time. Though I suppose we could snack on your weird grapes on a stick over there," he said, nodding back toward her counter.

"Anal beads."

Kennedy choked on his champagne. "I'm sorry?"

"For Lara's bachelorette party. I'm doing sex-themed food. Pinterest said those are supposed to be anal beads, though whether they're close to the real thing, I confess I couldn't say. Do you know?"

"Jesus," he muttered, looking like he'd wipe his brow if he had a handkerchief on hand. Which, knowing Kennedy, she was a little surprised he didn't.

"I figure it's the thought that counts. The real star of the show's going to be the bananas, with strawberries as the tip, and then a little dollop of whipped cream, you know, so it looks like—"

"I get the picture," he interrupted, sounding a little strained. He nodded at the dress. "What do you think?"

She looked down at it. "It's really beautiful—"

"Don't say 'but,'" he said, taking a step closer. "Let me do this. It's been a hell of a month for you. Let me take you to the ballet and feed you French champagne and buttery potatoes, or oysters, or whatever the hell you're in the mood for."

"Kennedy." She forced herself to look at him. "I'm sorry I didn't call. Or text back."

He nodded. "I understood."

"No, I don't think you could," she said quietly, looking once more at the dress, her heart aching a little. "That night on the boat was . . . spontaneous. Sexy. And I'll always remember it, perhaps a little more often than I should, given our working relationship. But I'm not looking for a repeat."

"Because of Jack?" he asked cautiously.

"What? Jack? Oh no. No, it's not that. It's just . . . I've been giving a lot of thought to what I want out of my life, especially my romantic life, and it's changed."

"How so?" he asked, watching her closely.

"Love at first sight is silly. I mean, it can happen, but there's no guarantee that it's permanent. Circumstances change; relationships shift . . ." *People die.*

She didn't say the last part, but the flash of understanding in his eyes told her that he knew. Knew that her dad's death had changed her perception of love. For so long, all she'd wanted was what her parents had, and it had genuinely never occurred to her that it could be taken away.

"Anyway, it means you're off the hook. I'm not going to demand love letters or a marriage proposal. And I was thinking, with you working with Christian now, it might be a good time for us to try that friends thing for real. We could play chess again, or . . ." She broke off when his face remained impassive. "It's your turn to say something."

"Well." He sipped the champagne. "I'd like to know if the dress fits."

She inhaled for patience. "That's your response? Because, by the way, you don't just buy women dresses and champagne unless you're hoping to talk them out of the dress later in the evening."

He rolled his eyes to the ceiling in exasperation. "I'm trying to be a nice guy . . ."

"Ian and Matt are nice guys. You know how they show it? They bring me back Starbucks whenever they go out for an afternoon caffeine break or take me to lunch on my birthday. They don't show up on my doorstep with . . ." She looked at the dress. "I don't even recognize this designer. How much was this?"

"Kate."

She looked up. "What?"

"Do you want to go to the ballet with me tonight or not?"

She chewed her lip. She did. She really did. She was guessing the seats were excellent, because Kennedy Dawson wouldn't bother with a live performance of any kind unless he had the best seats in the house. The champagne was delicious; the dress was the most gorgeous thing she'd ever seen . . .

"You promise no weird seductive stuff?" she asked, eyes narrowed.

"I'll try to contain myself."

"Good. Because I'm finally getting over you. I need to get over you. And it won't work if you're too nice."

"Noted. Go change," he said with an exasperated nod toward the hallway.

"Okay, fine," she said, the allure of the dress and the ballet too much to pass up.

Nothing to do with the company. Nothing at all.

"I'm taking this," she said, holding the champagne over her head as she went to change. "I'd tell you to make yourself at home, but I don't know how you're going to do that with the lack of grand piano and weird antiques."

"I'll try to entertain myself."

She nodded, then pointed her champagne flute at him. "Don't you dare eat my anal beads."

He let out a laugh—a loud, spontaneous, honest-to-God laugh. The sort of laugh that was so real, so rare, it'd have nearly been her undoing.

But only if she were still in love with him, of course.

22

Kennedy had enjoyed many a night at the opera, the theatre, and yes, the ballet. And though he'd probably seen more impressive shows, with impossibly-hard-to-come-by tickets, seeing the ballet with Kate surpassed them all.

She didn't just watch the ballet; she *lived* it, slightly forward in her seat, at times seeming to hold her breath.

He'd brought her tonight to make her day a little brighter, to take her mind off her dad, and he liked to think he succeeded. But perhaps the more surprising part of the evening had been the effect on him.

Kennedy had done plenty of dating in his adult life. Plenty of one-night hookups, as well. But unlike Matt and Ian, who'd made a career out of the bachelor life before meeting Sabrina and Lara, Kennedy hadn't shied away from relationships. He'd embraced his bachelorhood, dabbled in the playboy lifestyle, but he never angled for that to be his forever. He wanted to get married someday. It had always just been on a theoretical level, with some faceless "someday" bride. Someone beautiful, from his world, with common ideals. Someone easy, who wouldn't demand too much.

He hadn't realized until Kate had emerged from her bedroom dressed in the bright-pink dress, her smile unabashedly joyful, just how dispassionate his past girlfriends seemed in comparison. Or perhaps it wasn't the women. Perhaps it was Kennedy who had been dispassionate, thus indifferent to the women who came in and out of his life without causing much of a ripple.

But Kate . . . She was one hell of a ripple. She'd always been, if he were honest.

Kate was the one who made him think twice, who challenged him. She didn't do anything in half measures—she jumped into the deep end unabashed, always. Her confidence was alluring as hell, because it didn't come from a new haircut or a master's degree. It was a sureness in who she was, not just in her willingness to go all in but her *determination* to.

Until now.

Kennedy had known the moment he'd walked into Ian's office on Monday that something was different with Kate. He'd been prepared for it. Nobody came out of the loss of a beloved parent unscathed, and her lack of response to his messages had warned him that she was struggling.

Seeing her had confirmed it. Outwardly, of course, she'd been the same Kate. Same outward confidence, same effortless competence. But her eyes were different.

Gone was the direct, ever-observant gaze of a woman who knew what she wanted and was always assessing the most effective way to get it. Instead, the Kate in Ian's office had been guarded. Not quite withdrawn but cautious. Even her posture had been wary, as though braced for the next life blow.

It had killed him, even as he understood it. Just like he understood that she was trying her hardest to pull away from him before they had a chance to get started.

Kate loved her parents, but she'd worshipped their relationship. He was willing to bet that though she'd probably understood on a rational level that she'd eventually lose them, she'd likely never thought about what that meant for her vision of marriage.

Loving someone—all of the way loving them—might come with plenty of Disney-worthy feels, but it also came with a shit-ton of risk. Risk that they'd leave you, and you'd be incomplete when they did.

Ironically, just as Kennedy was starting to catch on to the appeal of those Disney bits, Kate saw the risks. It wasn't ideal, to say the least, but Kennedy was ready for it.

He'd just have to show her that the risk was worth it. Hence, the ballet.

She inhaled the late spring air as they stepped out of the theatre. "That was . . . I don't have words. Thank you."

"You're welcome."

She looked up at him. "Did you like it?"

"I did."

"Did you *love* it?" she pressed.

"I loved it."

"Was it your favorite?"

He laughed. "So persistent. Okay, fine. Gun to my head, I slightly preferred *The Sleeping Beauty* from last year."

"I was in *The Sleeping Beauty* when I was little," she said. "I was the Fairy of Temperament, also known as Violente."

"Sounds terrifying."

"Yes, I'm sure my fourteen-year-old self in a tutu was immensely intimidating."

"I think you at just about any age could be intimidating," he said, glancing down. She looked slightly less tense than she'd had all week, which was exactly what he'd been hoping for when he'd dropped a rather large chunk of cash on front-row tickets opening weekend.

"You should know that I take that as a compliment."

"You should know I meant it as one." He offered his arm. "The restaurant's just two blocks away. You good to walk in those shoes?"

"Sure. I've got you to keep me steady," she said, hooking her arm in his and then patting his biceps affectionately, the way she might a brother.

Kennedy did not like that.

Baby steps, he reminded himself.

He had to coax the old Kate out slowly, to convince her that he was worth it. That *they* were.

And though she wasn't ready to hear it, Kennedy had absolutely no intention of them being "just friends." Friends first, yes. He was going to be the best damn friend she'd ever had.

And then he'd convince her he could be a hell of a lot more.

◆ ◆ ◆

Kennedy was determined to keep his hands to himself tonight, but Kate was making it difficult. He'd always thought that the description of one's eyes rolling back in one's head was a weird exaggeration. But he witnessed it firsthand as Kate took a bite of her scallop dish and moaned.

Kennedy shifted in his chair.

"Oh my God," she said when the initial wave of food ecstasy finally passed. "I don't think I can survive another bite of this."

She opened her eyes and looked at him, and he hoped like hell she couldn't see the heat consuming his body just by watching her.

"Seriously," she said, cutting off another piece of the luscious scallop and dragging it through the buttery sauce. "You have to try this."

"I'm sure it's delicious, but I'll decline," he said, cutting into his chicken.

"Oh right." She set down her fork. "Shellfish. I forgot. I'm sorry."

He glanced up with a smile. "Why are you sorry? You ordered what you wanted to eat; I ordered what I wanted. We're good."

"I know," she said, picking up her fork. "I guess I'm just surprised that I didn't remember when I ordered. Remembering details is sort of my jam."

"At work, maybe. It's Saturday night. Give yourself a break."

Kate took a sip of her white wine. "I suppose. Plus, I guess I'm off the hook from remembering your details even at work. You're Christian's problem now."

He lifted his red wine in a silent toast, then put it down when he saw the expression on her face. "What's wrong?"

She took a deep breath as though gathering courage, then leaned forward slightly, meeting his eyes. "Why did you do it? Why did you volunteer to take on Christian?"

Kennedy kept his tone carefully impassive, knowing she wasn't ready for the real answer to that question. "Someone had to."

She blinked quickly, then gave a jerky nod before turning her attention back to her food. She cut off a piece of scallop with more force than necessary, then dropped her fork once more. "Did I not do a good job for you?"

Shit. This was harder than he'd anticipated—giving her the space she needed to heal without letting her think he didn't care. At the hurt on her face, he nearly cracked. Nearly told her just how much it had killed him to actually *volunteer* to spend less time with her at work, all because he hoped against hope that it would lead to them spending *more* time together—outside of work.

But he wasn't entirely sure she wouldn't get up and run from that, so he explained as best he could without laying *all* of his cards on the table. "Kate." He waited until she looked up. "You were the best damn assistant anyone could have ever asked for. I wouldn't have even considered volunteering if I didn't know Christian would be learning everything from you. But I also knew this was what you wanted—to work for two people instead of three."

"So you were just being nice?"

He suppressed a growl of frustration. "Don't sound so surprised."

"I'm not. Not after . . . Kennedy, I never thanked you," she said on a rush. "I'm a little embarrassed, actually. That day when Dad—" She closed her eyes, took a deep breath, then opened her eyes to meet his again. "You were there. You went above and beyond, and I appreciate it more than I knew how to say, apparently."

"You're welcome."

"Just like that? You're not going to give me crap for ignoring you or for not acknowledging it sooner? I treated you horribly, and—"

"You didn't. I didn't do it for me, Kate; I did it for you. I wasn't after thanks or a blue ribbon. I just tried to be what you needed at that time. That's all it was."

"It didn't bother you when I didn't reply to any of your messages?" she asked tentatively.

"It did," he said slowly, choosing his words carefully, trying not to betray how much it had bothered him. "I was worried about you. So were the other guys. Lara and Sabrina, too. We're used to seeing you every day. And we care about you. So yeah, it was hell not knowing what you were going through, not knowing how we could help."

She glanced down, looking ashamed. "I'm sorry."

"Don't be. We understood. But I'd love to know why."

"Why did I go silent?"

He nodded. "The first couple days, I can understand. But it was nearly three weeks."

It hurt.

"It wasn't well done. I know that. I guess . . ." Kate fiddled with her napkin. "I think I was embarrassed that I wasn't handling it better. I'm not used to being the weak link, the one who can't sleep at night and yet doesn't want to do anything all day *but* sleep. I told myself that I was hanging out in Jersey for my mom's sake, but she basically kicked me out. Did I tell you that?"

When she looked up, he shook his head.

"Yeah," she said with a self-deprecating laugh. "I mean, she did it gently, mama bird–style, and I'm glad she did. But it was embarrassing as heck to realize that far from being the one who takes care of anything, you're the one people are worrying about."

"Should we be worried about you now?" he asked quietly. He already was, but he also knew Kate was stronger than any person he'd ever met. For now, he just needed to make sure she didn't shut him out.

"I'm okay," she said slowly. She picked up her wineglass but instead of drinking, she stared down at it. "I miss him. A lot. I just want the ache to stop. The pain of realizing I'll never see him again."

He hurt for her, but Kennedy didn't offer any platitudes. He didn't tell her it would get easier or that the pain would lessen over time. She already knew that. She didn't need words.

She needed a distraction from her pain. And he was determined to be the one doing the distracting.

"What are you doing tomorrow?" Kennedy asked.

She paused midchew, then swallowed. "Um. I don't know. More penis stuff, I guess."

His wineglass paused halfway to his lips. "Dare I hope you're referring to Lara's bachelorette shenanigans?"

"My penis agenda is none of your—"

"No," he interrupted. "I hereby ban the phrase *penis agenda*. Actually, let's just go ahead and take the word *penis* off the table altogether."

"What do you want me to call it? What about—"

"No," he said again. "Just no. Are you free tomorrow or not?"

"Why?"

"Free or not," he said, refusing to give her any chance of wiggling out of what he had planned.

Kate rolled her eyes as she took another bite of her scallop. "Fine. No. I don't have anything going on tomorrow."

"Good. I'll pick you up at eleven. Dress casual."

She paused with her fork in her mouth, then pulled it out and frowned. "What?"

"There will be no penises, so don't get excited."

"I thought we couldn't use that word."

"Loophole. If you have said body part, you're allowed to say it."

Her cheeks turned slightly pink, and she took a sip of her water.

Kennedy hid a smirk, fairly certain that her blush had more to do with arousal than embarrassment. But her next words had him sobering.

"Kennedy, what are we doing here? I told you I wasn't . . . I don't want . . ." She broke off, looking frustrated that she didn't seem to know what she wanted or what she was trying to say.

His chest tightened with hurt for her, frustration for himself. But she came first, always.

He reached across the table for her hand, the ache in his chest easing slightly at the way her fingers folded instinctively around his.

"Do you trust me?" he asked quietly.

She hesitated only a moment, then nodded.

Hope soared. "Good. I'll pick you up at eleven tomorrow."

23

Kennedy showed up twelve minutes early. Of course he did.

Kate picked up the phone and pressed the button to let him into the building without bothering to say hello, one hand still wrapped around the handle of her round brush.

Not so long ago, her thick, straight hair had air-dried or was hurriedly brushed through with a regular old brush and blow-dryer. The new haircut required a bit of TLC to look full and bouncy, but she didn't mind. She would have styled her hair for any Sunday brunch plans. Really. It had nothing to do with looking her best for Kennedy.

At his knock, she opened the door and immediately sighed as she looked at him. "I should have known."

"What?"

"You said dress casual!" she accused.

He looked down. "This is casual. I'm wearing shorts."

"Uh-huh. Be honest with me—do you have those dry-cleaned, or at least pressed, every time you wear them?"

He looked at her like she was crazy. "Of course."

Kate sighed again. "Whatever. Come in. But I'm not changing to match that," she said, waving a hand over his perfectly pressed navy shorts, wrinkle-free white button-down, and boat shoes that were either never worn or kept in weirdly pristine condition.

She, on the other hand, had taken casual to heart. Denim shorts that were at least a half decade old, slim-fitting black tee, and adidas Superstars.

"I think you look great," he said as she headed back to the bathroom to finish her hair.

"Shut up," she called back. "I'll be ready in a few, make yourself at home, you know the drill."

Which was a little weird that he did. Weird to think that just last night they'd been in almost this exact same position—her primping, him patiently waiting to take her out. Weirdest of all, it felt strangely natural, as though they'd been doing this for years.

She tried a minute more to get her hair to do the bouncy curled-under thing, but it just wasn't cooperating today. Kate tossed the brush aside and pulled a hairband out of the drawer, deciding for a messy bun instead. It better matched the outfit.

"Okay," she said, coming out of the bathroom. "I'm ready. Or at least I think I'm ready. I could say it with more confidence if I knew what we were doing." She looked pointedly at the navy duffel in his hand. "What's in there?"

"Don't tell me you're one of those people who can't handle surprises."

"I'm *absolutely* one of those people who can't handle surprises. I'm the one who plans them, not receives them. Not knowing is annoying."

"Says the woman who planned my surprise birthday party."

"Yeah, but that wasn't my idea. I merely steered your girlfriend in the right direction so you had something to eat besides oysters."

"And yet that ice sculpture . . ."

She shook her head. "I tried, Kennedy. Really, I did."

"How hard?"

Kate laughed as she grabbed her purse. "She was persistent. How is Claudia, by the way?"

"No idea," he said, opening her front door.

She paused in the process of dropping her keys in her bag. "Really? You haven't talked to her?"

"Do you talk to your exes?" he said, pulling the door closed behind them.

"My exes are all super old news." She turned to lock the door, but Kennedy, in his usual take-charge way, pulled the keys out of her hand and did it for her.

"What about Jack?" he asked, looking at her out of the corner of his eye as he put the key in the lock.

"Oh, well him, yeah. I guess he's an ex. He's great. But then, you already know that."

Kennedy's hand stilled. "You guys talk?"

"Sure. He called on Friday to offer his condolences, see how I was doing."

Kennedy's scowl deepened for a fraction of a second, but then it cleared. "He's seeing someone, you know. A Broadway dancer."

"I know. He told me. We talk, remember?" Kate said sweetly as they headed downstairs.

"You're not upset that he's got someone new?"

"I don't really have a right to be, do I? I mean, I was making out with his brother just a few days after he and I broke up."

They stepped out onto the sidewalk. "That's not an answer to the question."

"No, it wasn't. Oh, it's gorgeous out!" she said in surprise. "A perfect spring day."

He looked like he wanted to push the Jack thing further, but he relented with a slight sigh. "Yes, the weather cooperated nicely with my plans."

She gave him a dubious look. "*You* made outdoor plans?"

"I did," he said, lifting his hand to hail a cab. "What, you thought I melted in the sun?"

"No, I thought you melted at the threat of dirt," she countered, climbing into the taxi ahead of him.

"Seventy-Ninth and Fifth," Kennedy told the driver.

Kate rolled through her mental Manhattan geography and frowned. "Not much there. It's right by the park."

"Indeed."

"But what else—Wait. Are we going to the park?"

He glanced over. "You don't like Central Park?"

"I *love* Central Park! I thought you didn't."

"What sort of jerk doesn't like Central Park?"

"I told you, one who doesn't like dirt."

Kennedy patted the bag and then looked out the window. "Good thing I've got a blanket to sit on."

Kate gaped at him. There was only one reason someone took a blanket to Central Park. In all of her imaginings, and there had been plenty the night before, the thought of Kennedy planning a picnic in the park had never occurred to her.

"Why are you staring at me?" he asked, not bothering to look her way.

"Why Seventy-Ninth? The park starts at Sixtieth."

"All the tourists enter at Sixty. It's less crowded up north."

"It's also closer to your apartment. Like, really close."

"So?"

"So why the heck didn't you just have me meet you? I could have grabbed the subway. You didn't have to come all of the way south just to pick me up. What a waste of—"

"Kate?"

"What?"

"Be quiet." He smiled a little as he said it, still not looking at her.

Her mind raced. Friends didn't cab thirty blocks downtown, only to retrace their steps uptown. Friends didn't. But dates sure as heck did.

She wasn't sure whether the thought pleased her or terrified her. Maybe a little bit of both. But she'd meant it last night when she said she trusted him. She trusted him not to hurt her. So she stayed quiet.

Several minutes later, Kennedy paid the driver, and Kate couldn't contain her broad smile as they walked toward the entrance of Central Park, a little girl on a scooter nearly clipping their toes with a happy "Sorry" shouted over her ponytail.

"Sorry about that," a man echoed, speed-walking after the girl, a toddler on his hip. "Rosie, slow down!"

"Hurry up, Daddy!"

Kate's smile slipped just a little bit, the scene reminding her of long-ago weekends with her own father. Not at Central Park but at the little rinky-dink park in their neighborhood where the grass was always a little brown, the swings a little rusty, but the memories were pure gold.

Kennedy set his hand on her back, just for a moment, a casual touch that might have said *this way* or *watch out for the dog poop*. But the slight brush of his thumb along her spine and the lingering warmth told her he understood what she was feeling. It said *I'm here.*

"Do you do this often?" she asked as they stepped into the park. It was bustling, being a sunny weekend day, but even still, she felt the difference from the city just steps behind her and the oasis ahead of her.

"Sure, great running paths," he said as they weaved their way down the path, sharing it with strollers, walkers, and the aforementioned runners.

"No, I mean for picnics." They veered to the right down one of the many forks in the road Central Park had to offer.

"Ah. No. Can't say that I've done it . . . probably in a couple decades."

"Decades? So you did this when you were a kid?"

"Sure. It was actually an Easter tradition, weather permitting."

She looked up at him. "Huh."

His eyes were scanning the various grassy areas, probably looking for the perfect spot to settle, so when he looked back down at her, he seemed surprised she was watching him. "What?"

"I just can't reconcile the Dawsons with a messy picnic in the grass."

"Who said anything about messy?" he asked with a quick wink. "My mom had a whole arsenal of dedicated picnic equipment, right down to the red-checkered blanket she had handmade from some woman out in Nantucket. The picnic baskets even had a special pie carrier, perfect for our Easter picnic days."

"A pie carrier. Wow."

"Maybe let's not mention this to her," he said, patting his decidedly non-dedicated-picnic bag. "If she still has the old picnic stuff, she'll probably try to foist it upon me." Kennedy touched her upper arm, then nodded to their left. "Over there. There's a spot under the tree that looks flat."

Kate headed toward the spot he indicated. Together they spread out the navy blanket from his bag, and she happily kicked off her shoes and settled on the blanket, watching as he unpacked the rest of the bag.

"What's in those?" she asked as he pulled out two enormous canteen-style water bottles.

"Water, rosé," he said, pointing at one, then the other.

"Rosé, as in wine? Can you drink in Central Park?"

"I won't tell if you won't." He pulled out a stack of plastic cups. "If anyone asks, it's pink lemonade."

"I can't really reconcile you drinking pink anything," Kate said as he set a container of store-bought pasta salad alongside a baguette. "Wait, what is that?"

"Travel cheese board."

"Whaaaaat? They make those?"

"What did *you* eat on picnics, Henley? Cardboard?"

"Normal food. String cheese. American cheese on white bread with off-brand mayo. Fig Newtons—name-brand, obviously."

He pulled out a package of delicate macarons from a bakery Kate knew well. Not for herself but from buying hoity-toity gifts for clients. Kennedy caught the direction of her gaze and wordlessly handed over the package.

"Isn't this dessert?"

He gave her a *come on, we're grown-ups who can do what we want* look, and with a grin, she took the package. She went for a green one, guessing it was pistachio.

"Mmmmm." Her eyes closed, delighted to be right about the flavor.

When she opened them, Kennedy was frozen in place, giving her the same look as he had last night when she was eating the scallops. Knowing she was playing with fire, Kate couldn't help herself from extending the cookie toward him, surprised, and yet not surprised, when after only a brief hesitation, he leaned down and nipped a bite of cookie directly from her fingers.

Their eyes locked for a second before she forced a bright smile. "Amazing, right?"

"A little sweet," he said, chewing, as he finished unpacking the last of the food and paper plates.

Kennedy settled on the blanket beside her, lying on one side, as he reached for the rosé thermos. He looked . . . different.

This was relaxed Kennedy. Picnic Kennedy.

She didn't like it. She'd just barely figured out how to get over crusty Kennedy and had convinced herself that she didn't want her heart entangled with anyone, and then he had to go and be all *appealing*.

Kate forced herself to look away before she did something stupid, only to look in the entirely wrong direction. "Oh *jeez*."

Kennedy picked up the plastic cups and followed her gaze, going still when he saw where she was looking.

On the far side of the lawn was a couple who, while not naked or even half-naked, might as well have been. *Make-out session* didn't quite describe it. It was more like . . . foreplay.

"I don't think I've ever quite so clearly understood the phrase *get a room*," Kate muttered, somehow unable to look away from the amorous couple. She wasn't close enough to determine anything more than that the woman was blonde, the man brunette, but there was no mistaking the way his hand slid over her hip, the way her long hair spread above her head, unknowing, or uncaring, that it was in the grass.

Kennedy cleared his throat. "Wine?"

Kate tore her gaze away. A second ago, she was thinking, *Heck yes, wine.* Now her body was tingling, ever aware of his nearness.

"Have you ever?" she blurted out.

"Have I ever what?"

She nodded in the direction of the couple without looking at them.

His eyebrows lifted. "Made out in the grass?"

She smiled. "Yeah. Or, you know, kissed in public. Actually, never mind," she said with a shake of her head. "Stupid question."

Kennedy frowned. "Why is it a stupid question?"

"Because you're Kennedy Dawson. I believe I once heard you use the words *PDA* and *lowbrow* in the same sentence."

His frown deepened to a scowl. "You make me sound so . . ."

"Uptight?" she teased.

"Yeah." He looked down at the cups, then tossed them to the side before looking back at her, his gaze going from irritated to considering. "Though, now that I'm remembering, that's not the one word you'd use to describe me."

Kate froze, that night on the boat crashing down around her, remembering her outburst, her confession. Remembering that what had followed made the couple across the lawn look tame.

Every instinct in Kate's body wanted her to flee, but she forced herself to face the situation like an adult, even as she swore she could feel her heartbeat at every single pulse point. "Yes, well. That was before."

"Before your dad passed?" he asked softly.

Kate swallowed. Nodded.

Kennedy's hand twitched as though he might reach for hers, but then stilled once more. "So the feelings . . . the ones I was so blind to. Gone?"

Her heart began to pound. "I thought we agreed to put that night behind us."

"Actually, I didn't agree to any such thing," Kennedy said quietly, studying her. "I merely haven't pressed the matter. But I do have questions. When you're ready."

"All right," she said after a moment. "Hit me."

His gaze never wavered from hers. "Ian told me I missed my window with you. That you had feelings for me early on, but then they stopped. I want to know why."

She laughed. "No, you don't."

He frowned. "I do."

Kate hesitated only a moment longer before deciding to come clean. He wasn't her boss anymore. She was no longer in love with him. So why *not* clear the air?

"Fine," she said, folding her hands in her lap and looking at him. "You know that night when you and the guys made that dumb pact to not date me?"

He visibly flinched. "You knew?"

"That you guys were childish morons? Definitely. But it wasn't the pact that bothered me. It was what you said to convince them to agree to it."

He shook his head, indicating he didn't follow.

Kate took a deep breath. "You said, 'The little thing's hardly irresistible, but better safe than sorry in case any of us gets drunk and stupid.'"

His head snapped back. "I didn't say that."

"You did," she said simply. "Trust me, a woman doesn't forget hearing the man she loves say something like that."

His eyes closed. "Loves."

"Yeah, well." She kept her voice light. "What can I say, I was young and stupid. But on the plus side, hearing your thoughts helped me get over it *real* fast."

He rubbed his hands over his face. "I sure as hell don't remember saying that."

"It's fine," Kate said with a smile. "I'm well aware that I'm no femme fatale, especially not back then."

"It doesn't excuse me being cruel."

"Well, you didn't know I was there, so—"

"Would you shut up and let me apologize properly?" he said in exasperation.

She held up her hands. "Fine. I'm listening."

He eased closer but didn't touch her, his eyes intense on hers. "I don't know what the hell that idiotic version of me was thinking. But I do know what the version of me *now* is thinking. Has been thinking for weeks."

Kate swallowed nervously. "What's that?"

His hand lifted as though to touch her face, then dropped again, his fist clenching. "That I can't stop thinking about you. About putting my hands on you. About how we can't seem to get our damn timing right, because you're telling me that night on the yacht was the end of something, when for me, it felt like just the beginning."

She tried to calm her racing heart and couldn't. She'd waited so long to hear these words from him, and yet she couldn't forget just how much that initial rejection had stung.

"I'm sorry, Kate—more sorry than I possibly have words for. Back then, the man you heard didn't have the right understanding of the word *irresistible*, but the man sitting beside you right now does. And you should know—you must know—you are the most irresistible woman I've ever known." His hand tentatively touched her cheek. "Do you trust me?"

Kate studied him, studied his every feature, determined to read the truth.

She'd be lying if she said she hadn't been a little distrustful of Kennedy in the past. Or rather, maybe not distrustful of him as much as of herself when she was around him. That much was still true. He, of all people, had the power to hurt her. Not because he'd want to or ever intend to, but simply because she'd given him such a big part of her heart and hadn't gotten all of it back yet.

But . . .

This was the guy who'd never let her down. Who'd driven her an hour to her family's house, then handled the aftermath of her father's death, all without expecting so much as a thank-you in response. He was the type of person who took care of other people. Who cared for his own. So yeah, she trusted him.

Which was why Kate gave in to an urge she'd been trying to stifle for years. She leaned forward and kissed Kennedy Dawson.

24

Had he really gone years without kissing Kate Henley? Because right now, Kennedy couldn't remember how he'd survived the past month since he last had his lips on hers.

Kate sighed, her breath warm and sweet as it mingled with his.

Kennedy's hand went to the back of her head, and he lowered her slightly back to the picnic blanket. He followed her down, settling his body against hers. Everything had changed that night on the boat and in the weeks leading up to it. He'd realized that he didn't just want Kate, he needed her. She'd been all he could think about, the only important thing. He'd seen it happen with Ian when he met Lara, watched it brewing for years with Matt and Sabrina.

He'd thought he'd understood it on a rational level. Thought that even if that sort of all-consuming obsession with another person didn't happen for him, he'd known what they were going through.

He hadn't. Not until it had happened to him with Kate.

Kennedy now realized that he'd do anything just to be near her. Even if it meant making out in Central Park.

Especially then.

She was shy at first, her kiss chaste, her body tense, and he let her set the tone of the kiss. Eventually, when her hand lifted to the back of his head, her fingers tangling in his hair with a touch of frustrated urgency, he rewarded her by tangling his tongue with hers. Her small body arched up, her mouth opening to his.

Kennedy was right there with her. He lost himself in the kiss, forgetting they were in a public place, on the fucking grass. He hadn't even opened the wine, but he felt drunk on the moment.

Drunk on her.

His thigh moved farther over her, pinning her legs to the blanket, and Kate folded her arms around the back of his neck, pulling him in. Kennedy's hand drifted over her waist, over the shirt, because they were in a public place, for God's sake. He'd never hated clothes as much as right now, and before he could think through the wisdom of it, his fingers inched beneath the hem of her T-shirt, finding the bare skin of her smooth stomach.

As far as touches went, it was a chaste one, but they both moaned.

His hand stilled, and his eyes flew open as he lifted slightly, breathing hard as he looked down at her.

Kate's eyes fluttered open a moment later, her gaze as dazed as he felt.

"I don't know if I can keep this PG," he admitted, brushing a brief kiss over her mouth. As though proving his point, her lips moved against his, warm and clinging and passionate, and the kiss went from chaste to hot in the span of a heartbeat.

"So don't," she whispered, then bit his lip.

His fingers clenched against her waist once more before he groaned and tore himself away, rolling onto his back with a rueful laugh. "Jesus. I feel like a horny teenager."

Kate lifted her head. "Why'd you stop?"

The vulnerability in her voice clawed at him, and he knew she was thinking about his careless words from years earlier. Words he didn't remember saying, hadn't even meant. *Hardly irresistible.*

Fucking moron. She was beyond irresistible.

And he was beyond hard.

He rolled toward her. "I stopped because I was about five seconds away from screwing you in the middle of Central Park."

Her wide smile surprised him. Delighted him.

"*Screwing?*" Kate said, her tone amused. "There's a word I never imagined hearing from Kennedy Dawson's mouth."

"What?"

"The word *screw* to describe sex. It's just so delightfully improper."

He frowned, not particularly enjoying how amused she looked at the thought of him and sex in the same sentence. "What word did you think I used?"

She pursed her lips and considered. "Coitus?"

"Christ." He turned his head back to stare up at the sky.

"Copulation?" she guessed again.

"Stop." His eyes closed in bemused dismay.

"Fornication? I don't know. I just picture you being very polite and proper and tidy about the whole process."

His eyes opened. Screw the picnic.

Kennedy sat up and picked up the thermos and cups, shoving them back into the bag, along with everything else he'd already unpacked.

"Hey!" She sat up in confusion. "What are you doing?"

Kennedy stood, then reached a hand down to her. "Up."

She ignored the hand and scowled at him. "I thought we were having a picnic in the park."

"I've got something better in mind."

25

They barely made it inside his apartment before six years of wanting this man took over.

The second his door closed, Kate's fingers found the front of his shirt, his perfectly pressed, never ever wrinkled shirt, and she bunched it between her fingers. Her eyes locked on his, seeing the same heat she felt mirrored in his dark gaze as she slowly, purposefully pulled his mouth down to hers.

Kennedy bent his head, closing the distance of their considerable height difference, and the second his mouth touched hers, he took control. One hand pressed the center of her back, the other cupped the back of her head as he spun her around and pressed her back against the front door, his mouth never leaving hers.

He slipped a hand beneath her shirt, his thumb flicking teasingly over the clasp of her bra before moving to her waist, his fingers pressing hot into her skin.

Kate's nails dug into his shoulders, and his fingers tightened in response before sliding to her hips and holding her still. For several delicious minutes, he did nothing but kiss her—long, drugging kisses that left her helpless with want.

When she thought she couldn't take any more, she broke the kiss on a gasp. "I need to catch my breath."

"Later," he said, his mouth moving to her throat as he maneuvered her shirt up and over her head, tossing it aside.

He bit her bare shoulder, and she gasped.

"Still think I'm proper?" he ground out.

Before Kate could register what was happening, she was over his shoulder and being hauled out of the entryway. Not carried, *Gone with the Wind* style. Hauled, Neanderthal style. It was single-handedly the most erotic moment of her life.

Or maybe not.

Because then she was on her back in the center of his bed. *Kennedy Dawson's bed.* Something she'd fantasized about more times than she cared to admit, even to herself.

But before she had time to register that it was finally happening, that his bedding was as pristine and wrinkle-free as she'd thought, though crisp hotel white and not the dark gray she'd imagined, he was pulling his shirt over his head, kicking off his shoes, and watching her like a man about to devour his prey.

That was the most erotic moment of her life.

Kate started to scoot higher on the bed, but Kennedy caught her ankle and dragged her toward him. She let out a little laugh, which quickly descended to a moan as he leaned over her, his lips skimming along the slight swell of her breast above her bra.

Hooking a single finger into the fabric, he tugged it down just enough to expose her nipple to the cool air of the bedroom, followed immediately by the wet warmth of his tongue. His mouth fastened around her and sucked, his hands ripping away her bra and repeating the whole process with her other breast, until she was writhing and begging for more.

Kennedy lifted his head, his gaze finding hers as his hand went slowly to the waistband of her shorts. His eyes held her perfectly still as his fingers undid the button. Then he stilled.

Last chance.

Kate's thighs moved apart ever so slightly in invitation, and his breathing quickened. She heard the rasp of a zipper. His. Then hers. Heard him groan her name as her underwear joined their shorts somewhere on the floor of his bedroom.

Heard *her* shout *his* name as his hand slid between her legs, finding her wet. Her eyes slammed shut as pleasure rolled through her, but Kennedy didn't let her take the coward's way out. His hand stilled, waiting until she met his gaze before he resumed moving his fingers again, exploring slowly at first, then surer as he watched her every expression, lingering longer when she cried out. He circled in the exact right spot, and her eyes closed again. His hand stilled. Waited.

Her eyes popped open, and she glared at him. "Damn you, Kennedy—"

He slid two fingers inside her without warning, and she bucked upward. This time when her eyes closed, he let her, his fingers sliding in and out of her body with perfect rhythm, his thumb finding the perfect spot once more . . .

She was so close, so ready—

Kate was just seconds away from release when he pulled his hand away. She was mollified slightly—only slightly—to see the way his hand fumbled at the drawer of the nightstand, the way his hands didn't just open the condom wrapper but tore it.

This time when she scooted up the bed, he joined her there, levering his body over hers, settling his hips between her thighs, his cock nudging against her aching center.

"Yes," she whispered. Her eyes started to close, but she caught herself. She was learning his ways.

He rewarded her by sliding his hand over her hip, hooking his arm beneath her thigh, until she was all of the way open to him.

He entered her with a thrust so hard she moved upward on the bed, her hand coming up to brace against the headboard as she cried out.

"Okay?" he growled, withdrawing slowly and holding still.

Kate couldn't manage words, so she nodded. *Okay?* She was so much better than okay.

He thrust forward again, and Kate's nails dug into his back.

More.

He gave her more. He gave her everything.

She'd been so wrong. There was nothing clinical or restrained about the way Kennedy Dawson took a woman to bed. It was raw, intense, and mind-blowing, and yet it wasn't careless. Even as he drove into her again and again, he watched her face, cupped her head in one hand to keep from driving her too far up into the headboard.

He cares.

And though she didn't want it to, it was the caring that unraveled her.

It was the way he held back his own pleasure until she found hers, his hand sliding between them, circling slowly, tauntingly, knowing somehow that she needed to be coaxed, just a little more—

She came with a cry, her face lifting instinctively to the crook of his shoulder. His hand came to the back of her neck, holding her as she shuddered against him, then laying her back slowly as her body started to relax.

His mouth crushed over hers, kissing her as he thrust home once more, gasping against her lips as he found his release.

Kate felt a flicker of alarm at the realization that his release brought her almost as much pleasure as her own, alarm turning to panic as he pressed a kiss to her temple that felt entirely too tender for her heart to handle.

He pulled away slowly and unabashedly rolled off the bed and went to the bathroom. She heard the flush of the toilet, the running water of the faucet, and sat up, sheet clutched to her nakedness as she looked desperately at the door, wondering, *What now?*

She didn't do this. She didn't have afternoon sex with a guy. And definitely not with a guy she worked with.

Did she run off and deal with the aftermath later? Did she play it cool, like it was no big deal? Did she—

The bathroom door opened, and Kennedy walked to the dresser, pulling on a pair of black boxer briefs, then pulling out a T-shirt.

Kate said nothing as she watched him, then realized he wasn't putting the T-shirt on. Instead, he tossed it her way.

She looked down at it lying across her lap. "What—"

He shrugged. "Or stay naked. No complaints."

Well, when he put it that way . . .

Kate pulled on the shirt. It was gray, soft, probably expensive, and shock of all shocks . . . not even remotely wrinkled.

She took a deep breath and realized the benefit of sleeping with someone she'd known for years was that she didn't have to figure out next steps in her own head. Instead, she handled it Kate style. No games.

"So now what?" she asked, looking him right in the eye.

He looked unperturbed by the directness. Hell, he'd probably been expecting it. The whole *knowing each other* thing went both ways.

"I usually want two things after sex: a nap and food. It just depends which comes first."

"Depends on what?"

He looked at her. "You."

"You want me to . . . nap with you?"

He shrugged. "Or eat. Your choice."

Kate felt her heart squeeze, and she wasn't sure if it was with hope or panic. But there'd be plenty of time to sort all of that out later. For now . . .

She smiled and flopped back on the bed. "Are you kidding? Nap. I mean, how much are these sheets? Be honest, are they more than my annual salary? They are, aren't they? Did you know I got mine at Target? Thirty bucks."

"You don't say," he said, coming around the side of the bed and lifting the covers to join her.

"They're pretty nice," she said, rolling toward him. "Not as nice as these. But good for the price."

"Hmm." His eyes were already drifting closed. "I'll have to try them sometime."

"Will you?"

His eyes opened. "Hmm?"

Kate swallowed. "It's just that you sounded sort of certain that you'd be trying my sheets, and I was sort of thinking this was a onetime thing."

He smiled and kissed her forehead. "Go to sleep, Kate."

She couldn't. Not after she'd just done the unthinkable and had no-strings afternoon nooky with Kennedy.

And yet she did.

And damn if it wasn't the best sleep she'd had in weeks.

26

Saturday, May 25

"What am I looking at here?" Sabrina asked, picking up the wooden skewer of grapes and inspecting it.

"Anal beads," Kate said around a stuffed mushroom. "Duh."

"Nice," Sabrina declared, dropping said "beads" into the glass of champagne she'd just poured.

"Here, dear," she said, handing the flute to an approaching Lara.

"Oooh, pretty garnish," Lara said. "I love grapes. They're so elegant."

"Mm," Sabrina said noncommittally. "So elegant." She reached out to adjust Lara's crooked tiara. "How many drinks have you had, babe?"

In response, Lara pushed her glasses up her nose and then spun in a circle, the white tutu Kate had bought her for the occasional whirling fanning out around her. Impressively, she managed not to spill a drop of the champagne, despite the definite tipsy wobble she had going on. "I'm getting married in two weeks. Married!"

She shouted the last word, and Kate laughed at her friend's uncharacteristic giddiness. "Guess those drinks took effect," she said as Lara twirled away to join her best friend and former roommate, Gabby, on the couch.

Gabby had moved to London with her boyfriend a year earlier but had flown back to New York for the wedding festivities. The most recent of said festivities being one (or twelve) rounds of Moscow Mules from testicle-shaped cups. Kate had had two. Lara and Gabby? A few more.

"What's this?" Sabrina asked, gesturing at a basket on the counter.

"Hangover kit for tomorrow," Kate said, reaching out and pulling the basket closer. She pointed. "Excedrin, obviously. Bottled water. Gatorade. Saltines. Eye mask. Note card telling her that an egg sandwich on a bagel and coffee will be arriving at ten thirty a.m."

"You already told her that."

Kate gave Sabrina a look, then glanced pointedly at the couch where Lara and Gabby were singing a very off-key rendition of a Christina Aguilera song Kate hadn't heard in at least a decade.

"Right," Sabrina said. "A reminder would be good."

"Hey, Lara," Kate called over to the living room. "If you're going to dance, move that champagne glass away from the edge of the table, hon!"

Lara did so, lifting the glass carefully with two hands the way one would hold a chalice, and then setting it in the very center of the coffee table before flinging her hands over her head in a *ta-da, I did it!* gesture.

"Good job," Kate said as Lara went back to doing some very jerky dance moves.

Sabrina perused the open wine bottles on the counter before settling on a Sauvignon Blanc, pouring herself a glass. She held the bottle up toward Kate, who extended her glass for a top-off. She wasn't entirely sure it was the same white she'd been drinking before, but she was *just* tipsy enough not to care.

"How do we have so many open bottles for four people?" Sabrina mused.

At Lara's request, the bachelorette party had been kept exceedingly small. As an FBI agent, Lara was careful about who she cut loose around. Kate was honored to be among the select few and also relieved that she didn't have to deal with small talk. Normally, she could host a party, whether it be her own or her best friends', like nobody's business.

Lately, though? Lately, her brain had no room for talk of the weather, or the latest movies, or *oh-em-gee, what is Justin Bieber up to now?*

For the first time in a long time—maybe ever?—Kate wasn't up to dealing with other people's business. She was drowning in her own.

"It's good to see her happy," Sabrina said with an indulgent smile at the wildly dancing Lara.

"It really is," Kate said. "Ian, too. He's been like a little kid at the office lately. The other day he brought in candy for everyone. *Candy.* Not like fancy chocolates, but some bag of assorted crap. He went around to every office saying, 'One for you; one for you,' like a little kid."

Sabrina laughed. "God, I'd have killed to see that. Was he drunk?"

"Yeah, on love," Kate muttered.

She expected a caustic remark from Sabrina, who'd known Ian since they were kids and who was a pretty die-hard cynic. And then she remembered . . . no longer. Sabrina had joined Lara and Ian in the happily-in-love club, and though she hid it better than Ian, Sabrina was dopily drunk in love with her new husband. And Matt with her.

And just like that, Kate realized that she, the one who'd not so long ago had her kids and pet names picked out and had once doodled *Kate Dawson* on her notepad in a moment of weakness, had become the group's resident cynic. *No, not cynic,* she corrected. She was just . . . smarter now. A little less blindly trusting that it would all end happily ever after.

"It's good to see you happy, too," Sabrina said. "Or at least easing back that way after your dad."

Kate's head snapped up, and she found her friend watching her. "I still miss him," Kate said quietly, the pads of her fingers on the base of the wineglass, spinning it round and round on the counter without taking a sip.

"Of course you do," Sabrina said matter-of-factly. "You always will. But right now is the worst, and I'm glad you have someone by your side to help you through it."

Kate's eyes narrowed, and Sabrina's narrowed right back.

"What, you think I didn't know? That we all didn't know?"

"Know what?"

Sabrina shook her head. "You're a terrible liar. Even worse at playing dumb. You and Kennedy are doing it."

"Shh!" Kate glanced over to where Gabby was trying to teach Lara some sort of sashaying dance that looked like it would be complicated sober, much less way past sober.

"Oh please," Sabrina said. "Gabby lives on another continent and couldn't care less about our love lives, and Lara already knows."

"How?" Kate asked, aghast.

"Well, because I ran into Kennedy this week, and he was giving off the *I'm getting regular sex* vibes. The exact same vibes I got the second I saw you today. Which I suspect is exactly why you've been avoiding us all week. Or maybe that's just because you've been too busy humping?"

Screwing, Kate mentally amended with a little smile.

"Ooh," Sabrina said, leaning in. "I'm liking that smile. That means you're not just getting regular sex but good sex."

"Yes to the latter; no to the former," Kate said. "It's good. Really good. But not regular."

"Oh my God, it's true!" Sabrina's eyes were wide. "After all of this time, you and Kennedy finally hooked up."

"Wait! You said you already knew!"

"I mean, I had my suspicions from that glow you're rocking, but now I know for sure. Spill the details. When? Where? How many times?"

"Twice," Kate said, holding up two fingers. "Once last Sunday, and it was just spontaneous, and casual, and . . ." *Mind-blowing.*

"And the other time?"

"Wednesday," Kate admitted. "We were both working late, and he asked if I wanted to go to dinner."

"And then you did it after dinner?"

"We never got there," Kate said, trying not to blush as she remembered the very dirty things she'd done to Kennedy in his office.

"Nice," Sabrina said.

Had Kate not been looking at Sabrina, she might have missed the flicker of concern that went along with her approving tone.

"What was that?" Kate said, pointing at Sabrina's face. "That look."

Sabrina had always been direct, and tonight was no different. "I'm worried about you."

"Why? Aren't there studies showing that sex is life-affirming or some such?" Kate said, picking a piece of cheddar off the cheese board and nibbling the corner, even though she wasn't really hungry. "Besides, you're the one who told me to scratch my itch."

"Yes. But doing it more than once takes you solidly out of fling territory. Take it from me: more than once means something."

"It means that Kennedy has a really great body."

"Kate," Sabrina said softly. "I'm glad you're having good sex. Thrilled. But are you positive it's not more than that? You were in love with him once. You've said so."

"Yes. Once. But that doesn't mean I'm in love with him *now.*"

Her friend gave her a skeptical look.

"I still care about him," Kate admitted. "But I don't want a relationship. Neither does he."

"You sure about that?"

"Yes. I—Wait, what do you know?"

"Nothing. Really. It's just that after the night on the boat with you two—"

Kate stilled. "You know about that?" She hadn't told a soul. Not even her girlfriends.

"Kennedy told the guys, and Matt mentioned that something had happened with you two."

"Wait, *what*?" Kate blinked. "Why would Kennedy mention that to them?"

"I don't think it was a salacious gossip fest or anything," Sabrina rushed to reassure her. "I mean, Matt didn't get, like, details on your bra size."

Kate winced.

"Sorry. I just mean it wasn't a locker-room type of conversation. I think Kennedy told them because it mattered. To him. I think you matter to him."

You're mine now.

The memory of that night rushed back at Kate, bittersweet and tormenting.

She didn't know if she was ready for that tender, possessive version of Kennedy—if she'd ever been. She'd caught a glimpse of him that day at the park, and it had both exhilarated and terrified her. For now, she wanted the casual Kennedy. The version from this past week that had been sexy and flirtatious, even a little bit charming.

"We're on the same page now." *I think.* "We've gotten the sexual tension out of our systems, and now we can go back to just being colleagues and friends."

"Friends." Sabrina didn't bother to hide her skepticism.

"Yes. Like you and Kennedy are friends. Like he and Lara are friends."

"Okay, but there's a huge difference. Two, actually," Sabrina said. "We didn't use to fantasize about him putting a ring on our finger. And we haven't seen him naked."

"Well, I no longer want his ring on my finger, and the naked thing is just . . ." Kate tried for cool but couldn't hide her blush.

Sabrina noticed. "That good, huh? I mean, the guy works out. A lot."

"I don't kiss and tell."

Sabrina picked up a wine bottle. "Have some more of this, and maybe you'll get around to the good stuff. Better yet, have one of those Testicle Mules that Gabby and Lara downed like water."

"Yuck, we are not calling them that."

"Says the woman who brought anal beads to the party," Sabrina said, nodding at the grapes.

"Hey, *you* made her a tiara out of condom wrappers."

"Protection is important. Mostly I'm hoping we get to play pin-the-dick on Ian." She pointed at the cardboard cutout Kate had ordered online. Ian's face had been superimposed on a male model, naked except for a fig leaf.

"Yeah, but did you see they sent along, like, twenty different types of dicks?" Kate said. "I think the idea is for Lara to pick the one that most resembles Ian. I don't really want to know that. Do you?"

"Yikes, no." Sabrina winced. "I guess it's a good thing our girl seems past the point of being safely blindfolded."

Proving Sabrina's point, Lara had started playing Cyndi Lauper on the sound system. Women everywhere knew the opening notes of "Girls Just Want to Have Fun" usually went hand in hand with a headache the next morning. Especially if there was singing involved.

Which there was.

"How mad at us do you think Ian's going to be for letting his fiancée dance on the couch?" Kate asked.

The front door of Lara and Ian's apartment started to open, and Sabrina straightened. "I'd say we're about to find out."

Kate turned toward the front door just as Lara shouted Ian's name and vaulted off the back of the couch and straight into his arms. He stumbled back a step or two as Lara slammed into him and was steadied by Matt and . . . yes, Kennedy.

Kate purposely didn't look at him as she took in a tipsily affectionate Lara and Ian, whose singing along with Cyndi was a dead giveaway of his state.

"What in God's name did you give him?" Sabrina asked as Ian twirled Lara around their living room. Gabby clapped to the music from the couch, not even close to on beat.

"He mostly stuck to his usual Negronis, heavy emphasis on the plural," Matt said, helping himself to a mushroom as he wrapped an arm around Sabrina's waist.

Kate glanced at Kennedy, keeping her face carefully in the friend zone. "You do realize you guys are crashing a bachelorette party, right?"

"We did our best but decided the whole bachelor party was a bust when Ian started telling the stripper all about the wedding. In great detail. Then asked if she was cold."

"Oh dear," Kate said with a laugh. "Well, at least we know he'll be loyal."

"Lara, too," Sabrina chimed in. "I suggested a male stripper, and she asked if we could have Ian do it."

"And there's *my* nightmare fodder for weeks," Matt said with a wince.

"So what do we do with them now?" Kennedy asked as Ian and Lara moved on from Cyndi to ABBA. "Oh Jesus. Here comes the striptease."

"Come on, man," Matt called as Ian began twirling his dress shirt above his head. "At least let it be Lara who takes her clothes off."

"Is she wearing condoms on her head?" Kennedy asked.

"Nice, right?" Sabrina said proudly.

Kate took one last sip of wine, then decided it was time to call it. "All right," she said, clapping her hands and walking into the living room. "Lara, sweetheart, pull your skirt down. Matt was just kidding. Matt, Sabrina, you think you can get our girl Gabby here into the guest room?"

"I'm a guest!" Gabby said with a happy, slightly oblivious smile.

"You sure are," Sabrina said, wrapping an arm around the other woman and moving her in the direction of the second bedroom. "You want to brush your teeth?"

"Why are you spinning in circles?" Gabby asked.

"Matt, can you get her some water from the fridge?" Sabrina called over her shoulder.

Kate took care of Lara, reaching up and gently untangling her hair from the condom crown. "You ready for bed, bride?"

"Can Ian come?"

"Of course, my dear," Ian answered for Kate, extending his hand to Lara, who took it with a flourish.

Kate stepped aside, watching with a smile as Ian led his fiancée toward the bedroom, realizing they were long past caring that there were other people in their apartment.

"Don't forget my hangover kit on the counter!" Kate called after them.

"They'll be okay. He's a little tipsy, but I think he's more happy than he is drunk," Kennedy said quietly.

"Drunk on love," Kate said with a smile. "Lara, too."

Matt had joined Sabrina in the bedroom, and Kate heard them arguing with Gabby over the merits of sleeping in her stilettos.

She and Kennedy were alone. He looked down at her. "You have fun?"

She smiled and moved back to the counter to clean up. "I did. You?"

"Sure. Yeah. It was nice to hang out, just the three of us, instead of a big blowout bachelor thing."

"Yeah, I think Matt learned that lesson for all of you last year," Kate said, remembering how a particularly rowdy bachelor party, with an ill-placed *Wall Street Journal* photographer, was what placed Matt and Sabrina on their course toward coupledom, but not without plenty of bumps along the way.

"You don't have to clean up," Kennedy said as she started taking glasses toward the sink.

"It's okay. I don't want them to have to worry about it tomorrow when they wake up."

"They won't. I asked my cleaning guy to come by in the morning to take care of it."

Kate turned to stare at him, letting herself see him for the first time that night. She swallowed, because he looked . . . good. His hair was just a little more disheveled than usual. His dress shirt was white and should have been boring, but rolled up to his elbows to reveal his watch and strong forearms, it was anything but.

She tilted her head. "You hired a cleaner? Why?"

He shrugged. "Because I know you. Knew you'd insist on cleaning up for them."

"Because it's what I do," she said before she could stop herself.

He took a step closer. "I know. You take care of everyone. Everything. Who takes care of you?"

Her breath caught at the intense look in his eyes, but before she could process it, he stepped back, his expression reverting to unreadable.

"Cannon," Kennedy called over his shoulder. "We're heading out."

"Wait, what?" Kate asked. She and Kennedy weren't a *we*.

Were they?

Matt stuck his head out of the second bedroom door. "Sounds good. We'll be right behind you once we convince Gabby that now is not the time to text her eighth-grade boyfriend telling him what a mistake he made."

"Good luck with that," Kennedy said, setting a hand on Kate's back and nudging her gently toward the door.

"I know he let a good one get away," they heard Sabrina say cajolingly from the bedroom. "But trust me, that message will be so much clearer if you take a selfie tomorrow instead of sending that one you just took. Better yet, wait until the day *after* tomorrow."

Kate grabbed her purse and followed Kennedy into the hallway, but she turned toward him in the elevator lobby. "I'm not going home with you, you know."

"Okay."

"Just because we—Oh." She broke off when she realized he hadn't argued with her. She tried not to feel rejected. Or disappointed. "Okay."

The elevator door opened with a *ding*, and Kate stepped toward it.

Kennedy grabbed her hand and pulled her back. His head dipped down to hers, taking her mouth in a sweet, surprising kiss.

She stiffened, well aware that Matt and Sabrina could walk into the hallway at any moment. Not that it mattered. There apparently were no secrets in this group.

"I missed you," he whispered against her mouth.

Kate melted into him, kissing him back. *I missed you, too.*

And she had. She'd seen him just yesterday, but it had been at work, and now that she no longer worked for him directly, she didn't have an excuse to pop into his office. Their contact had been limited to polite good mornings and stealing steamy looks across the office when nobody was looking. In other words, everything she'd once daydreamed about and yet . . . better.

But is it enough?

He pulled back slightly. "You tired?"

"No," she admitted. She'd had a venti latte at four o'clock with the expectation of a late night.

"Come home with me."

She let out a little laugh. "I could have sworn I just told you—"

"Not for that, pervert," he said with a wink. "You owe me a rematch."

"A . . . what?"

"Chess," he said, pushing the elevator button again with his finger, holding her hand with the other. "I keep a board set up in my living room."

"Of course you do," she muttered.

"Come on," he said, pulling her closer. "Unless you've had too many drinks. Worried your skills might be compromised?"

Kate's eyes narrowed. "I'm mostly sober, but for the record, I could checkmate your ass even if I'd outdrank Lara and Gabby tonight."

He leaned forward, his eyes gleaming. "Prove it."

27

Kate headed up the bishop she'd just captured and waggled it at Kennedy. "What's it to be, Dawson?"

Kennedy stood, and her mouth went dry at the sight of his bare, tanned six-pack. He held her gaze as his hand went to his belt and paused.

She licked her lips.

Then he removed the belt. Just the belt. His pants stayed on.

He sat as he tossed it to the ground alongside his shoes, socks, and shirt. "Can I just say, strip chess is one of the better ideas I've ever had."

"Says the man who's losing."

"Says the man who has more clothes to lose than you do," Kennedy said, letting his gaze drop purposely to her bra-covered breasts.

Her nipples tightened in response, but Kate pretended to ignore them, and him, as she studied the board. It was true, though. She was winning the chess game, but he was winning on the naked front. Had she known her evening would take this turn when she was getting dressed, she'd have opted for something other than a dress. She'd have gone with pants. Socks. Cardigan. Camisole. Maybe two camisoles. Scarf. Parka.

"Your turn," she said, pretending a bored tone.

Kennedy took his time, reaching for his whiskey and taking a sip. Studying her, studying the board. Finally reaching for a pawn. Pulling back at the last minute. He moved his queen, and she winced as he slowly, purposefully picked up her knight.

They'd agreed that captured pawns didn't warrant a lost item of clothing—only the bigger players. Like the knight.

He slowly lifted his eyebrows in challenge, but he didn't gloat. He didn't have to. They both knew that after losing her strappy sandals and her dress, she had only two items of clothing left:

Bra. Panties.

She reached out and picked up his glass, taking a sip of his whiskey for courage. He'd seen all of her bits already. She knew that. But it was one thing to be naked in the heat of the moment, another to sit across a table from a man naked—or at least mostly naked.

She sat up as inspiration struck. "Do earrings count?"

His gaze lifted briefly to the small silver hoops in her ears. "If you need them to."

Damn. It was both the right and wrong answer. Had he said no, she'd have relished insisting that they did count. Instead, he left the ball in her court, left the decision up to her. She could play it safe, take out an earring in hopes that he'd make more missteps in the game than she would and end up naked first, or . . .

She could prove to him that being naked in front of him didn't faze her in the least. That it was just *naked*, not *vulnerable*.

Kate reached under the table for the waist of her coral underwear. Not her prettiest, but at least they weren't embarrassing.

"Bottoms first?" he said, sounding surprised.

She flashed him a cheeky grin, faking bravado she didn't feel. "I'll be sitting down. You can't see under the table. If I were to take the bra off . . ." She waved her hand at chest level. "Boobs all over the place."

His gaze heated and flared for a second before his eyes drifted downward to where her hands had started to ease off the bikini-cut panties. "Coward."

Kate's eyes narrowed. "Excuse me?"

"This is the second strip show tonight I've been robbed of seeing. That hardly seems fair."

Naked. *Not* vulnerable.

"Well, we can't have that," Kate said, her bravado a little less faked this time as she slowly stood. Once more her hands went to her waist, watching the way his gaze tracked the motion. The way his fingers clenched around the knight piece still in his palm as her thumbs slipped beneath the elastic.

Kate pulled them down to midthigh, then did a tiny shimmy, letting them fall the rest of the way, fluttering to the carpet at her feet. She kicked them aside.

She didn't realize she was holding her breath until she heard Kennedy swallow.

"Well, then. I guess that makes it my turn," she said primly. Kate started to move back toward her chair when Kennedy's fingers closed around her wrist.

He yanked her forward, and a second later, she was on his lap—straddling his lap.

"Kennedy!" She wiggled, jostling the chessboard in the process. His hands found her bare waist, holding her still.

"You had to know," he said as his lips found her neck, "there was no chance I wasn't reaching for you."

Kate's head fell back with a moan as his mouth moved down her chest, and she admitted to herself that she *had* known. That no matter what she told Sabrina about getting him out of her system, she'd wanted him from the very second he'd walked through Lara's door tonight.

Way before that.

His mouth skimmed over her bra, his tongue licking her nipple through the lace. She whimpered, and his hands went to her bra clasp.

"Wait," she managed around a gasp. "This is cheating."

He stilled, his cheek pressed between her breasts, breathing hard. "What?"

"It's breaking the rules," she said, nodding to the chessboard. "You haven't earned the loss of my bra. And I have to capture another piece before you lose your pants." Her hand slid down over the clothing item in question, and she pressed her palm to his hardness.

Kennedy groaned harshly. "I forfeit."

"I don't accept," she whispered, caressing him. "I like rules."

What she liked even more was prolonging this, ever aware that each encounter between them could and should be the last, and she wasn't entirely sure she was ready for that.

Kate started to pull off him, intending to finish the game, but Kennedy had other ideas. One hand cupped her butt firmly, holding her against him, the other pulling her face down for a kiss.

She sank into it. Sank into him, letting her lips and tongue communicate all of the things she didn't know how to say, even to herself.

"I'll follow your rules," he said against her lips. "But I'll play on my terms."

She pulled back slightly in confusion. "What—"

He hooked a finger into the front cup of her lace bra and held her gaze as he tugged it down. Then his head dipped, capturing her nipple in his mouth with a firm suck.

Her back arched, her hands coming to his head, as his fingers pulled down the cup on the other side, a little rougher this time, and licked that nipple as well. Back and forth he went, and somewhere through the haze of passion, she realized his game. Their strip-chess rules dictated her bra and his pants stayed on.

Technically.

His mouth returned to hers, kissing her passionately as her hands found the button of his pants. She unfastened them, he groaned his encouragement, and together they wrangled his pants and briefs down but not off.

Kate looked down her body, taking in the strangely erotic sight of her breasts spilling over the top of her bra, his pants bunched around his thighs. Her fingers wrapped around him. Stroked.

"Yes," he growled.

She did it again, and he rewarded her with a lick at her nipple, a thumb on her clit. With torturing, teasing hands, they brought each other to the brink, his eyes on hers the entire time, until finally, when they couldn't take any more, he wrestled a condom out of his wallet. She didn't care that it was cliché he carried it with him, didn't know if he always did or just since they'd started hooking up, and she didn't care.

Correction, she didn't want to care. But it was darn hard when he lifted his eyes to her, his gaze dark and intense as he brushed her hair away from her face in a tender gesture that belied their frantic fumbling from moments before.

Kate held her breath, pausing for a drawn-out moment, trying to reclaim her heartbeat. Trying to reclaim her *heart*.

The realization caused a ripple of fear, and she reached for him, positioning him at the entrance of her body before sinking down, slamming her eyes shut as she did so. He murmured her name, a question on his lips, but she shook her head, her hips moving urgently over his.

Kennedy hesitated a moment longer, then his body made the decision for him, hands greedily moving over her as he lifted her, then pulled her down again, his hips slamming up to meet hers in a furious coupling.

He maneuvered his hand between their bodies, his fingers rubbing just above the spot where they were joined. She cried out, and he joined her at the precipice, thrusting into her hard at the exact moment she clenched around him.

Her orgasm was as turbulent as it was satisfying, and, too weak to do anything else when it was over, she slumped against his shoulder, her breath coming in near sobs.

She'd wanted fast and furious, and she'd gotten it. No tender love-making here, just good old-fashioned, no-strings screwing.

But as her heart rate slowed and her breath ceased coming in gasps, she registered . . . *him.*

The way his arm wrapped around her possessively, his other hand running over her hair in a caress meant to comfort. She felt a single tear run out of the corner of her eye and knew from the way his hand froze for a moment that he felt it hit his shoulder.

But then he resumed his gentle stroking and didn't ask why she was crying.

She suspected that she didn't have an answer. Not even for herself.

28

"You nervous?" Kennedy asked.

It was a rhetorical question. Ian had been pacing around the dedicated "groom's room" for a solid twenty-three minutes now.

"You know what? Why don't we revisit that question when *you* get married, see how *you* like it," Ian snapped, putting both hands on top of his head and taking a deep breath. "Sorry. I'm on edge."

"No worries," Kennedy said placatingly. He'd had plenty of friends and a brother get married. This wasn't his first rodeo.

Though he purposely ignored Ian's mention of his own wedding. Partially because it was hardly the time, but also because that day was seeming a long way off lately.

Kennedy was trying like hell not to get depressed by that fact.

"I was terrified at mine," Matt said from where he sat backward on a chair, his casual posture completely at odds with his groomsman tux.

"We know," Kennedy said. "You barfed on your tie. I gave you mine."

Matt saluted him with his bottle of water. "Thanks for that. Don't know that Sabrina would have loved me wearing one from the hotel gift shop. Though *What Happens in Vegas* would have been great in the photos, right?"

"I'm not going to puke." Ian stopped pacing long enough to pull a curtain aside and look out the window. "I don't think."

Kennedy batted his hand away. "Knock it off. You're not supposed to see the bride."

"She's not out there." Ian glanced at the guys. "Is she? I thought the girls were getting ready in the master bedroom upstairs."

"They are, but she's got to come down at some point to get in place for the processional."

"Processional?" Ian looked at Kennedy.

"Or, you know, whatever. The march."

"Dude, don't call it a *march*," Matt said, crumpling up his bottle and tossing it in the trash. "Ian, you've got to breathe through your nose. Kennedy's going to be mad if he has to give you his bow tie."

"Not really," Kennedy said. "I brought a spare. Big thanks to Lara for letting us wear standard black bow ties instead of having to wear pink, or lavender, or whatever color dresses the bridesmaids are wearing."

"Champagne," Ian said, tugging at his collar. "The dress color is apparently champagne."

Kennedy actually knew that. He'd seen it hanging in Kate's bedroom earlier that week. Though at the time he'd been so damn relieved that she was letting him in, he hadn't given two shits about the dress.

"Breathe," Matt said again. "In less than an hour the hard part will be over, and you'll get a drink, probably some sort of bacon-wrapped scallop deal, and you'll get to kiss your girl every time someone clinks on a glass, which will be a lot."

"I want to kiss her now."

"Yeah, well, then you should have eloped instead of having a big fancy wedding in the Hamptons," Kennedy countered.

Though, truth be told, it was shaping up to be a damn good wedding. The house they'd rented as their "bridal-party headquarters" was spacious and air-conditioned. The hotel where the guests were staying was walking distance from the beach where the ceremony would take place. And though Kate had insisted they rent a tent in case of rain, there was nothing but blue skies and sunshine.

Kennedy was happy for his friends. Elated. And if he were a tad jealous, he'd deal with that later.

There was a quick knock at the door, and the wedding planner, a pretty, smiley blonde named Brooke, stuck her head in. "You guys ready?"

Ian stepped toward her, his gaze slightly manic. "Is Lara ready? Have you seen her? How is she?"

Brooke smiled, unperturbed by his rapid-fire interrogation. "She's ready and eager to become Mrs. Bradley."

Just like that, Ian's shoulders relaxed, and his face broke into its usual easy smile. "All right, then. Let's do this."

Kennedy wouldn't admit it to a soul, but he liked weddings. Liked them even more when he was able to stand beside his best friend, offering his support on the most important day of Ian's life thus far.

Liked them best of all when the woman who had completely consumed his every thought for the past few months was coming down the aisle toward him.

It wasn't his wedding. Kennedy knew that, obviously. But for one heart-stopping moment when Kate appeared and began her walk down the aisle, he imagined an entirely different situation—her walking toward him, not as a bridesmaid walking in the general direction of where the groomsmen stood but Kate walking toward Kennedy, bride to groom.

She looked beautiful. The dress was a shimmering light-bronze color, strapless and fitted up top, full and flowing down to her knees. Her hair was back in a simple knot that suited her small features perfectly, and when her eyes lifted to his just for a moment, Kennedy's breath caught.

Mine. She was his.

Kate took her place on the opposite side of the pastor, turning toward the aisle and smiling at Sabrina, who was following behind her in a matching dress. Kennedy shifted just slightly back so he could keep Kate in his line of sight.

It was only the change in music announcing Lara's arrival that dragged Kennedy's gaze away from Kate. He smiled, not only at the radiant bride in a simple white gown but at the dopey grin on Ian's face.

"My eyes are definitely not watering," Matt whispered for Kennedy's ears only.

"Ditto," Kennedy said out of the corner of his mouth, relieved that his weren't the only eyes stinging with the threat of happy tears.

Lara reached the end of the aisle, pausing to hug her father, a tough-as-shit FBI agent whose usual scowl was nowhere in sight as he kissed his daughter's cheek and handed her off to Ian.

Kennedy's gaze caught on Kate once more as Lara stepped into place beside Ian, and he felt his heart crack at the expression on her face. Her eyes were wide and full of tears, but she wasn't looking at Lara and Ian. Her eyes were on Lara's father as he took his place in the front row beside Lara's mother.

He knew that it was hitting her then, and hitting her hard, that her father would never be there for this moment in her life.

Oh, Kate.

Her bottom lip wobbled, and it took all of his self-control not to step toward her. *Hang in there, love.*

Kennedy was endlessly grateful for Sabrina in that moment. The other woman had noticed Kate's distress and set a hand on her upper arm. Kate touched Sabrina's hand with a grateful smile, then inhaled and turned her attention back to the bride and groom.

He didn't. He kept his gaze on Kate, willing her to look at him. To lean on him, just a little.

She didn't look his way the entire ceremony.

And even as one part of his heart soared for these two friends who'd just exchanged vows, another part of his heart broke.

Because he knew what he'd just witnessed: Kate Henley had shut down entirely, shutting him out in the process. For good.

29

Saturday, June 8

"Okay, if you're not going to do something, I will."

Kennedy didn't look up from where he stared at his untouched champagne on the table. "Sabrina. You look stunning."

"Save it," she said, dropping into the chair beside him. "What are you doing over here?"

He flicked his gaze at her. "You thought I'd be doing the chicken dance?"

"That's the Macarena. You can tell, because Matt's right in the middle of it." She pointed to where Matt was dancing his heart out, standing in between a laughing Ian and Lara, as they all did some ridiculous dance with their hands that Kennedy had maybe learned at one time but couldn't be bothered at the moment to remember.

"What is going on?" Sabrina said, leaning closer to him. "Did you and Kate get in a fight?"

"A fight? No." He lifted his champagne. "We'd actually have to speak to have a fight."

"Yeah, I noticed you're getting the cold shoulder. Who *is* that guy?"

"That one? Not sure. There've been so damn many," Kennedy said, forcing himself to glance in Kate's direction.

Sure enough, she was chatting it up with some beefcake of a guy. And actually, Kennedy did know this one. He'd met Lara's cousin at the rehearsal dinner the night before. Sort of a douchebag, but Kate didn't seem to notice. Or care.

Just like she didn't seem to care that his assistant, Christian, was gay when she'd flirted with him. Or with Jarod Lanham when she'd laughed hysterically at everything the man said. Or that kid who looked all of twenty-three.

She wasn't making a spectacle of herself. She wouldn't have done that to Lara and Ian. But anyone who knew her well, as Kennedy and Sabrina did, knew that this wasn't normal Kate. Her eyes were too bright, her laugh a little bit brittle.

Kennedy glanced at Sabrina and expected to see her watching Kate as well. Instead, Sabrina was watching him, her gray-blue eyes concerned. "You're worried about her."

He thought about denying it. Telling her to mind her own business. But Sabrina was important to him. They didn't go back as far as she and Ian, and there'd never been any chemistry between them, but they'd clicked on a friendship level from the very beginning.

And right now, he needed a friend.

He nodded. "Yeah. I'm worried about her."

"You care about her."

He nodded again. Shrugged.

"No, I mean, you *care* about her, Kennedy."

Kennedy looked at her. "Of course I care about her. I care about you. And Lara. And the guys, when they're not being annoying."

"And because I care about *you*, I'm going to call bullshit. Your feelings for Kate are nothing like your feelings for Lara and me. And I know you, Kennedy. I know that beneath that gruff exterior of yours, you feel deeply."

"No psychobabble, please," he said with a wince.

"Tell me I'm wrong."

"What do you want me to say?" he snapped. "She knows I'm here, but she's gone out of her way not to talk to me or even acknowledge my presence."

"Why?"

He took another sip of champagne. He may be annoyed as hell with Kate right now, but he wasn't about to expose her vulnerabilities to others, even a friend like Sabrina.

But Sabrina knew her friend well. "It was Lara's father walking her down the aisle, wasn't it?" Sabrina asked. "I could tell she was upset. Poor thing."

Kennedy didn't bother to argue. Of course she was upset. Anyone who'd lost her father a month and a half earlier would be, but it was extra brutal for someone like Kate. Sabrina thought he felt deeply? He had nothing on Kate. Despite her efforts over the past few weeks to keep everyone—most of all him—at a distance, it wasn't who she was. Kate didn't do anything in half measures. She threw herself one hundred percent into everything. Her work. Her friendships.

Love.

Hadn't she told him as much? That she was holding out for the head-over-heels sort of love that he'd always thought was fictional?

He knew better now.

The trouble was, Kate loved with all she had. And she grieved that way, too. Just as the old Kate had once believed with her whole heart that true love was out there waiting for her, the new Kate was just as determined to shut herself off from the pain.

"It's not like I've asked her to marry me," he muttered.

Sabrina blinked slowly and stared at him. "Sorry. What?"

Shit. "Nothing. I just . . . I couldn't possibly have moved any slower with her. I've been trying to give her time and space, and the whole thing blew up in my face."

"I thought that's what might be happening," Sabrina said with a sigh. "I have to take a little responsibility for it, too. I more or less told her to bone you to get you out of her system."

He gave her a look. "Thanks for that."

"Well, at the time, I didn't know you were in love with her."

Kennedy didn't bother to deny it. "I didn't know it, either."

Sabrina sighed again and scooted closer, resting her head on his shoulder. "I'm sorry, Kennedy."

He pecked a brotherly kiss on the top of her head but didn't say anything.

"For what it's worth," she said after a long minute of silence, "I've always thought you two were meant for each other."

"Me too," Kennedy said slowly, a little surprised at how easy the admission was. "But looking at her now . . ."

Kennedy winced as the song turned to a slow, drippy ballad, and Kate tugged Lara's cousin onto the dance floor. Watching her laugh with another man had been hard enough. Seeing another man's arms around her was a whole other kind of agony.

"I know. Which is why we need a new plan," Sabrina said, standing as Matt headed toward their table to retrieve his wife for a dance.

"What are you thinking?" Kennedy asked tentatively. Normally he didn't particularly relish advice on his personal life—or at all—but Sabrina had made a lucrative career out of fixing other people's problems. If he was going to listen to anyone, it'd be her.

"I'm thinking maybe we were wrong about her needing space."

"And?"

Sabrina studied her friend on the dance floor before glancing back at Kennedy. "She's a little broken right now, but deep down, Kate still wants someone who's not afraid to go all in—someone willing to put it all on the line. For her."

"I know." He said it quietly.

Sabrina put her hand on his shoulder. "Be that guy."

◆ ◆ ◆

"What is your problem?" Kate snapped at him as he pulled her away from the reception. "Blake and I were dancing."

"Dancing is a stretch for what that was," Kennedy grumbled. "His hands were about six inches too low for dancing, and the only movement I saw was you rubbing against him."

"Oh, nice," she said, trying to tug her wrist free from his grip. "Playing the part of the jealous boyfriend? Seriously?"

"Yes, *seriously*, Kate," he said, spinning back toward her just in time to see surprise register on her face. "Tell me, what exactly was your plan here tonight? What was the goal? To dump me without actually having to say a word or look me in the eye?"

She blinked quickly, but not before he saw the flash of guilt. She knew she'd behaved badly, and it mollified him. Slightly.

His chest still ached.

"I've been rude to you," she acknowledged, crossing her arms. "And I'm sorry, truly. But I can't *dump* you, Kennedy. We're not dating."

There it was. Proof that his *give her space* plan had been solid in theory but fucked in practice. He'd given her too much space, too much wiggle room, and he was losing her. *Damn it.*

"Kate." He stepped toward her, ignoring the fact that sand was getting all up in his shoes, and blocking out the sound of the reception, the bonfire in the distance, even the drunken college kids who had just gone racing past them. "I know today was hard on you."

She stepped back, her eyes suspiciously bright. "Don't be ridiculous. I love weddings. I'm thrilled for Ian and Lara."

"I know you are. I also know it was hard for you to see Mr. McKenzie walk Lara down the aisle."

She swallowed and looked toward the water, and he saw her eyes were shining.

He dragged a hand over his face. There was nothing worse than knowing she was hurting and he couldn't help, but he was hurting, too.

"I'm not trying to pressure you, Kate. I don't want to rush—"

"Then don't," she said at a near shout. "I've been clear with you, Kennedy. I don't know how to be clearer. I don't want . . . this." She gestured between them.

"You used to," he said, hating how desperate he sounded. "You told me that night on the boat that you used to."

"Past tense, Kennedy."

"Bullshit," he said, anger kicking in around the pain. "You can't look me in the eye and tell me these past months have meant nothing to you, that we haven't come damn far. I've seen the way you look at me, Kate, and I know damn well you've seen the way I look at you. You can't tell me you don't feel what I feel every time our eyes meet, every time we touch. You're hurting right now, and I get that. You need more time, and I can do that, but you've got to give me something, Kate. Tell me to wait, and I'll wait as long as you need. I'll wait forever, but don't *end* this."

Kate's eyes were bright with tears, and for a heart-stopping moment of hope, he thought she'd tell him what he wanted to hear— what he needed to hear, more desperately than he'd ever needed anything.

Instead, she backed away, and his hopes crashed down around him. Wordlessly, she shook her head.

He swallowed. "So, what, the past few weeks have just been you fooling around?"

"You *knew* that it was." Her voice pleaded with him to understand. "What do you want from me?"

He stepped closer. "I want access to the old Kate, the one who believed in love at first sight, who would never settle for 'fooling around.'"

She shook her head and looked down at her feet. "I can't—"

"Kate." He tried one last time, gently lifting her chin until she was looking at him again. "You have to know that's why I jumped at the chance to have Christian as my assistant instead of you. It's because I knew full well I couldn't date my assistant. And I want to date you. More than anything."

"But it won't last. Everything ends one way or another, because that's life."

"Is that what you'd tell Lara and Ian or Sabrina and Matt? Or would you tell them to go for it? That they can't just quit on the good stuff in life because they're scared of the bad."

A tear leaked out of the corner of her eye.

Kennedy moved slowly, reaching out and cupping her face, relieved when she didn't move away. "*We're* the good stuff, Kate. No, I didn't hear angels singing the first moment our eyes met, but that's got nothing to do with you and everything to do with *me*. You know me. Things take me a while. I think too much; I'm always up in my head. I may not feel as quickly as you, but I do *feel*, Kate.

"You once said you wanted someone who'd fall hard and fast for you, and while I know I let you down on the *fast* part . . . I did fall, Kate. I've fallen all the way."

He swallowed. It was the closest he'd ever come to saying he loved a woman, and he willed her to hear it.

She searched his face for a long moment, and Kennedy held his breath.

"Good speech, Dawson." She said it quietly, but it hit him like a slap anyway. "But we've just screwed a few times. Don't romanticize it."

His hands dropped, his arms falling limply to his sides as pain splintered through his entire midsection.

Kennedy loved her. More than anything. But she wasn't the only one who needed to self-protect from hurt. And right now, the one with the power to hurt him was *her*.

So Kennedy forced himself to nod. Step back. Turn. And walk away.

30

"Wolfe Investments, this is Kate."

She tucked her phone under her ear as she repositioned the egg on her Starbucks breakfast sandwich so it was centered.

"Kate. It's Christian."

She licked cheese off her finger and put the English muffin back on top. Then shoved it away. She wasn't hungry. Hadn't been hungry in more than twenty-four hours. Not even for cheese.

"Hey, you sound awful," she said to her protégé. "Did Genevieve give you that nasty cold? I *told* her last week she should have stayed home."

"I guess," he said glumly. "I'd come in, but—"

"Don't," she ordered. "Nothing is more annoying than the moron who brings his snot into the office to show what a trouper he is, and then takes out the whole office with his cooties."

"I know. But I'm so new, and it feels lame to ask you to fill in for me this soon. I've only been there a few weeks . . ."

"Don't worry about it," she said, though her decisive tone was wavering as she realized what Christian's absence would mean. She'd have to fill in for him. As Kennedy's assistant.

She hadn't seen him since *that* night, and the thought of coming face-to-face again . . .

Her stomach roiled with queasiness. She swiped the breakfast sandwich into the trash before she barfed.

Kate flicked her mouse to wake up her computer, desperate for a distraction. "I still have access to Kennedy's calendar, but is there anything I should know?" She carefully kept her voice professionally indifferent.

"Well, that's actually the good news," Christian said after blowing his nose. "Kennedy's out today."

She froze. "Out?"

Kennedy was *never* out. He took maybe one vacation a year, usually a golf trip. But spontaneous days off? Never. As far as she knew, the guy didn't even get sick.

"Yeah, he just texted me an hour ago and said he was taking a personal day," Christian said, blissfully unaware of how atypical that was for Kennedy. Even more unaware of why Kennedy was taking a day off.

I did fall, Kate. I've fallen all the way.

"I've already called and rescheduled all of his meetings," Christian was saying. "So other than manning the phone, you should be Kennedy-free today."

Oh, she'd be *Kennedy-free* a lot longer than that. She'd made sure of that, hadn't she? She didn't think one could ever come back from her *good speech, Dawson* bombshell.

"There's a folder on my desk of stuff to be filed," Christian was saying. "But Kennedy made a point of saying it was low priority, so it can probably wait until tomorrow."

"I'll get to it if I can," she said absently. She knew the routine. Kennedy had fully embraced the digital age and kept electronic copies of everything in the cloud. But Kennedy, being Kennedy, also kept hard copies of things he deemed especially important. It was a good sign that he'd asked Christian to file them. It meant he trusted his new assistant.

"Thanks, Kate. I appreciate it."

"Of course. Let me know if you think of anything else, but mostly focus on getting better, okay? Lots of sleep."

"Yes, ma'am."

She hung up with Christian and stared unseeingly at the computer screen. She took a sip of coffee. It had no flavor. Since when did *coffee* have no flavor? Kate mentally slapped herself. She wasn't going to be that girl. This was her decision. She was the one who'd made the smart call, rather than the emotional one. She would be smart. Independent. Maybe take up kickboxing.

"Kickboxing, Kate? Really?" she muttered to herself.

She tried to focus on her computer for real, and as she went through her normal routine of checking the guys' calendars, it hit her . . .

None of the guys were coming into the office today. Ian was on his honeymoon in Paris. Matt and Sabrina had decided to extend their stay in the Hamptons after the wedding.

Kennedy was *out*.

Which meant Kate was good and truly alone at the office. She couldn't remember the last time that'd happened, if there even *was* a time.

"Well," she said, sipping the coffee again, then frowning because it was tasting even blander by the moment. "A quiet day. That's exactly what I need after a busy weekend."

But by ten a.m., Kate realized quiet was the *last* thing she wanted. The last thing she *needed*. Solitude left her alone with her thoughts, and her thoughts, as they were, were agonizingly brutal.

The night of the wedding kept playing like a nightmarish montage. Not the wedding itself, obviously. It had been a beautiful ceremony. But she couldn't deny that seeing Lara's dad walk her down the aisle had been excruciating. She'd known it was going to hurt, but she hadn't been expecting it to feel like her legs had been kicked out from under her, like her chest had been crushed. And having Kennedy standing just a few feet away through it all, looking at her like . . . like . . .

I did fall, Kate. I've fallen all the way.

Even if it were true, she didn't want to fall back. She didn't think she could stomach the pain of loving someone all the way and then losing him.

Especially Kennedy.

Desperate for a distraction, she called her mom.

Eileen picked up on the third ring. "Hi, honey."

"Hey, Mom!" She forced brightness into her tone. "How are you?"

"Good! Actually, Janine and I were just walking into the salon to get our nails done. Can I call you later?"

Rejected by her own mother. "Of course!" Whoops. Her tone was too bright and hit on a false note.

Her mom noticed. "What's wrong?"

"Nothing, just a long weekend."

"Oh right, the wedding! How was it?"

"Amazing. Absolutely perfect," Kate said. "But seriously, go do your thing. Call me when you get a chance—no hurry."

This time she managed to achieve her usual calm, in-control Kate tone, and her mom let her off the hook. "Okay, talk soon. Love you."

"I love you, too," Kate said before hanging up and finding herself once again surrounded by uncomfortable silence. Even the phones were unusually quiet.

By lunchtime, she'd finally cracked and had begun talking to herself again.

"This is what you wanted," she reminded herself as she pulled her prepackaged Whole Foods salad out of the fridge. "You wanted space, and you got it. You wanted to learn how to rely on yourself for happiness, not someone else, so this is good practice."

She nodded at herself, as though that would make the pep talk more convincing, when in reality, even to her own ears it sounded like a cliché movie about some loser woman who'd gotten knocked down by life and, instead of coping with it, had turned into some irrational weirdo.

Kate managed only three bites of salad before shoving that aside as well, her appetite still nowhere to be found. Caught up on her inbox and still looking for something to occupy her mind, she went to Christian's desk and picked up the navy file folder. She'd given all of the guys their own color files a couple of years ago to make things easier on herself. Ian was orange, Matt was green, and Kennedy was navy. She dealt with a lot more navy folders than she did the other colors, since Kennedy liked to print out just about everything in addition to his various cloud backup systems. She'd protest more, but she liked that he also donated an obscene amount of money to reforestation, so maybe it all evened out.

She grabbed the folder and the keys to his office, noticing it was thicker than usual. Knowing him, he'd been holding on to the to-be-filed stack for a while, probably making sure Christian was legit before trusting him with any personal documents.

Kate smiled to herself, because it was so Kennedy.

Her smile slipped, because even that reminded her of that night.

You know me. Things take me a while.

She shoved the key into the lock, pushed open the office door, and tried to ignore the wave of *Kennedy* that hit her. She went to the wooden file cabinet along the right wall of his office and, after unlocking the cabinets, began putting everything in place. She'd done it so many times, she was more or less on autopilot, knowing which folder to put each sheet in based on letterhead or logo alone.

She picked up a piece of ivory paper, blinking down at the letterhead in confusion. Not because she didn't recognize it, but because it definitely didn't belong in Kennedy's files. It was from Columbia University, and Kennedy was a Princeton guy. And yet it was definitely addressed to *Mr. Kennedy Dawson*.

Still baffled, she scanned the contents, realizing that she'd gotten this same memo herself late last week. It was a generic form letter informing those affiliated with the school that the admissions, alumni, and administration offices had all been temporarily relocated during renovations. Kate had gotten the memo because she was an alumna of the business school.

Why would Kennedy get one?

Pointlessly, she glanced over her shoulder, and then, before she could think better of the invasion of privacy, gave in to the need to know. She opened up one of the drawers, to the *C*s, searching for Columbia. She didn't find it, but there was a folder marked *C*—a plain manila folder, not navy, the way it should have been if it was a folder Kate set up for him.

Kate sent up a silent apology for snooping and then pulled out the folder, somehow already knowing that her instincts were correct. The *C* stood for Columbia.

The stack of paper inside was relatively slim, but the impact of what she found nearly knocked her off her feet. Dazed, Kate walked slowly backward until she found herself sitting in Kennedy's chair, reading the contents over and over until it finally sunk in.

Ian hadn't paid for her MBA tuition. *Kennedy* had.

Why had Ian lied? Why had Kennedy? It didn't make any sense, but there was no denying what she'd read. Kennedy had written an enormous check years ago, paying for her entire degree with one signature. There was no indication that he'd split the cost with Ian, no mention of a transfer of funds.

Kennedy had given her that gift. And hadn't said a word about it.

Kennedy might not have fallen in love with Kate the way she had with him, at first sight, all in. But he *had* cared when she'd assumed him indifferent.

I think too much; I'm always up in my head. I may not feel as quickly as you, but I do feel, Kate.

Of course he did.

And suddenly Kate realized that she'd made the most massive mistake of her life.

31

Kennedy stared down at the chessboard. Moved the white pawn forward, then moved it back. Then he realized that he wasn't white; *she* was.

And she'd never be playing with him again.

He crossed his arms and glared around the room. What did people do on days off? It was too nice out to stay inside and watch TV. He wasn't depressed, for God's sake. He could go for a walk to the park—Nope. That made him think of her. Just like work made him think of her. Same with food. Drink. Breathing.

Shit. Maybe he was depressed after all.

Good speech, Dawson. Don't romanticize it.

The sound of dozens of chess pieces clattering to the ground snapped him out of the flashback, and Kennedy looked down, stunned as his brain caught up with what he'd done. In a rage, he'd swiped the chessboard to the ground.

Kennedy Dawson didn't do rage. But then, he didn't really do love, either, and look where he was now. Head over heels for a woman who didn't love him back.

He started to bend down to pick up the pieces but stopped. He'd do it later. Right now, the mess suited him. So did the anger.

Kennedy headed toward the kitchen, intending to call his brothers and see if any of them could make time for a weekday round of golf. Chasing a tiny ball around while playing the world's most frustrating sport sounded like just the thing.

A pound at his front door had him pausing in the hallway and reversing course toward the foyer. His front door was wood but had glass paneling at eye level so he could see who was on the other side. At least, normally he could. He didn't see anyone right now, which meant the other person would have to be . . .

Very short.

Kate.

He knew it. Sensed it. Hated how much he hoped for it.

Kennedy ordered his dignity to ignore the insistent pounding. Let her wait. Let her hurt like he was hurting.

He opened the door.

Kate's fist paused midknock, and she dropped it to her side, then lifted her hand to adjust her headband, betraying her nervousness, but he was fresh out of sympathy.

"What do you want, Kate?"

"Why'd you buy my dad that fishing trip?"

He didn't even pretend to know what she was talking about. "What?"

"Right after I first started at Wolfe. My dad had to cancel his annual fishing trip with his friends because the place they'd always stayed at was closed. You rented a house for them. Why?"

Kennedy shook his head, vaguely remembering the occasion but certainly not remembering the details. "I don't know. It seemed important to you, because it was important to him. I had the ability to help, so I did."

"And what about when I said I wanted to go back to school. That was important to me, too. You had the ability to help . . . so you did?"

He opened his mouth with the default lie that Ian had paid for it, but she lifted a finger in warning.

"Are you sure you want to lie to me right now?"

Kennedy tiredly ran his hands over his face. No. He didn't. What was the point anymore?

"Why?" she asked quietly, reading his silence for the affirmation it was.

He shrugged. "Like you said, it was important to you. So I guess it was important to me, too."

She nodded slowly. "Okay. But then why let Ian take the credit for it?"

"I've asked myself that a million times," he said honestly. "I still don't know if I have an answer. It just seemed important somehow."

"That I didn't know you did something nice for me? No, not just *nice*." She shook her head. "Over-the-top generous, Kennedy. Even for someone with a lot of money—and I know you have a lot—paying for my tuition outright was *beyond* generous. Why not just let Wolfe cover it? They have education assistance for employees."

He was already shaking his head. "I didn't want you tied to the company. For all I knew, you'd start business school and realize you wanted to do something else with your life, something outside of Wolfe. I wanted that to be an option for you."

"You wanted me to leave Wolfe?"

"No," he said sharply. "God no. I just wanted you to feel like you could, if you wanted to. I wanted you to be happy."

"Ah," she said lightly, even though she didn't sound like she understood. "But you didn't want me to know it was *you* who'd ensured that happiness?"

"Not really," Kennedy said warily, because she had that look on her face—the one where she knew she was one step ahead of whomever she was dealing with. Which meant she was one step ahead of him, and with his defenses as low as they were around her these days, he wasn't entirely sure he was up for this conversation.

"Why?"

He shook his head.

"Try, Kennedy," she whispered. It wasn't a plea, but it was close.

This was important to her, and because *she* was important to him . . .

"I didn't want you to like me because of that," he said in a rush. "I didn't want to win your affection or your respect because I paid your tuition. I wanted you to like me because of *me*. To like me just as I was—uptight, crotchety, and all of that."

"But I *did* like you," she said softly. "Way too much."

"Well, I didn't know that," he said, his voice a little cross. "All I saw was that you were easy with Matt and Ian but on edge with me. I figured you disliked me because I wasn't charming and easy to talk to the way they are."

"Because I heard you call me plain—"

"About that," he interrupted, because if they were going to have this out, they were going to have it all of the way out. "It was recently pointed out to me that I was the one who insisted we make the pact to stay away from you. Did you hear *that* in your eavesdropping?"

She frowned and shook her head.

"Ian and Matt apparently didn't need the pact because they were never in danger of hitting on their assistant. *I* was the one who needed it, who needed to be reminded to keep his hands to himself. Does that sound like a man who thought you were plain? Or in any way resistible? Because it sounds to me like a man who needed his friends' help in resisting."

"Revisionist history." She gave a flippant wave of her hand, but he reached out and gripped her wrist.

"No, Kate. It's not. I *noticed* you. I did. Even if I didn't consciously realize it at the time. And yeah, it bugged me that you never seemed to like me like you did the other guys. You think I don't realize that I can come across as cold? That I lack Matt's charm and Ian's wit? That despite being older, I come behind Jack in both looks and personality?"

"Stop it," Kate said firmly. "Stop saying those things. I didn't fall in love with Ian, or Matt, or Jack the moment I saw them. I fell in love with *you*."

Kennedy's breath caught, but then he remembered that she fell *out* of love with him just as easily.

"Why are you here?" he asked tiredly when she didn't say anything more.

"I wanted the truth about why you paid my tuition."

"You could have called."

"Um, no way would you have picked up. You're mad at me."

He let out a deep breath. "No, I'm not. I just need time to get over you. You had years to get over me. I think I deserve at least a couple days."

"Well, you're not going to get it, because I didn't." She stepped closer, and his fingers gripped her wrist tighter.

"You didn't what?"

"Get over you." Her words were quiet but confident, and they packed a hell of a wallop. She met his eyes steadily, wilting slightly when he stayed silent. "You're not saying anything."

"Well, no, Kate," he said gruffly. "I sort of laid it all out there, and you tossed it aside pretty easily. How do I know you're not going to change your mind again tomorrow? Or the next time I say something clueless that hurts your feelings, because God knows it'll happen? Or the next time things get tough?"

"Now see, I knew you were going to say that," Kate said, tugging her hand free so that she could rummage around in her purse. Before he could register that she'd pulled out a dark-red velvet box, she was down on one knee.

Kennedy's stomach dropped. "What the—Are you nuts?"

Undeterred, she opened the box. Not slick and practiced with a flick of her thumb but with two hands, clamshell-style. "Kennedy Edward Dawson. Will you marry me?"

"Get up." He bent down, trying to lift her, but she wiggled away.

"You have to answer. It's rude not to."

Rude. She'd come to his house, told him she was in love with him, and proposed, all without giving him a chance to catch his breath, and he was rude? This time when he reached down, he caught her, hauling her up easily. But by the time he set her back on her feet, all of her bravado was gone.

"Please, Kennedy. You don't have to marry me. Just give me another chance. *Please.*" Ring box still clutched in her hand, she reached up and tugged on his shirt, her hands a little shaky. "I love you. I don't know how I possibly thought I was over you, when you're all I've thought about, all I've ever wanted."

He caught her chin and held her gaze. "I want you *all in*, Kate Henley. I can't do this if you're not."

She smiled smugly and issued her challenge. "Then make me Kate Dawson."

Kennedy's heart soared at the thought. He pulled her closer. "I love you."

She bit her bottom lip as though trying to hide a smile, then failed completely, because her face erupted in a full grin. "You love me?"

"Yeah." He cleared his throat. "A lot."

He brushed his lips against hers, softly, not yet completely confident this wasn't a dream. But then she kissed him back, and he poured his heart into the kiss and felt her give hers right back. And though he had every intention of finishing the kiss upstairs, there was one last item of business . . .

Kennedy tugged the box out of her hand and studied the traditional but expensive-looking ring, knowing from the name on the box that it was no cheap corner-store buy but a huge investment. He felt a lump in his throat, knowing how terrifying the gesture must have been for her.

To keep her from feeling embarrassed, he grinned at her. "I'm a traditional guy, Henley. You really think I'm going to let you rob me of a proposal?"

"Not really," she said. "It was more of a grand gesture. Actually, you know, now that I think of it, why don't I just take that back—"

Kennedy wrapped an arm around her shoulders and began pulling her forward as he held the ring well out of her reach. "*Very* amusing. I think I'll just hold on to this."

She pulled to a stop outside the living room. "What happened to your chessboard?"

"Ah." He glanced at the mess. "Female woes."

"Apparently. Can I interest you in a game? Distract you from this silly girl who forgot her own heart for a while there?"

"Maybe later. I've got a long game that I'm playing right now that's taking all of my concentration."

She shrugged and kissed his shoulder, and the casual, sweet gesture of affection made his throat clench with emotion. *God.* It was official. He was as whipped as Ian and Matt.

And he'd never been happier.

Epilogue

Saturday, July 20

"Happy birthday!"

Kate paused in the doorway, grinning at the gathering of her friends and family.

Lara had walked in with Kate, and she linked their arms. "Not surprised, huh?"

"Not even a little," Kate said. "Kennedy knows better than to totally rob me of planning my own birthday party."

"You and your planning," Sabrina said, linking her other arm. "But hey, it's your birthday. Whatever floats your boat."

"Well, it's not totally without surprises," Lara said slyly, nodding at an older woman approaching them.

"Mom!" Kate pulled her arms free of her friends and rushed over to hug her mother. "What are you doing here?"

"Oh, your fella arranged for me to come into the city. Found someone to watch the puppy and everything. Brought me here in a fancy car, put me up in a fancy hotel. He even arranged for me to have my hair done. See?"

"It's fabulous," Kate said, kissing her mom's cheek, relieved to see that she looked genuinely happy.

The shadow of losing Kate's dad faded a little more every time she saw her, and Eileen reassured Kate with every visit that life really did go on—it was just a different stage of her life. Kate liked that and hoped that someday her mom might even find a new partner for this new stage.

"You know you didn't have to come all this way, though, right? I know you hate the city, and this isn't even a birthday ending in a zero."

"I wouldn't miss it," her mother said. "Oh! Look, prime rib . . ."

She dashed off toward a buffet table, just as Kennedy approached, a slight smile on his face.

Kate flung her arms around his neck, kissing him full on the mouth, unabashed they were in the middle of a crowded room. "Thank you," she said against his lips.

"You already knew it was happening. You're the worst surprise party recipient ever."

"I didn't know about Mom, though. Best surprise ever."

"You sure about that?"

She laughed and pulled back. "Seriously? You think you can top my mom?"

Kate's smile froze in confusion as she realized everyone was watching them expectantly.

She frowned. "What am I missing?" Then she saw it and laughed. "Oh my God, an ice sculpture!"

"They're very in right now, didn't you know?"

"I did. What the heck is that?" she said as she got closer. "It's very . . . phallic."

"Yeah . . . Didn't really think that through. It seemed like a good idea at the time."

"Oh! It's a king!" she said. "From a chessboard."

"Nerds," Ian said from behind a fake cough.

Matt chimed in. "You know, if either of you wants to play, I've actually beaten a grand master. I'd love to take either of you on—"

"Oh, Matthew. Please be quiet," Lara said, tugging him away from Kate and Kennedy.

Oblivious to her friends, Kate stepped closer to the ice sculpture. "There's something inside it. What . . . Oh. *Oh my God.*"

Her hand went to her mouth as she registered the solitaire diamond ring encased in the middle of the ice.

She whirled toward Kennedy, but he was already on his knee, smiling up at her with a cocky, confident smile. Which was probably fair, considering he was already wearing her ring. He hadn't taken it off since the night she'd given it to him. The guys occasionally gave him crap for having a "guy's engagement ring," but he only ever smiled.

"Told you I'd get my proposal my way." Without looking away, he tilted his head toward the ring in the ice. "Marry me?"

Her heart felt like it was bursting from her chest as she grinned down at the only man she'd ever loved. "*Yes.* All in."

Kennedy smiled wider as he stood and wrapped her in a hug that lifted her off her feet. Their friends clapped and cheered around them, but as Kennedy lowered her back to the ground, his word was just for her. "Checkmate."

She looked up at him. "Really? What did you win?"

Kennedy's eyes were warm and adoring as they locked on hers. "Your heart."

ACKNOWLEDGMENTS

It takes a village to turn a story into a book. To my village, you know who you are, and I'm more grateful than I can possibly express.

Special shout-out to my editor, Kristi Yanta, for rearranging your entire life to fit revisions for this book in your schedule. I could not (and would not) write it without you, so Kate, Kennedy, and I are immensely grateful!

To Maria Gomez and the rest of the spectacular Montlake team for working all of your usual magic.

And of course, to my readers, for making any and all of this possible.

ABOUT THE AUTHOR

Photo © Anthony LeDonne

Lauren Layne is the *New York Times* and *USA Today* bestselling author of more than two dozen novels, including *Hot Asset, Hard Sell,* and *Huge Deal* in her 21 Wall Street series. Her books have sold more than a million copies in nine languages. Lauren's work has been featured in *Publishers Weekly, Glamour,* the *Wall Street Journal,* and *Inside Edition.* She is based in New York City. For the latest updates, be sure to check out her website at www.laurenlayne.com, and follow her on Instagram @laurenlayneauthor.